A ... rm.
A BOOK ... VOICE.

Hand to Hand is a grassroots publishing and purchasing innovation that saves resources and money. It asks each reader to pay just $5 to help defray the author's publishing costs, and to pass the book to another reader who is also willing to support it and pass it on. This ensures its journey from hand to hand and builds community between readers and authors through use of the honor system.

Here's Why: 1) Books are smart technology—portable, durable, tactile and organic. And they carry culture. But when owned, they are relegated to shelves. Earth's resources and the author's voice are lost. Hand to Hand Books believes that most readers care for both things. **2)** Authors are normally paid between $1 and $2 per copy. To better support the source of the art, all Hand to Hand Books income goes directly to the author, who pays all publishing costs. **3)** Readers save money by spending only a fraction of the cost of a new book. They also foster community through discussion of the book and its reader-distribution plan in person and online.

http://TheTroubleWithWisdom.com

To Begin: 1) Sign in on the next page to document the book on its journey and **2)** donate $5 on the website using the PayPal button. Or send a check to Hand to Hand Books, P.O. Box 123, Dorset, VT 05251. If you have comments, please share them on the website.

To Continue: Consider the next reader, and then pass on both the book and the awareness of stewarding it in this paradigm. You can proliferate new seed copies by guiding friends to order them through the website or via Hand to Hand's email: **h2hbooks@sover.net.**

To End: The Readers' List describes the journey of the book. To assess the paradigm, Hand to Hand Books requests the final reader (when the copy disintegrates) to detach it and to send it to the above address.

Options: If you choose to own a copy in the regular way, you can order one for $20 plus shipping through the website or via email.

Comments
Write On...

The Trouble with Wisdom

Readers List
(The Hand to Hand Journey of This Copy)

Name	City, State (& Country)	Date
1)		
2)		
3)		
4)		
5)		
6)		
7)		
8)		
9)		
10)		
11)		
12)		
13)		
14)		

A NOTE TO THE FINAL READER:
When this copy disintegrates and can no longer be passed on,
please carefully remove this page and send it to:
Hand to Hand Books,
P.O. Box 123, Dorset VT USA 05251
Through this, we can assess the viability of the paradigm.

201

Readers List Continued
(The Hand to Hand Journey of This Copy)

Name	City, State (& Country)	Date

15)_____

16)_____

17)_____

18)_____

19)_____

20)_____

21)_____

22)_____

23)_____

24)_____

25)_____

26)_____

27)_____

28)_____

29)_____

30)_____

A NOTE TO THE FINAL READER:
When this copy disintegrates and can no longer be passed on,
please carefully remove this page and send it to:
Hand to Hand Books,
P.O. Box 123, Dorset VT USA 05251
Through this, we can assess the viability of the new paradigm.

The Trouble with Wisdom

Thomas Henry Pope

Published by Hand to Hand Books
P.O. Box 123
Dorset, Vermont 05761

Distribution by Hand to Hand Books
and by readers
Printed by Shires Press
4869 Main Street
P.O. Box 2200
Manchester Center, VT 05255
www.northshire.com/printondemand.php

ISBN-13:   978-0-615-30646-9

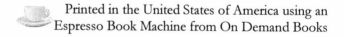 Printed in the United States of America using an Espresso Book Machine from On Demand Books

To my two fathers:

Harold, who taught me the love of language

and

Chokyi Gyamtso Trungpa, Rinpoche,

who taught me the love of everything else

Prologue: March 1959

Alone on the mountain with no sheep or goats to keep him warm through the brutal Tibetan night and fleeing the atrocity he had witnessed in his monastery down below, the mute shepherd-monk Samten bent over to retch. Instead he discovered his voice.

He had run uphill for over an hour right through twilight. Spent, he hammered a stone through a frozen rivulet and drank like a highland gazelle with his neck stretched long and his cheeks in the water. The cold of it numbed the roiling in his belly. But when he stood again to draw in the thin serving of oxygen, he found his diaphragm clenched tight. With wide eyes he watched the disc of stars above him tip and wheel. Turning with them, he stumbled and fell hard onto rocks beside the water. When a vision of a radiant Buddha appeared in his mind, he presumed the worst and prepared for death.

But it was not Samten's time. His breath returned, and with it came a new determination to press over the mountain to warn the sister monastery in the valley beyond. When he stood a second time, a wave of nausea took him. He gagged and shook, but the too-fresh images of desecration and blood erupted out of him, not as vomit, but as a long, spastic bellow.

For weeks throughout the highland range of Eastern Tibet, rumors of unthinkable acts had passed from yak herder to tenant farmer, to trader, to monastery cook, to monk, to high lama and to government official. But most Tibetans discounted what they heard. They couldn't believe that their neighbors to the east were capable of attacks in cold-blood and comforted themselves with the knowledge that stories become embellished through repeated telling, Senior lamas attributed the tales to people sensing for the first time the presence of an outside, technological world. And they counseled everyone to refrain from fear and gossip and to renew their aspirations to the ideals of generosity and compassion.

But words coming from Samten—now that was a miracle, and the lamas in the Naked Red Lady Mountain monastery listened to him carefully. The smooth acceleration of activity that followed the meeting was the single capability in which the ossified, hierarchical culture of Tibet excelled. Every person in the lay and monastic community knew his part. Within fourteen hours of Samtem's arrival, one hundred and seventy-five monks and eighty-seven peasant households had prepared for the escape of their lamas.

At ten p.m., seven rugged Tibetan ponies stood packed off to the side of the main courtyard in a blue wash of moonlight—wooden saddle frames draped with brilliant yak wool rugs; silver studded harnesses; equine headdresses of embroidered silk cones and trails of ribbon, each indicating the rank of the rider; saddle-bags; leather canteens embossed with religious symbols; wool blankets; and holsters for a butter lamp and a riding crop. They bobbed their heads to adjust the caparisons and clopped their hooves on the smooth cobbles in anticipation of setting out. A young livery monk steadied each pony. A superior in the stables checked every binding and strap.

Through a side gate in the raked-back outer walls of the compound, a parade of porters loaded provisions for a long journey onto a score of yaks: bundles of every size, and crates with hand-cast metal hardware loaded with official garments, clothes for all weather, a small library of liturgical manuscripts, paintings of teachers and deities, paper, ink, brushes, tea, banners, bedding, tents, collapsible tables, kitchenware, gifts to ease the party's burden on those who would host them, and gold and silver to replenish all these things as the need arose. From any other point of view, such fanfare flew in the face of the intention to flee, but the nineteen-year-old abbot of the monastery, Chokyi Lodro Ngawang Selpo, Rinpoche, gauged that any deviation from eight hundred years of tradition would have needlessly upset those who were being left behind.

The abbot emerged from his residence with four reincarnate lamas, his secretary, and his bodyguard-monk. At the top of the wide stone stair that connected the great meditation hall to the courtyard, he halted. Only during his enthronement six months before had the space ever blazed with more butter lamps. He looked at the round faces of his people—scarlet cheeks and dark eyes.

"Stay steady," he said, only to find in the next breath that his words had fled. He felt the pulse of blood in his neck. Not a body moved. Even the babies were quiet.

He cleared his throat and tried again. "The life we cling to is . . . " There in a sphere of light he saw his little brother in the arms of his uncle. And over there, the old boot maker, Dundrup. And there, Chintso, the girl who once inspired him to question his monastic vows, now married and pregnant, leaning into her husband Gyaltsen, the handsome salt trader.

"This life we cling to is . . . is a dream. It can't be grasped." The meaning of the words settled on him like a lead cloak. To steady himself, he put a hand on a huge, red column that supported the mass of carved rafters and gargoyles above his head. "Please remember this. Those who harm others don't know they're tightening the ropes of their own suffering. When the soldiers come, let them see your kindness. Think only of their well-being." And to his monks he said, "Rely on what you've been taught. Your aspiration will carry me."

In the long silence that followed, images that Samten had spun out in his stammering and miming swelled in the abbot's mind stream: the snake of dust coming up the clay track from the river; Mao's troops trudging in hard-heeled boots under crisp banners flapping the Chinese character for "peace"; villagers lining their way in welcome—monks and lamas too—holding their white offering scarves; two Chinese officers on horseback throwing handfuls of little wrapped candies; Tibetans, young and old, playfully diving for them in the dirt; the gates of the monastery being opened and the elite guard entering; the sudden turning of the scene from cheerful to threatening; in full view of everyone, the rounding-up of the lamas and senior monks; the barking of commands that they renounce their elitist way of life and enter the communist family; Samten's abbot earnestly replying that Buddhists wish for the peaceful coexistence of all peoples; the Chinese commander seizing a novice monk, pointing his pistol at the boy's head and renewing his command for all the hierarchy to renounce their evil oppression of their Tibetan brothers; the abbot pleading for compassion for the child and the commander shooting the abbot in the head at close range; the selecting of teenage monks to shoot their teachers or to be shot themselves; the elders forgiving their students and the boys weeping as they complied; some shouting Buddhist mantras as, instead, they turned the weapons on themselves; the commander bellowing at their impudence and dragging a young woman into their midst, threatening to kill her unless they stopped their martyrdom; a young lama coolly assassinating the commander and then himself; soldiers firing at everyone wearing a robe; the seizing of girls and women and their shower of shrieking . . . at which point, Samten climbed down from his hiding place on the roof of the great meditation hall and began his escape uphill.

As the abbot mounted his pony in the courtyard, his old teacher suddenly called out from the main residence door. He hobbled across the space with a small bundle, leaned his weathered head close and said softly, "Rinpoche, my heart son, we almost forgot these." He peeled back a fold of blue and gold brocade to reveal the two scepters of the lineage, the keela and the dorjay. "You can't leave these here. The Chinese will melt the gold down for their teeth. At least with you, they have a chance of not being lost." He raised his yellowing eyes to the young man he had trained in every intricacy of mind and administration.

"You should be on this pony. Not me," said the abbot. "You have the polished wisdom."

His teacher shrugged and said, "But you're too valuable. They know that capturing you will strangle the will of this part of Tibet. And humanity can't afford to lose the gifts you're on the verge of mastering." He scrutinized his student. "Besides, I couldn't endure the trip," he said at last. "It's an old man's place to stay. I'll help here in the morning."

The abbot inhaled to argue, but seeing his teacher's resolve, he closed his mouth. "I'll take them with me," he said finally, sliding the bundle into his saddlebag. "And I'll return them. Somehow, I'll return them." He leaned over in his saddle. His teacher hooked a hand behind the abbot's neck. They pressed their foreheads together.

Then Chokyi Lodro Ngawang Selpo, Rinpoche, left through the main gate on a life's journey that took him over the Himalayas in midwinter, into renown in India, Europe and America. He taught simplicity and compassion as medicines for the Technological Age. In his later years, as the conditions for catastrophe strengthened, he dropped out of sight and lived with an outcast family in New England. When he knew his end was near, he entered a mountain retreat, composed one work of wisdom for survivors of the Dark Age and died without a witness.

1

Vermont

Twenty-Eight Years after the Unraveling

A winter moon rose late and breathed cold life into The Valley. Roused by the light, a buck, bedded down in his high-range recluse of spruces grown twisted in the wind, leapt up and snorted. Farther down the slope, an owl hunted the tangle of hardwoods and shadow. Three nights before, grinding and roaring, the river had shed its load of ice. And on the road beside the water, harnessed like an animal, a man (both healer and murderer) pulled a cart heading for the far side of the world. The two lineage scepters of Selpo, Rinpoche rode next to his skin concealed in holsters fit into the notches behind his upper arms.

He was used to being his own horse and he was built for labor, with powerful legs fluid under load. His breath condensed and his lips moved with his thoughts. Sometimes he even spoke outright. The light of the moon, a gift to any traveler, shimmered on his blue-black hair—a dead-straight mass pulled back to a horsetail—and it shined in his eyes. Asian eyes, black, from his mother's mother. A half step behind, sifting the man's talk for sounds of concern, a German shepherd, wearing saddlebags, walked with his head down, tuned to the message of boot heels. From their years together, man, dog and cart moved as one thing.

The road pulled away from the river and cut through the most fertile land in the North Country. A half a mile at its widest, The Valley was cradled between slopes of gray slate that had been ground into voluptuous curves in the last glacial age. The Indians had named the place The Hills Like Women Lying Down. But beside the road, woods were retaking the old farm fields. Poplar and sumac had invaded first. Now maple, birch and hickory stood twenty feet high. Still, around the ruins of the farmhouses, immense crowns of lilacs and rhododendrons waited for spring.

War had breached what a thousand seasons could not. Finally exposed, the hand-hewn timber frames were dissolving in the rains. When he was a boy, the man with the cart knew those houses, and knew the people who lived in them: McGowan, Herder, Sipple—Scot and Brit folk whose ancestors had come to the New World centuries before. Most were gone; they'd fled as soldiers in various uniforms pushed south and north and south again. True, some people had joined in with one side or the other or had been disposed of for simply defending their homes. Those who couldn't travel—the old and the weak—had died hiding in the hills; there were encampment ruins and bones up there.

After some miles, he came to the junction of a road to the west and felt the significance of his turn to that bearing; it would be his heading for a long time. He began to climb. When the hill hemmed a lively stream in close to the road, he and the dog paused for a drink. They noted its scent of stone and hemlock but didn't tarry long enough to let their second winds wither. Leaning into his harness, a smile spread in him. He was soft from winter but knew pulling would make him strong again.

They came to a line of steppingstones across the stream that led to a stand of ancient maple. The man felt the draw of the place and paused a second time. He wanted to enter—to listen with the sense of a deer to the voices of water, to stand like a tree, and to walk like an elephant—things the old Tibetan monk taught him on some of their outings there after he had been pulled from school in the village to avoid the beatings by the local children. His stomach tightened in the memory of a little boy's introduction to prejudice. He saw the load on the dog, remembered his mission and walked on.

As the dawn inched forward, the trees took hold of their cellular memory. "Pump! Pump life force into purple buds, beyond counting." And the air stirred. New saplings grew in the traveling lanes and the wheels of his cart jumped and rattled in fresh-cut gullies. "It's a good thing we're leaving here," he said to the dog, "else I'd have to start spending my time clearing roads." He looked at the fading stars and guessed he would make the meeting site close to sunrise.

The Valley Folk knew him as 'the son of those people from away.' The one who murdered Curtis and who atoned year after year hauling a cart. The one with the strange name. Zhampa. The Tibetan word for traveler or mule or bridge; they could never remember which. He carried seed in his cart around those hills, seed that kept hunger from turning country people into raiders. And he atoned with his skills as a healer; no one was refused his attention. The Valley Folk were glad for Zhampa's service. Twice yearly he traveled to far-flung hamlets—to the east in the fall and west in the spring—carrying news out and back, and, with it, a sense of belonging in an unraveled world. He brought seed and remedies, and returned with things like tools and thread, things given in exchange or found along the way. Mirrors and hooks, jars and wire. Yes, they were soothed by his deliveries, but they worried. How long could his body last?

Sensing they had come to rely on him too much and would make his departure difficult, Zhampa kept his plans to himself. And he left after midnight. The three people who had discovered he was leaving swore to keep his secret. And that night in March they headed to join him at Homer's Ledge, a slate cliff overlooking The Valley, a half mile off the road at the top of the rise.

Zhampa arrived sweaty from the long pull. He unhitched himself and the dog from their loads, then, sitting cross-legged on the precipice, watched the morning come. Light from the rising sun filled an overgrown meadow to the north. It spilled over the top of the old hedgerow into fields lower down. The beauty of it was seductive. "Oh, no," he said under his breath. "I won't." The dog raised his head a moment and looked at him intently.

Below, a red tail hawk rode the first down draft above the trees. It flew toward his family farm on the opposite slope, then veered south along the river. His father Eric DiOrio had cut that farm from the forest upon arriving in the area. A bowl of fields in the woods, sitting on a fold of earth above the valley floor. Zhampa eyed the house, the two barns, the ponds and the network of stone walls. Off to the left the best couple of acres a man could hope for had produced the seed that became the salvation for a whole generation in the North Country. And beyond them, the hundred year-old red oak stood guard for the three graves he had dug. From below, the complex was naturally hidden, sequestered at the base of the steep skirt of the mountain and accessible only through the mouth of the Hollow.

The place had been an island in the long stream of suffering . . . except, of course, for that February morning in the worst part of the Unraveling. Zhampa pursed his lips and his eyes fell on the remains of the place up the road toward the village. The buildings of Curtis' farm were burned flat, the fields a wasteland that had become a good place for blackberries. He shook his head. He would be glad to not have it as a reminder.

His eye traced the path above the DiOrio farmhouse. Past the row of compost bins stepped into the hillside. Past his mother's ginseng grove on the edge of the woods. On up the mountain skirt past the roof of the cabin his father had built to hide the old monk Rinpo, when the government sequestering of non-Christian groups first began. And higher still to the fan-shaped cliff the Valley Folk called the Scallop. He focused there on an auspicious deformity in the rock, the retreat cave where the monk had spent his last years in meditation. My Jewel of Refuge, Rinpo had called that south facing place. He checked behind his armpits for the scepters; they rode well in their leather holsters. Then he felt under his horsetail for the handle of the machete. It lay flat and concealed along his spine in its sheath. He had slit and re-enforced his shirt and vest to allow the blade coming out in a hurry. And he'd ground the edge sharp enough to shave hair.

In the spread of the hills, he saw the bodylines of women lying down. The burgundy tips of the endless tree-scape brushed against the blue Vermont sky. He marveled how The Valley had survived in that ruined century. The rugged land and the unpredictable climate made it a near-perfect place. Populations scrambling for warmth and food had taken their desperation elsewhere. The argument to leaving washed over him a last time. He could live there simply for the rest of his days—farming, delivering seed and healing people. But he'd made up his mind: If not now, then not at all. "I'll be too old, if I wait another winter," he said to the farm. And he flashed on Rinpo's advice:

Take your place in the flow of things.

The morning lay nearly mute. Still he failed to hear Oakley below him climbing the steep slope that ascended to the ledge, or to see him through the bare trees. Oakley had gifts in the forest that far exceeded his own, and his route was always confidential. It was the style of the man. Part heritage and part his way of coping with a life lived on the extremes. But something caused Zhampa to look over and, eighty feet below, a man carrying a huge pack with a tump line was scaling the cliff. Zhampa snorted in awe. Oakley'd come cross-lots straight up from the valley floor. And then up the rock.

"He's feeling his oats today," Zhampa thought. Moments later a ripe smell wafted up. A pair of gnarled and blackened hands with the ring finger gone locked onto the stone near his feet. A head with matted hair appeared wearing a triumphant grin. Years before, Oakley had left his front teeth on a barroom floor and without them, a smile gave him a cobra look. He bounded up in two quick moves, dropped his pack on the rock and hunkered down beside Zhampa. He was barely breathing hard.

"Your back is my business, Chief," Oakley said. The way he turned that ritual phrase—a leftover from his time in the Muslim Wars—always made Zhampa smile.

Though the land before him was brown and gray, Zhampa considered all the seasons as a man would when leaving friends. The green of summer days. The yellow and scarlet of autumn. Leaves blowing free in a gray world and covering the forest floor in a carpet of crackles. Geese wedging the sky east and west on their way to the Chesapeake and the Gulf. In their wake, he visualized the land waiting for snow; then it coming, gently at first; and then it pounding from the northwest. Wood stoves whistling inside the houses.

A lift of air brought him back to the present. His buttocks were cold. He shifted his flesh, then took three long breaths. "I don't know we'll see this place again," he said. Oakley opened his mouth to speak, then closed it. He sucked his lips in and nodded.

They heard Mercedes neigh as he came along the old carriage road—at that time just a path in the woods that bore off north to the village along the ridgeline. Mercedes was a glorious animal, a Morgan-Belgian, loaded that morning with two sets of panniers and the huge canvas tarp. A bow rode unstrung in a holster along his neck. Gabe, the young hunter, was leading him; his body was strong as a bullock's. Wisps of steam rose from the almost perfect globe of his head.

"Look at him, willya?" Oakley said.

"Go easy on him, Oakley."

"Not sure easy's the best way."

"You can't fault him. He's shaped for his time. And Jesus, he's got a lot of talent per pound."

"Talent needs direction, Chief."

Zhampa thought a moment. "There's two of us. We can handle him."

"Don't you get it? He wants his stripes. Wants to be what we are. The ugly part."

"I know." Zhampa's voice came tense.

"It's normal for a young buck to wonder what it's like to kill somebody. But he's found out that even the girl's got her stripes. Figures we three're good luck and he's next."

"That was different," Zhampa said, clipped. "She had no choice and you know it. She'd ha' been dead."

Oakley stilled. Then to someone who wasn't there he said, "Soldiers have never had a choice."

To Zhampa the boy was beautiful, but with Oakley's words ringing, he wondered if some paternal instinct had blinded his judgment. About the stripes he said, "He has no idea how heavy they are. It's our job to keep him from crossing over."

"He's loose, Chief. He's gonna foul us up."

"You'd have me send him back?"

"No dammit," said Oakley. "We need his bow."

"Okay then. We're his teachers. That's the size of it."

"I'll bet you he's gonna try to find a gun. It's all he thinks about."

"He promised me. No guns. He knows how I feel."

Oakley tipped his head in forced acquiescence "Just don't put him on my squad."

Zhampa laughed. "There's only four of us. You want separate quarters, too?"

Oakley looked away.

In the next instant they caught a flash of light in the woods below. Zhampa squinted in thought, then relaxed. The metal frame of the little solar panel had reflected the sun—old equipment from his father's day, but durable, still able to charge the cores for the two headlamps as they went. Celeste had made a special holder for it on her pack.

"The younger generation's bringing up the rear," he said to Oakley.

"Wish we had a couple more of those," Oakley said about the headlamps.

When the sun reached twenty degrees, the party was complete: Zhampa, a mixed-blood puller of carts; Oakley, the old scout; Gabe, an orphaned boy who could catch anything that moved; and Celeste, Zhampa's stepdaughter, a redheaded woman who carried a slew of her mother's gifts. As the others rested, Zhampa looked over at the Scallop, pondering the papers Rinpo had left for him on his retreat table, papers that predicted the Unraveling and that called him to action.

> *This is the darkest hour of a Dark Age, but don't waste time weeping. . . . Take the scepters home, Zhampa. Take them to the far side of the world, back to Tibet where they were forged. Though they have little value here, in the hand of an Enlightened One, their power is beyond concept. Take them to the monastery at the base of the Naked Red Lady Mountain. They will be expecting you and will know what to do. Take your place in the flow of things. Think beyond your valley. Do this for the welfare of all beings and for those who will come in the Next Age.*

The final time they were together, Rinpo had pulled the twelve year-old Zhampa close to him on the ledge outside the door of the retreat cave. He'd placed his finger to his lips and rolled the god scepter, the dorjay, in his hand. The overcast of the day swirled and parted. With the keela, the knife scepter, he sliced open the sky. Zhampa had stood transfixed by the lama's explanation of the image that rippled in the space outside the skin of the world. In that moment he promised Rinpo he would reflect on it every day. But a month later when he went off to the boarding school for gifted children, the image began to fade. Crowded out by the clamor of classes, rivalries and girls, his promise became unkept. In college the workload of medical studies helped erase all but the memory of something strange happening that day. Finally, the Unraveling and his murder of Curtis obliterated his interest in such things. For three decades Rinpo's intention awaited discovery. Papers written in longhand sat on a table in a cave in a corner of America.

Zhampa shook his head. He had labored for the last three years to understand what Rinpo had left him. Still, as he made ready to carry out Rinpo's command, he was uncertain of the line between reality and dream. At last he readied the dog, hoisted his pack and harnessed himself to the cart.

"It's a beautiful sight," he said to Celeste, whose eyes were glued to the farm. He headed over the shoulder of the hill on an old hunter's trail. Coco trotted at his heels.

2

No one spoke going down the mountain. Zhampa contemplated the point in the road west of the Seven Villages where he'd have to choose which shore of the Great Lakes to take. In a last scribbled note, Rinpo had advised: *As you travel, keep to the north whenever possible.* But concerned about wintering on the Canadian prairie, Zhampa wanted the southern shore. Of the others, Oakley walked in the lead, reading the sky and the land, gleaning information about food, shelter and direction for that day and the next. Gabe gave him wide berth; his jaw muscles worked. Maybe the two had already had words. Celeste's brooding was expected. Behind were spots of refuge, places thick with spearmint and elderberries, and private swimming holes. Ponds the beavers built, barns for her animals and, of course, the herb and medical workshop. Zhampa's journey had left her no good choices.

"We'll be wandering blind before we're thirty days out," he had said to her.

"I'm not staying here without you," she said.

"But you'll be safe here. It's a good life now. You can handle all the systems. And you know seeds as well as I ever will."

"It's too much work for one. And there's no partner for me here." The dish she held had trembled. "And who's to say danger won't show up in The Valley again."

Celeste's mother Claire had brought her to the DiOrio farm early in the fifth spring after the Unraveling. Unsure of what they would find, they made their way gingerly through the woods and concealed themselves at the base of a giant sugar maple. For an hour they watched for activity. When the sun was soon to set, Zhampa—stripped to the waist, olive-skinned and muscled across the shoulders—emerged from the greenhouse and walked up close with flats of plants. He knelt, making nests in the soil for plugs of cabbage. The sight of him brought Claire to life. She brushed Celeste's hair with her fingers and tied it up in the back. She knocked the leaves off both of them. Leaving their bundles, they climbed over the stone wall into the field. The garden soil was black and soft and, distracted by the skill of Zhampa's hands, Celeste stepped on a stick.

Hearing the crack of wood, Zhampa looked up. He tipped his head and was still for many seconds. Claire and Celeste were standing outside the fence, a green pointillism of new leaves behind. Vulnerable, watching for response from him, creating destiny, he thought, and acceding to it all at once. They were dirty but looked beautiful in that light. Claire wore a simple muslin dress, made formal with a few repairs. She had oversize boots, empty hands, and the grace to stand there waiting. The child was the miniature of her mother, a forefinger in her mouth, blinking. Without breaking eye contact, Zhampa rose.

"Claire," he began, but no other words would come.

"Jack's gone," Claire announced across the distance. "Some counter-militaries took him two years ago. Conscripted him." Her jaw tightened and her words trailed off. She glanced at her daughter and then surveyed the far hill line. She shook her head at something beyond sight.

"I never heard from him," she said. "Then last fall word came he'd been killed." She turned to look at Zhampa. "They ripped him from me. They threw his life away." A moment passed. Then her voice rising, she said, "I just didn't want to risk it up there another winter alone. Thought maybe you could use the help." She paused again. She looked at her daughter. "Maybe you're with someone."

Zhampa jerked into motion. He waved a finger at the gate, walked over and opened it. Approaching her, his breathing was loud in his ears, his face hot. Slowly he took Claire's hands and, feeling her permission, he wrapped them around his back. She released herself into his body.

"I'm not," he whispered into her hair. "Thank God, I'm not. I've never stopped thinking about you."

Dizzy, he held her a long while. Finally remembering the child, he dropped to one knee and leveled his eyes with hers. He brushed a whip of hair back from her cheek, and examined the knot in the back.

"You're lovely," he said. Celeste did not look away.

"She's absolutely lovely," he said to Claire. And then to Celeste he asked, "Would you like to come down to the house to see Whizz? I'm sure he'd love the company."

"Who's Whizz?" Celeste asked.

"Whizz is the cat here. He's a big fur ball, and he loves to be scratched."

Celeste nodded with drama, as if trying to shake a hat off her head, and she let Zhampa hold her hand on the walk down. Under his other arm, he carried their two bundles.

And they moved in. Twice that summer Zhampa made the four-day trip to the higher mountains, bringing back their valuables—blankets, pots, a few books, some silver, a bolt of fabric, a wind chime, a hand-operated flour mill, a picture of Jack and a cloth rabbit worn from cuddling.

Ten years later, as she lay dying, Claire whispered to them both, "Take care of each other." They had, the best they could, but Zhampa still blamed himself for Celeste's abduction.

Ahead lay soft, undulating territory, with deep soil and small streams. Once woods, cropland and villages had occupied that land in gracious proportion, but even before the Unraveling those communities shriveled with the changes. In the years of his seed deliveries, Zhampa wasn't surprised by the disappearance of the few souls that had dared to hang on.

"We'll have to be careful about travelers around the Hudson," he told the others as they camped in a bosk of cottonwoods that first night, their boots drying in a circle by the fire. "The folks who use the river aren't the same as we're used to. Might be coming from tougher places." He bent down to check the biscuits in the reflector oven and stirred the coals with a stick. His high cheekbones shone in the light.

"How many days 'til we get there?" asked Celeste. "A week?"

"No. Four, I'm hoping. Depends on the mud."

"Actually we got snow ahead, Chief," Oakley said.

It came the next day. Storm clouds swept over a pale sun. As the air cooled, they pressed toward an isolated shed; snowflakes the size of fingernails padded the world silent. Two days later, when they set out again, the roads were soft and slick, but the sun was warm and they reached the river at dusk, six days out.

The two southern bridges along that fifty-mile stretch of the Hudson had been destroyed in the fighting. But in an abandoned mill town, water poured over a falls on a river bend. The deep water hugged the near bank, and years before, Zhampa had figured out how to cross over the remains of the steel bridge built there in the previous century. Twisted girders still linked the shore to the middle abutment. From there he would wade through the shallow section of river where the second span had dropped below the falls.

That year, ice flows and a whole tree were packed up over the girders. Having unloaded Mercedes, Gabe rode him bareback upstream to find a slow place to coax him across, while the others cleared the ice and debris with axes. By midday, all the gear and the dog were settled on the foundation rim of the middle abutment. The current wasn't swift there, but a chest-deep pool had been hollowed out right off the platform. Letting loose an involuntary whoop, Zhampa leapt in with his pack held overhead, bulled his way across to shore and built a roaring fire on the far bank to warm himself between trips.

In late afternoon Gabe appeared dry and grinning. He'd had to go quite a spell up-river, he said, and had had a run-in with three fellows who wanted to take his horse.

"Guns?" Zhampa asked.

"A rifle," Gabe said. "A rusty old club. Didn't look as if it'd been fired in forever. And I figured they prob'ly didn't want to waste a shot on me, but just in case, I didn't stay 'round long enough to find out. They saw my bow, too, and I guess they figured I could bite back." He smiled through pride-pursed lips.

"Prob'ly no ammo," Zhampa said.

Gabe shrugged. "I took off north and went a few more miles to a smooth section and found some stones out into the water. Got Mercedes most of the way over and suddenly we both dropped in over our heads. Had to swim the last." His pantomime of shock made Zhampa smile.

"I dried off at my own fire," he said. "And those same losers were cussin' at me from across the river on my way back."

"Shit!" Oakley said. "They saw you?"

"Yuh." Gabe's eyes moved to the base of the fire and Celeste stiffened. Her fingers wrapped around the handle of the knife that hung between her breasts.

"Think, asshole. Think. Never be seen twice." Oakley shook his head and his voice was hot. "We got to go, Chief. They could be coming down-river to cross. They must know this spot." Objects began flying with precision from his hands into the cart and the open bags. He kept checking the far shore.

Zhampa knew it was best to pay attention when Oakley moved like that. "Let's go," he said.

Celeste jumped in with the tasks, but Gabe hung back. They shoveled dirt onto the fire and went off double-time, not yet fully dry, staying on pavement when they could, to leave no trail. If Oakley slept that night in the cinderblock building they found in the edge of the next town, it was sitting up by the back door with his knife in his lap. When the sun rose, they were long gone.

They made a beeline across the thirty-mile stretch of asphalt, wasting neighborhoods and city centers that stretched from the old resort lake in the north through Albany and south. Crossing this region on his annual trips to the Seven Villages, Zhampa had witnessed the evanescence of things. Something—he presumed tanks—had chewed the pavements raw; water and frost worked the cracks deeper. During the fighting or the exodus that followed, fire had blazed everywhere. The carcasses of buildings moldered in a brisk growth of wild plants. He had scavenged through every one that was upright, but had found little. Cabinets, doors, flooring, and glass had all been taken. So at his lead, the travelers put their shoulders to their loads, hushed their talk and marched until they came to a stream running in its natural bed and trees that were older than any of them. They set up camp quickly and slept hard, leaving dinner for the morning.

They were five days cutting through the southern foothills of the Adirondacks, and a cold rain forced them to hunker down for a sixth. There they nursed a fire under Gabe's tarp. Celeste baked a bannock and Oakley dug out a pair of winter-slowed bullfrogs. While Zhampa was preparing some of the previous fall's cattail roots for the pot, two young men worn down to the bone stumbled out of the undergrowth. They were moving against the current, they explained, because things to the south had continued to be unbearable.

"We left in the middle of winter about ten weeks ago," said the older of the two. "Wanted to get out of there before the roads dried. Figured we'd be south of the snow line the whole way and still keep ahead of the spring thieves."

"There were three of us," said the other. "My woman, his sister," he said, motioning toward his partner, "was with us, but she died about twenty days back. She came down with a fever and we couldn't get her warm."

The youths became quiet.

"Where was home, boys?" Zhampa asked.

"Outside of Cumberland," said the brother of the dead girl, pulling at his straggly beard.

"Cumberland. Cumberland, Maryland?"

The brother looked vaguely at his companion and the latter offered, "Mister, we just know it as Cumberland. It's beyond Philly."

"Yeah. No matter. Go dry off by the fire. We have food enough to share."

Because Mercedes clearly made the boys nervous, Zhampa knew they were unlikely to find a fit in any of the communities in the North Country. Every settlement had a story about the stress of newcomers. Best to let fate sort out the big issues, he concluded. So he said nothing about the bridge or river. Instead he instructed Gabe to show them how to use a fire bow and to give them one of theirs. In the morning they left the pair with the memory of a good fire and deep sleep.

A westerly wind brought cumulus clouds as they came to the first of the Seven Villages. At each farm, mowed fields and split rail fences surrounded a stable of groomed horses. Mercedes flared his nostrils and quickened his gait. Gabe started to yammer, until finally Celeste asked, "You thinking you might have found a new home?"

"Hell, no," the hunter said with a snort. "I'd get bored hanging around with chores to do all day."

Zhampa's early arrival, and with companions and gear for a long trip, was big news in the Seven Villages. It told of the passing of the era of the man coming with seed. Everywhere they went, they ate well—bread, corn cakes and pork dishes. They slept comfortably in hay barns.

As was customary Zhampa set up a clinic in the middle-most hamlet, and the injured and the ill came in a steady stream. They lay on his table and let him manipulate their joints. He took their pulses and read their irises. He stuck his hairbreadth needles into energy points. And he prescribed herbs as treatment. He moved smoothly in the big parlor-turned-hospital, speaking in low tones to his patients and conferring with his two apprentices. Delhia was making great progress in the healing arts, he felt. Her intuition guided her hands, as if she were milking energy from the air itself. Her people would be well cared for after his departure, which allowed him to set aside a tension he hadn't known he carried.

On the morning of the fourth day, the rain stopped. Those families that could get away gathered for a farewell picnic for Zhampa. They came on foot and in an assortment of horse-drawn vehicles. Baskets, utensils and blankets were unloaded. Instruments and fire-blackened pots appeared. The children swirled like dry leaves in a wind. Older girls moved as a service army, instructing the young men to carry tables and split wood. A great blaze was kindled.

Not permitted to help, the travelers wandered and chatted with the older folk. They sipped a garnet-colored applejack and they watched two pigs being rotated over a fire of coals. The smoke and tang of burning fat filled the air. Late in the afternoon, a newly betrothed couple struck a metal gong fashioned from an old oil tank end cap. Commotion stopped. Parents forcibly held the little children as an old man stood on a chair and addressed the gathering. He spoke, almost chanted, a grace of sorts, not to a Christian god but to an overarching deity who was, "Manifest among us," he intoned, "in the light and the trees and in the power of the soil. Manifest in the wind that brings us the rain and the seasons. Manifest in the hearts of our elders, in the smiles and blushes of our young adults, and in the hands and feet of our young. Manifest here for our taking all the days of our lives. And hear me now. Nothing, I say, nothing, no words uttered by man or woman can describe adequately the wonder of birth and life and the final dissolution of all things back into the earth. Earth from which new life will come again . . . if we only take care of it."

As he spoke, teenagers slipped away from the clutch of people, holding their stomachs in silent laughing. Adults nodded at his words. Others waited politely, eyeing the feast on the tables. With the prayer ended, these souls, Oakley and Gabe among them, rushed for the food. The old scout made a stealthy exit with a heaped bowl and a tankard of drink. He settled in the leafless orchard where the sun sliced through the black shapes in long diagonals, a place where he could see everyone, but not hear their talk.

Gabe sat across from several young women. He wore his hunter's face and said little.

Before the food was finished, a series of toasts began. Testimonials and praises to Zhampa—who he was and what he symbolized. As people spoke, he chewed his cheek and looked at the ground. He stumbled through the few sentences he gave in response to their calls for 'Speech, Speech' and felt embarrassed by the quizzical looks on the faces near him. But Celeste put the world back right by offering a toast to the goodness of the folk of the Seven Villages. She thanked them for their hospitality, then launched into a stunning tribute to "My father," she called him, "who in spite of all the wonderful things he's done so far in his life, has his greatest service yet to come." Fearing the alcohol might make her say too much, Zhampa flashed her a look.

"I'll follow you wherever you go," she said raising her glass to him. And during the cheers, she sucked heartily on it and mixed back into the crowd.

After the food was devoured, the dancers exhausted, the dishes cleared, and the awnings furled, a sea of hands and hugs offered what words only mimic. Farewells and invitations—should the travelers return—were hooted into the night, as the back ends of wagons moved into darkness on their way home.

3

The knife that hung around Celeste's neck was not given to her. Seven months after her mother died—the summer she turned sixteen—she'd gone alone out of the Hollow in search of herbs to make a tincture for bleeding lungs. Zhampa milked the goats when she didn't return in time to do it. By sundown he began looking for her. In the morning he discovered her walking stick and four sets of footprints but lost the trail in a hard rain. He enlisted two Valley men to help, but they found no leads. Throughout that summer he circled through the North Country looking for her. One family in the eastern direction had been victim to a party of four, but the description of the woman didn't seem to fit. She was tough, they said, and they misjudged her build. They didn't remember seeing red hair, so he looked no further.

But it was Celeste they had seen. She had been made servant and concubine to a trio of young murderer-thieves. When it dawned on her that pregnancy would make her expendable, she used blue cohosh, tansy and Queen Anne's lace to work with her moon. To ward off their brutality she honored them and feigned willing wife to three. And she studied their every habit.

Over the weeks, they pushed eastward, consuming the meager supplies of others. In Indian summer they came down upon a neighborhood of three pitiful houses in the sandy lands of New Hampshire. Her captors terrorized the families, and executed the two men who resisted. When they laughed at their crimes, Celeste clapped her hands, imitating joy. Though there was little of value in the houses, they made off with several crocks of home-brew and camped beside a waterfall up a gravel trail. That night she served a stew and drank some of the alcohol. The men became loud and boastful by the fire and when the smaller two stood to pee in the falls, she whispered to the strongest, "I want you for the whole night. Help me bed these two, so they'll sleep like stones and not disturb us."

Excited, he challenged his friends to a contest of drink, offering Celeste as prize. The unsuspecting two drank until they couldn't speak, and when they dropped into hard sleep, she lay down with the last. When he, too, slept, she rolled him off and over, slipped his knife from his trouser sheath and cut him deep through the neck arteries and vocal box. He surfaced from dream, locked eyes with her, raised a clumsy hand as if to make a point, then garbled and fell back, body and soul traveling separate ways. And because of the sound of the falls and the liquor in their blood, his companions slept through their own murders.

She returned what little she could to the survivors of the three homes, but they were most cheered by the news that she brought. In gratitude they packed her the few things they could spare and gave her bearings to Vermont. With the murder knife as talisman around her neck, she made her way back to the Hollow by the harvest moon, her former life a tray of dropped crystal.

Since then, that knife had tapped her solar plexus with every step she had taken. It tapped out a new rhythm as she and the others rode horses out of the Seven Villages toward that fork in the road that Zhampa had imagined for many months. Stuart, a sandy-haired youth rode along with them, leading them to the edge of his world, where he was told by his father to bid them farewell and bring the horses home. In that new order, Celeste found herself sandwiched between Oakley and Zhampa in the rear and Gabe and Stuart in the lead.

Under long gray skies the hills gave way to a tableland made interminable by the shag of trees thriving along countless wallows and leaden creeks. Circling north of two small cities, they cut through a devastated place of houses packed close.

"How many people used to live around here, do you think?" Gabe asked.

"Don't know," Stuart said. "A ton, I guess. Looks like they loved living on top of each other. Funny with all the land there is." He rode quiet a minute, then said, "Pap says everybody forgot how to grow food. Relied on deliveries."

"Forgot how to hunt it," Gabe said. "Must have been tough when things fell apart."

"Pap says there was so many guns it was a shooting carnival."

"What's a carnival?"

"Don't know exactly. Worse than war, though. He says places where people bought stuff were cleaned out. Then neighbors fought each other for the stuff they'd stolen. A man would kill for a pair of boots. When it got cold, people made for the warm country. He wasn't down this way, my pap. Came from the east, but he said the stink of rotting bodies was in every wind for a year or more. Didn't matter where you were. It settled on the land with the rain, and the snow too. One long brown stink."

"Must have been worse here. Wasn't like that in Vermont."

"We weren't born yet. . . . Hey, d'you ever see a car go?" Stuart said pointing to rusting a hulk along the road.

"No," Gabe said.

"Me neither," he said. "Not sure I want to."

"I'm happy right here on Mercedes." Gabe stroked his horse's neck. "I wonder what it's like down south. I kinda want to go."

"I'll stay north," Stuart said. "My pap and my ma say it's safer."

"Wicas said that, too. Better off staying where it's tough."

"Wicas your pap?"

"Kind of. Taught me everything," Gabe said.

Zhampa heard Wicas' name in the wind and nodded. His relationship with Wicas started out badly but got steadily better when the bachelor discovered Zhampa's healing skills and his seed stocks. Wicas was tough as gristle, but he showed his heart in the ease with which he scooped up Gabe when his parents were killed. He schooled the boy on weather and signs, on trails and trees. He pointed out the dens of the bear, where the badger lived. By the time he was ten, Gabe could give a fair count of the ducks, geese, and hawks within twenty miles of home. Wicas taught him the deer herd, showed him how to bring down the weakest. They swapped their kill with those who grew crops, though for them a vegetable was more a thing of color than of necessity.

Zhampa flashed on the day Wicas breathed his last, his face gray and waxy, his body stretched out in the wagon wrapped in a putrid blanket. Gabe, a rugged little thirteen, had driven Wicas over himself in a downpour, carrying the old man for treatment for the cough that killed him.

"Take me to the healer," Wicas had wheezed out to the boy. But, he'd waited too long.

"Anyway," said Stuart, "my folks wandered against the flow and finally joined in with the families in the Seven Villages."

"I don't need to farm," Gabe said.

"No? Huh. There's more than one way, I guess."

"Oh, yeah." Then Gabe gave a long discourse on hunting.

"May come in handy someday, this bow stuff," Stuart said.

"You know it will. Listen here. Never kill in the same place. Spooks 'em too much. It's not what you think. They're as smart as you and me. They remember where one of their own goes down. . . . "

Two days later they crossed a river and walked the edge of a long marsh. They camped in a wood and fell asleep to the chorus of peepers.

Zhampa awoke to a low growl from Coco and Gabe's voice. "Mister, you so much as twitch and this arrow will go clean through you. And before you start bleeding, a second one will pin you to that cart." On the edge of the camp, Gabe stood in slanting shafts of amber light, his bow in full-draw. Before him a lanky figure was frozen bent over with his hands on Zhampa's gear. "Not even an eyelid." Then to the others, he said, "We got company."

"You armed?" It was Oakley's voice, his frame standing where he had slept.

"No." The man's voice was short of air. "Yes. I mean, no."

"Which is it?" Gabe said.

"Don't shoot me."

"Wait, Gabe," said Celeste.

"You got one more time to get it right," said Gabe. "Do you have a gun?"

"Yes, but there's no bullets in it."

"Celeste," Zhampa said, "put the head lamp on him. Let's see what we got."

"I heard the horses shifting, Zhampa. Woke me up. Good thing I had the bow down."

"Yeah, Gabe. Nice work."

The man's hair was long and black, months foul; his face gaunt above the beard. His shoulders boned up through the wool of his long-coat.

"Are you alone?" Zhampa said.

The man replied by sucking in his lips and nodding.

"There are no others?"

"Not that wouldn't take pleasure in killing me."

"Where are they?"

"In the city."

"What city?"

"Rochester."

"How far are we from there?"

"Five miles from where the houses begin. They don't come out here."

"Who are they?"

"You the mayor of Rochester or something?" Oakley asked.

The man coughed a laugh. "There's nobody living there anymore. Just the gangs that roam the streets."

"Why don't you put your gun out here very slowly," Zhampa said, "so we can get rid of that detail."

The man untied the cloth rope that replaced the function of buttons and fished in his garments for a small pistol.

"Yeah, Chief. He's right. It's not loaded."

"I told you. Haven't had bullets for three years. That's why I'm on the outside and they're on the inside."

"They have ammo in the city?" The man nodded. "Okay, thanks Gabe. But keep your arrow notched. What's your name?"

"William."

"Why are you here?"

"I'm hungry."

"No, I mean, why not leave? There are other places."

"I can't live out there." He waved a hand away from the city. "There's still cans in the houses sometimes. And cats when I can catch 'em."

"Nice," said Stuart. Celeste groaned.

"There are other cities," Zhampa said.

"Not that way," William said pointing west. "They're all gone."

"How so?"

"White lighters, of course. Where have you been?"

"We live in Vermont," Celeste said. "Zhampa, can we let him sit down? Can we all sit down?"

"White lighters?" Zhampa said. "Have you been there?"

William shook his head. "Don't need to go. Nobody's ever come here from the west."

"Buffalo?"

William shook his head again.

"Pittsburgh?"

"No. Not for more than twenty years. The Globalliance took out the America that worked."

"So it's true, Oakley."

Oakley nodded. "I guess we knew it in our bones, Chief."

"That pretty much makes the decision for us, doesn't it? We're going north across the lake."

No one slept the rest of the night and being close to the city, they lit no fire in the morning.

"So you know the land outside the city?" Zhampa asked William.

"Yeah, it's my safety zone. I go back into the neighborhoods when I have to forage. Their scouts make a lot of noise when they move, so I've figured out how to come and go."

"And they're armed?"

"People left a lot of guns lying around."

"And how many gangs did you say?"

"Two main ones. And there's always subgroups and overthrows. That's what happened to me."

"You were a leader?"

"For a long time."

"Here's an idea, William. We feed you for a couple of days, you lead us to the lake."

William didn't think long before agreeing.

"How do you know we can trust him?" said Gabe. Celeste and Stuart leaned in to hear the answer.

"How about if I draw you a map," William said, "and when things aren't as I draw, then you send me packing."

"That takes care of the daylight. At night we'll tie him foot to foot to you, Gabe. You both willing?"

Gabe finally nodded. They broke camp and traveled east of the city and north toward the lake. William's landmarks ran true and they camped when he said they were close to the water. As Oakley and Zhampa made ready to explore the shore, Celeste came to them. "I won't stay with three men," she said. Both men nodded.

Later, seeing she was leaving with them, William said, "If she were mine, I'd have her cut her hair and wrap her tits tight. A woman is a prize gangs will kill for."

"But you said they're not interested in the lake. And we're—what? Twenty miles east of Rochester?"

"I'm guessing. Suit yourself."

"I'll cut it," she said. "And thanks."

Around sundown on the first of May, Celeste, Oakley and Zhampa set off on foot with two days food to see the lake at first light. Zhampa swung his machete for hours cutting a path through apple orchards overgrown with vines. It was well after midnight when they heard the muffled sound of waves in the still air. When they pushed through the brush, the lake opened before them under an almost-full moon. Celeste had never seen a body of water without another shore and, starting at dawn, she sat mesmerized as they scanned for boats. They saw none.

Finally Zhampa said, "I'm out of my league here, Oakley. How are we going to cross this?"

"No problem, Chief. Just need a good boat. David Oakley, US Marines. Honorable discharge May sixteenth, 2028. Rank, Second Lieutenant. Part of our training was at sea. Small sailing vessels, . . . Sir." He finished with a two-finger salute, as if tossing a cigarette.

"I thought I knew everything about you," Zhampa said with a laugh. "Okay, Lieutenant, which way would you suggest we start?"

Oakley pointed west.

The walking was tough; three-foot wide beaches of rolling stones edged by a sheer four-foot bank topped with brush. Occasionally concrete steps led to the remains of summer homes, but there were no signs that there had ever been boathouses along that shore. They grew grim at their prospects. On the second morning they climbed a lone bluff with straight drops to the water and on the heights several mansions with overgrown grounds lined up with views to the north, black holes where their windows had been. The biggest of these sat on a promontory sticking out into the lake. A path led down to the water on carefully set switchbacks. At the bottom, a sheltered cove.

"Boat house, Chief." Ancient willows concealed a two-bay house with its lake-side aspect collapsed. Tucked inside the debris a twenty-one-foot open cockpit day sailer hung in a sling.

"*Felicity*. Rochester," Zhampa read.

"Four in this boat?" Oakley said. "With all our gear? Risky."

Felicity's hull was sound and her mast was folded down lengthwise with its rigging intact. Oakley said it would be easy to raise it again. And when they discovered the sails missing, Celeste suggested they use Gabe's tarp.

By mid-afternoon they had much of the waterside of *Felicity*'s boat house cleared of debris and Oakley took off for the inland camp to get the others and the tools to cut a beam that was too large to move out of the way.

The following morning they split into teams: Oakley and Zhampa cut out the beam, saving it long for use as a spar hanging out over the water. Oakley carved a hole in the far end of it and drove in a section of galvanized pipe. Celeste and Stuart sewed patches on the tarp. Gabe and William searched for cable and something to use for a pulley. Around noon a spliced length of cable and chain was fastened to the stern of the boat sling and given two turns around a rim of a small tractor wheel, lying flat over Oakley's pipe. The other end was rigged to a pair of Stuart's horses on the opposing beach of the cove, and with every small step of his team, the boat in its sling inched down the concrete ramp. When it floated free, everyone cheered.

"Not leaking much," said Oakley. And after raising the mast and tightening the rigging, they celebrated over a meal of pike. Next, they laid *Felicity* on her side in shallow water and cut the tarp into a sail. Lacking fittings, they bound the grommets to the boom and mast track hardware with triple-wound baling wire that Oakley had insisted on carrying. And with that, Oakley took her for a trial sail in the protection of the cove and then out onto the lake.

"She's a pretty good boat," he said as he glided back in. "Still didn't see any others out there."

"How's the wind?" Zhampa said.

"Not bad."

"By my map, I figure it's a little over fifty miles, straight across. Could we make it in a day?"

"I think we should try a night crossing, Chief. The wind'll be down and we'll be harder to see if there's other boats out there."

As they began working on their loads to fit into the boat, Gabe announced. "I'm not going."

Zhampa glanced around. Celeste was nodding to herself. "What do you mean, 'not going?'"

"My horse and I are one thing. We don't get separated."

Zhampa slapped his head. "It didn't even dawn on me, Gabe." He thought a moment. "We need you. If we split up, our chances for success stink."

"Mercedes can come to a great life on our farm," said Stuart. "I'll take care of him 'til you get back."

Gabe hrumphed through his nose. He looked at Zhampa, and then at Stuart. "They're not coming back."

"What's your plan?" Zhampa said. "Back to The Valley?"

"William and I are going to make a land run."

Celeste looked at William "Land run? To where?"

"We've been talking. William's got unfinished business in the city. Then we're going to pick up some rifles, cross the lake further on and meet up with you along the way."

"But you heard for yourself," Zhampa said. "The land west of here is ruined."

"He hasn't been there to find out. You haven't been there. I want to find out if there was White Lighters. I've been hearing about them my whole life."

"Well, suit yourself, Gabe," said Zhampa. "But like I told you, if you get guns, just stay on your own. Find your own adventure."

"Gabe," said William, "I've changed my mind. I'm not going with you."

The hunter wheeled on him. "What? We talked it all out the other day."

"Yeah, we did. And you're a stinger with a bow. But we're dreaming. We won't survive the city." He turned to Zhampa. "I'm asking to come with you. If Gabe doesn't take the place, can I come?"

Gabe dismissed the lot of them with the back of his hand and looked to loading his horse. Zhampa dragged Oakley up by the boathouse and talked as passionately as he knew how. After, he took Gabe across the cove. His arguments and even his lie about Wicas's deathbed request to watch out for him changed nothing. He was wasting his breath on the boy. He warned him again about crossing over the line and told him the poison that killing brings. But in the end, he saw Gabe was much like he himself used to be. Sure about things he knew little of. He realized that young men were wound to move a certain way. So on the shore of that great lake, after awkward words and silences during the packing of Felicity, the band of six became a band of four. Gabe and Stuart made ready for opposite land routes. The two riders waited until late afternoon to see the boat off. Felicity was out about two miles and seemed to moving well with two and a half more hours of daylight when Stuart headed overland back to his precious hills with his father's tie of horses following behind. Gabe accompanied him to the top of the rise. He said farewell, looked out to see a twenty-mile vista of lake and land heading west, and with no threat from the sky, pushed Mercedes toward the city.

4

William became ill as soon as he set foot in *Felicity*. Oakley tried to pacify him in the calmer waters of the cove, but William wasn't prepared for swells of the lake, the lifting and falling, nor for the spanking of wave crests along the hull, for the boiling song as she parted the lake, and certainly not for the pitch of the boat or the tacking as they made their way up wind—beating one way, then turning hard, the main boom sliding overhead and the wind catching her sail, pulling her leeward gunwale recklessly down to the water.

"A boat's built to float, Mister," Oakley said, looking away. But they were heavily loaded. Even he was cautious about where everything sat. The cockpit was full. With each tack, bodies, packs, the dog and the contents of Zhampa's cart complicated the climb to windward. Tension defeated grace.

Once underway, Oakley said little. He looked at the sail—its free edge and how it rattled, and by the mast to check how it was catching the wind. He looked at the waves and the ripples that scampered up their backsides, and over his shoulder at the shore to see their progress.

When William let out a woof at seeing a *slosh* of water in the bilge, Oakley said, "If it gets bad, we'll bail."

On the main lake, the wind came more from the northwest and Oakley changed course to make the most of it. *Felicity* got out of sight of land with the last of the light. The breeze held, allowing her to make good speed through the first quarter of night. Later, it faltered, then quit, leaving her bobbing in the waves. The sail flapped, the boom creaked in constant motion. William descended into vomiting. And the smell of his retching made Celeste sick. In response, Oakley tied off the tiller and snored in his spot. Eventually Zhampa, too, fell into bobbing dreams, with a hand clenching the harness of the cart, which was lashed upside down on the little deck in the bow.

He awoke to the resonant smacking of water along the hull of his dream—his neck stiff, Celeste lying on his leg, William breathing fetid air close by, and Oakley at the tiller. Underway. Sailing. Crossing Lake Ontario. Yes.

"It's about four, Chief. We have weather," and he gestured his head west without looking there. The moon had a red cast and was burying itself in a ridge of gray cloud, low to the horizon.

"What's our direction?"

"Same, but the wind's changed. From the South. We're on a run. I'm starting to think that it'll be good to see that shore line."

"How far have we come, do you think?"

"Hard to tell. Prob'ly twenty-five miles when we ran out of wind. We've been under way for a little more than an hour. Call it eight miles."

"Thirty-three. Another twenty or so. How worthy is this little tub?"

"Not good to speak disrespectful of the boat you're in, Chief. She's not bad . . . in a moderate wind." Then he did look west and at the sail and ahead. And they spoke no further until the light and the increased hum of the water alongside woke Celeste, and William after her. They both seemed to understand the shape of things and asked no questions. All eyes forward. *Felicity* heading downwind, almost as fast as the waves.

Clouds arrived, low and writhing, and, with them, more push from the wind. The boat strained. Then for a short time, a confusion of sunlight illuminated a long expanse of gray froth before them. And a band of purple brown.

"We got a landfall, Chief."

"Looks more like we got ourselves a race," Zhampa said. "Celeste, William, let's think here. The last hundred feet is the important part."

"I can't swim," William said.

Zhampa paused. "You're going to learn today. Right now we need to figure how to save the gear. Particularly the spoilable stuff." He organized them to bundle and wrap the seed and the food.

When they had closed to within two miles of the shore, Oakley headed *Felicity* to the northwest. "I'm seeing a low ground there, off to port," he said as he trimmed the sail. "We need a beach. Hang on. It's going to be a little rough." *Felicity* pounded as the swells rolled under her. Then came the rain—not heavy, but wind-whipped. But as the shore approached, Oakley hollered, "Don't like what I'm seeing, Chief. Breakers too far from shore. Too shallow, too soon." He turned *Felicity* back hard to the north running before the wind again. "We'll have to take our chances with the steeper land."

"William. Celeste," Zhampa said. "Tie your boots onto your packs."

With two sharp reports, like windows snapping in an arctic cold, the boat lurched to starboard. Wind poured by the mast through a trough in the sail.

"Our bailing wire's popping," Zhampa said.

Felicity dragged and a wave broke over the stern, putting six inches of water into her bilge. William let slip a wail. Oakley's knife flashed at the main sail sheet and, one-handed, he threw six feet of rope to Zhampa.

"Shove that through the grommet if you can," he said, "and pull like hell." Zhampa looped the rope around the mast and through the tarp. Together, he and Celeste closed the sail some. *Felicity* picked up speed.

"Here comes the land. I'm steering us to the left of those rocks. Little sand flat there. Our best shot."

Fifty yards from shore, *Felicity* scraped the bottom with her keel, knocking everyone off his feet. Coco pawed the air. The next wave lifted her and shot her forward, out of control. Oakley had the tiller hard over. She wanted to broach into the hollow of the breakers, but she surfed oddly on the next wave and straightened out for shore.

"Get ready to jump, but keep your hand on her," Oakley said. "We'll ride her in. Now. Everybody out."

"William, in front of me," Zhampa said. And William went. Zhampa behind with a handful of his coat. Celeste over the other side. Coco up, barking but still on board. Oakley milking the steerage and then finally he, too, over the stern, all of them chest-deep in the foam and the rip, hanging onto *Felicity* and then as the next wave came, all lifted and dropped again. And again. *Felicity*, done with her task and lifted aft by the next swell, caught her bow in the sand; her stern swung hard to starboard, crosswise to the surf and laid that gunwale toward the shoreline. Coco and two packs flew into the water. Everything tumbling.

"William," Zhampa said, "take these. Get on the beach." When Celeste cried out that she was pinned to the hull by the waves, Zhampa pushed through the breakers around the bow, only to see Oakley carrying her like a bundle around the stern, running her up on land. Things were in the water. A cart wheel floating, an ax underfoot. With hardly a word they formed a baggage brigade—Zhampa, Oakley, William in the water up to his thighs and Celeste on the sand, hobbling and grunting. Coco beside her, concerned, barking, whirling.

Celeste and William rigged the unused part of the tarp into an awning in a poplar grove a hundred yards inland. Zhampa and Oakley made trips to *Felicity* to get the cart body, Oakley's rope and things that washed up.

In the morning the rain held off under dark skies and to the sound of the waves crushing *Felicity* into the shore, all hands helped to sew the sail back into a tarp. Coco took off hunting for himself as he would do—seeking rabbit, squirrel and frog. Ten minutes later they heard him barking up the hill. Something in the sound struck Zhampa. He leapt up and ran in that direction. Oakley took off, too, pulling the hatchet from the fire log without breaking stride. He headed into the woods in a line tangent to the sound. William looked around for cover and Celeste released the snap on the sheath of her breast knife. A second dog yelping. Then a rifle shot and silence.

Zhampa broke into a clearing to see Coco flexed and motionless. His teeth were clamped on the throat of a crossbreed pit bull, its body jerking, its eyes rolled up as if to catch a glimpse of a daytime star. Zhampa saw the figure and the rifle, but went to his dog. He kneeled and put his hands on the body. At his name, Coco opened his jaws, breathed out a groan, and died. Zhampa heard the rifle fall to the ground. A pair of small, weathered hands appeared opposite his, one on each dog. Only when the voice broke into full-throated grieving did he realize the shooter was a woman. Two people, two dead dogs. Nearby, the causal rabbit.

That was how Oakley found them, coming up into the clearing from behind with his hatchet out ready to use it in short strokes to cleave harm from his friends and how he caught a rare glimpse of Zhampa without his armor. Eyes wide like a young boy's, looking at the vacant face of the dog and snapping his head to shake the reality out of his consciousness. He threw off an appeasing touch of the woman. "Not again," he yelled. "Not again. God damn, not again."

Oakley sheathed his hatchet and walked into the woman's line of sight. He motioned that she consider leaving Zhampa alone, which she did after lingering on her own loss. Gathering her rifle, she followed Oakley down the hill.

Zhampa had nothing to offer Coco at the end. Wanting nothing of people, he set off uphill, weaving and slipping on the leaf mold of the forest floor, hugging the carcass, the head lolling over his shoulder. A bench of land with a strong rock behind and a view of the lake called him. He lay the body down and stuffed the innards back where they had been. When the rolling overcast sky reminded him of Rinpo's magic on the retreat ledge, he reached under his shirt and unbuckled the holster that held the dorjay. Its finely cast surfaces rocked in his palm; the weight of it pleased him. Suddenly hopeful, he swirled it at the clouds in the same motion the monk had used. But they rolled on toward the east. Remembering more, he put his finger to his lips, asking that the dog keep the secret. He rolled the dorjay again. Nothing. He pointed it at the body, squeezed it, then shook it to get its power to flow. When Coco continued to be dead, he kicked the ground and yelled, "How hard can it be?"

Finally he settled, cradling the head in his lap, reviewing his memories with the dog and his memories of other deaths. As Coco's body became cold, he noticed the trunk of a birch tree in his sight line, welted and torn at the chest-height of a man and pondered what could have done it. Near it on the ground lay a limb as thick as his wrist, newly snapped off with the bark shredded and the sapwood splintered. He didn't remember striking the one with the other until another loss some three years later.

When it was time to leave, he stood and looked down. "Good thing you got to go early, Buddy. Saves you all the trouble." Then he bellowed at the sky, "We're all going to die on this trip, aren't we?" He winced. The flesh in his throat was raw.

The woman was short and wiry. Tight curls pushed out of her hand-knit cap. "I'm Annabelle," she said to Zhampa before the others could introduce her. She didn't offer a hand.

His friends were subdued, causing him to think that they were in trouble. Celeste handed him a cup of tea and rested her other hand on his arm.

"I'm sorry about your dog," he said to Annabelle.

She nodded. "They needed two rabbits."

"We're going west and won't linger in your land. If there's something we can do though, to make up for this bad start, let us try."

"They've told me," Annabelle said motioning toward the others, "and there are things you can do for us."

"Us? Your family?"

"No, for the Lake Clan. All the way through."

"The what?"

"You've sailed into the Lake Clan Rosary."

Zhampa looked at his companions. They nodded, encouraging him to hear her out.

"What does that mean, Lake Clan? Are we in trouble?" he asked.

"It's a network of hostels and guides. For travelers. These lakes and shore trails are a highway. Have been for centuries. We've organized a new way. We can make sure you get through. But if you bring trouble, we can send you right back where you came from."

Zhampa tuned his ear to the waves. "We'd have to swim," he said. "Our boat's wrecked."

"Yeah, I saw you coming. It was obvious you didn't know what you were doing. I figured you for refugees, coming up to safety. You're not the first."

"Hostels? There are places to stay?"

"All along the lakes. On this side anyway." She placed the cup she'd been holding on a fire pit rock.

"What's in it for you?"

"A percentage of what you're carrying. You'll see. It's a good system. You keep us going and we protect you."

"I told her we don't have goods," Celeste said. "That we're traveling light."

"But they'll take labor," said Oakley.

"What do you mean 'protection'?" Zhampa asked.

"You travel with permission. No stamp, no travel. Parties without stamps from each post get shut down every step of the way. We got a penal code that makes you think twice." She looked at everyone carefully to make sure they'd heard.

"What's your policy on weapons?" Zhampa pushed his chin toward her rifle.

"Those of us who run the network are all armed," Annabelle said. "Travelers give up their guns before they start. They get 'em back at the end, if they've behaved themselves. People find it's better to comply and fit in. It's been working so far. Sixteen years since we set it up."

"She knows we're unarmed," Oakley said, "except for knives and wood tools."

"They tell me you're a healer." Annabelle said. "Herbs. Acupuncture. The Chinese stuff. Me, my ears pricked up when they said the old chiropractic's one of your specialties. We don't get doctors coming through much. You'll do fine along the trails."

She didn't ask their ultimate destination. "Too many have died minding the business of others," she said. "But if it's passage you need, I'll get you started. The Lake Clan will get you to the far end of Superior, and then you can go wherever you want."

Zhampa and Annabelle buried their dogs side by side. The following morning they moved to her hostel home to wait for her husband to guide them west.

5

"Chief, you look like puke in a cup."

"I'm not sleeping."

"Not eating much either, from what I see."

They sat on boulders on the bluff near Annabelle's home. Below them the lake lay easy with small waves.

"Is it the dog?"

"It's everything."

Oakley looked over. "I'm listening."

"You ever stopped to think about all the death we've seen?"

Oakley nodded.

"You feel guilty?"

"What about?"

"Surviving."

Oakley cast about as if checking to see that they were unobserved. "You've helped a lot of people, Chief."

But Zhampa was shaking his head. "I killed a man."

Oakley shrugged. "I know."

"But he was sitting down, godammit. I didn't even let him stand up to defend himself."

Oakley looked at his feet. "Others have done worse, Chief." He chewed his lip. "At least revenge has logic to it."

"Gives me dreams. Dreams I can't sleep through."

"Yeah."

"Do you dream?"

"Everybody dreams."

"I mean the kind that keep coming back."

Oakley glanced over, mouth sour. "All the time," he said. He pulled a blade of spring grass and parted it into long threads with his thumbs and index fingers. After some seconds, his voice low and clear, he said, "I dream awake."

"Awake?"

Oakley balled the strands in his fingertips and squeezed until green juice dribbled down his thumb. His nostrils flared. "When you've been in the hell part of war—not the flag-waving, 'Aren't they brave young heroes' crap, not the speeches of ultimate sacrifice for God and country or the stirring-taps-and-honor-guard-emotional-blanket shit that honey-coats new widows and numbs the guilt of the white-livered hawks who sent you there—but the every minute shredding of your sanity by trying to be a good boy with a future in a free-fire zone without knowing who the fuck the enemy is, or where he is, or the real agenda behind the conflict. Shredded by wondering if the poor woman hoping to buy a couple of oranges in a mud-walled market is really a wild teenage boy with visions of spending his eternity fucking virgins when he blows you up; by having to kill people because they jerk funny one time when they see your automatic rifle and the look of terror in your little boy eyes; and by being praised as patriotic for doing it by REMF's who sit safely behind a thousand miles of red tape or, worse, by some dickhead in the White House where the cherry blossoms hang in perfectly groomed trees, who have no understanding that the chunks of brain and bone matter of the toddler you just blew away—because it came into view at the wrong second—will never come off your clothes in a million years, 'cause you see them every morning when you look down to take a pee. And they still glow red when you close your eyes." He pulled up a handful of grass. "That's how I dream, Chief. Awake."

Zhampa measured the silence in waves breaking on the stony beach below. Oakley had never talked about his soldiering. He had never said more than twenty words in a row. Celeste had been forced into barbarism just for minding her own affairs. Next to theirs, Zhampa's crime was unnecessary. Revenge is conscious. He chose to kill Curtis.

But Oakley wasn't finished. "After you been through that, there's no 'Right' to be found. Anywhere. I wish I'd died with my buddies. The war's over for them. Believe me, I tried. Took the meanest missions they had. Just couldn't get killed. Started spooking the whole battalion. Finally the REMF's took me out. Said I was a perfect soldier and that I was enjoying it too much. I threw away all their medals and went to find my own way."

More waves on stone.

"Have you?"

"I function. But there's no healing that."

"Why are you here, Oakley? What made you come?"

"Because you need somebody at your back. And I need you at mine. And 'cause maybe getting the dorjay home will keep others from doing what we did. A mission with hope in it."

A great ketch with a full spinnaker made its way eastward on the lake. They acknowledged it with a pointed finger and a nod. Annabelle had told them about the vessels. "Every lake has them," she said. "Ours keep to the northern shores. They're mostly for VIP's and the bigger cargo. I've put your doctor credentials right up top on your papers. They'll get you on board. The water's good this time of year. The winds are strong, and it's before squall season. You'll have to walk the narrows, though. Everybody does. Gets a little sticky with the boats from the other side."

"The other side?" asked William.

"What do you think? We're alone in the world? The southern shores are bouncing back. But there's no network over there. Georgian Bay is ours and in Superior we each stay on our sides."

Annabelle's husband Michael returned leading a trio from the east. He was sinewy, as graceful on his feet as Zhampa was strong. Their route to Tranquility Harbor at the southern end of Georgian Bay avoided the old engineered highway, which was impassible with dead vehicles, Michael said. They walked small country roads north and west. Away from the shore the land grew flat, suitable for farms, there to take advantage of groups passing through.

The first of the summer traffic filled the evening camps. The Lake Clan guides in their red jackets carried the weapons and stood guard in shifts through the night, vigilant to things both inside and outside the camp. Without discussion, traders of long standing took the best seats around the fire. The farms along the route bartered in berry preserves, sourdough loaves and dried beef. And after Zhampa treated a traveler for intestinal worms, food flowed to his party for his services.

Two days out, at a crossroad with an old sign pointing south to Toronto, William wrestled with his past; safely in a new environment, he began pining for the one he had left. But he stayed on and their camp that night was crowded: three squat men from the Maritimes with a load of ivory; an Ojibway family heading west to join another branch of their clan; a pair of upcountry French Canadians with bulging packs that they scrupulously guarded, who sat apart rattling away in their incomprehensible dialect; a Señor Renaldo, an ambassador from Spain before the Unraveling, who enthralled everyone with stories from distant lands; three women— two barely twenty—whose commodity seemed to be themselves heading for work on the bay. Celeste watched their every move. In that large company of men, she was not alone.

"Lake Clan Rule allows women to work that way," Michael told Zhampa the next morning. "You can't regulate that part of nature very well. Besides handling real crime is hard enough."

The last day before reaching the bay they came upon a small party heading east, two men among them moaning, bloody bandages where their right hands had been.

"Stealing," Michael said when they were out of earshot. "Father and son from the look of them."

"That's punishment for stealing?" Zhampa asked.

"It's a horrible crime."

"A worse sentence."

"Oh, no, my friend. Life's fragile these days. Makes stealing almost as bad as murder. And we have to respond to crime, otherwise we're not civilized." He walked in silence a moment. "There's been too much death, you know, so we don't kill criminals. Jails don't produce anything, and we have no surplus to support people to run them. So we treat crime this way and go on."

"Treat it?" Zhampa said.

"It works. Labels criminals. Deters others. It's the *hand* that steals. So the hand goes."

"What do you do for murder?"

"Both hands. They'll never kill again."

"Or survive."

"That's up to them. Collaborators lose an ear. Liars and trouble-makers, their tongues."

"Wish I'd thought of it," William said. "Let's people know where they stand."

Tranquility Harbor was misnamed, a small town in constant motion—a collection of inns, a market, a couple of piers and two boat yards. For boats arriving late, a night crew unloaded and loaded for the trip west. Food in the saloons came with beer and a rough whiskey. Everyone's papers were checked as they entered the town. Oakley paid for their first night's lodging by joining a project to rebuild a stone foundation wall. While waiting the two days for the sixty-eight-foot two-masted schooner *Fearless*, Zhampa opened a clinic, and Celeste and William helped store goods in the holds of two cargo vessels.

Celeste was delighted to find that the captain of the *Fearless* and two of her crew were women. Captain Lucinda said her father had raised her on board ships and that after the Unraveling she took to wind power easier than he did.

"Close to half of the Lake Clan sailors are women," Captain Lucinda said in the brief conversation they had as the last of the ship's stores were loaded. "Have you sailed much?"

"One time," Celeste said. "And we ran into a storm."

"Well, sometimes the weather is beautiful. And it looks good for tomorrow. But we can never tell."

Heading out of Tranquility Harbor, Captain Lucinda showed her skill winding her course through tight channels between spruce-laden islands with shores of solid granite. The open waters of Georgian Bay made William sick and, on the third day out, the wind picked up, so that they all welcomed the scheduled stop in Parry Sound. When rain and wind kept them on the pier another day, Oakley went off alone to climb some of the steep slopes inland. In the morning his bunk was cold. Going topside, Zhampa ran into Captain Lucinda.

"I got bad news," she said. "Your friend is being held by the Marshal of the Court."

"What for?"

"Sexual assault." She let the words sink in. "His trial will be at noon."

"Ridiculous," Zhampa said.

"Unfortunately," Captain Lucinda said, "we're setting off as soon as everything is belayed. Will you be staying with your friend?"

"Of course. Today, you say? How can there be a trial so soon?"

"Parry Sound is the central port in the Bay. The judge is in town. They generally meet right away. It's normal."

"Women aren't his thing. I know the man."

"I'm sorry, but you'll have to gather your gear and the young couple."

"They're not a couple," said Zhampa. "And where is Oakley now? Where is the court?"

"They look like one to me," Captain Lucinda said. "The Barleycorn Pub serves as the court. But I don't know where he's being held."

"Not at the court?"

Captain Lucinda shrugged. "We don't have jails."

Celeste and William stayed on the pier with the gear while Zhampa looked for Oakley. He found the pub. It was locked until 'about 11:00,' the sign said, and the upstairs windows were dark and unbarred. Zhampa asked everyone he met where a prisoner might be held but got no consistent information about where to go.

"There's no one place, Love," said a lady shopkeeper. "Come back later. Perhaps one of my customers will know something. Sexual assault, you say?"

"No, I didn't."

She flicked her eyes as if struck with dust. "Well, I must have heard something. It's an awful thing. Awful crime. For your friend's sake, I hope he didn't do it."

"He's innocent."

The shopkeeper puckered her lips and lifted her eyebrows in a way that said, "He's probably guilty of something, otherwise he wouldn't be in that fix."

Zhampa, Celeste and William moved the cart and packs to the storeroom of a boarding house. When they returned, the pub was full; people even stood on the steps. But they forced their way inside. Moments later a door opened. The crowd stirred. Oakley, hands tied and hobbled, was led to the front of the room and pushed down onto a bench facing a large wingback chair. He didn't acknowledge the looks or the voices. As soon as he sat, a guttural whisper rolled back from the front. 'Missing a finger. The ring finger.' Heads wagged and faces became stern.

"What difference does it make?" Zhampa asked a man next to him.

"Sex with underage girls. He's got a history, that one."

"It was a war injury." But the man was already talking to someone else.

"I'm going to work my way up front," Zhampa said to Celeste. "See if I can have a word with him." But before he'd made it halfway, a side door opened. The crowd gave way to allow a tall woman with gray braids to come forward. She took the chair and leaned over to speak with a man who stood at attention to her right. Next she looked around the room, at Oakley, at his bindings, and at his guard.

"I am judge of the Central District, Melinda Thomas. This court is in session." She looked at Oakley. "Sexual assault is a serious charge. If you're guilty, you'll know the sting of justice for the rest of your days."

Heads moved in response to her words.

"Mister Marshal," she said, "tell the court what you heard and what you understand."

The man at attention spoke so all could hear. "A young woman was assaulted last evening. We have two independent witnesses that say it was the accused. They caught him in the act."

"And you have the witnesses?"

"Yes. And the woman, of course. They're ready to testify."

"What's your name?"

"Oakley. David Oakley." Hearing the defiance in the voice, Zhampa pushed closer.

"Mister Oakley, if you're guilty, save us the trouble of going further by saying so now. It may help your situation."

Oakley gave a slow shake of his head.

"Produce the woman," the judge said.

The marshal pushed his way to another room and returned with a cowed girl.

"Tell the judge your name," he said.

"Bonnie."

"Speak up. Everyone must hear."

"Bonnie," she said again. "Bonnie Mayhew."

"Do you know this man?" the judge asked pointing to Oakley.

The girl turned hesitantly and stole a glance at Oakley. Zhampa recognized her. She was one of the three women from the trail. "Yes, Ma'am. He's the one."

"I asked you only if you recognized him. Not for a verdict. How do you know him?"

"Barely. Saw him east of Tranquility Harbor . . . and last night." Her voice dropped.

"Were you working?"

"Last night?"

"Yes."

"No. No, Ma'am. But of course, I might have considered it, if . . . "

"Did you speak with him?"

"No," she said with more emotion. "I never saw him. He grabbed me off the street. Pulled me into a doorway."

"A doorway. Of a house?"

"I can't remember. I'm new in town."

"Did you scream?"

"Of course, I screamed, but the wind was wailing."

"And?"

"He raped me."

"In the doorway?" The judge pondered. "That's not easy."

"Yes. From behind."

"Did you scratch him or hit him? Did you try to defend yourself?"

"He was very strong and he held my arms back. Look at him." And she pointed a finger. "I've got bruises on my face. And on my neck and shoulders." Her hand fluttered near the spots she spoke of. "I thought he was going to break my arms clean off."

Her testimony hung in the hushed air.

"Then what?"

"Just as he finished, two men came and ripped him off me. They beat him good. Tied him up and took me back to my room."

When the judge dismissed her, the marshal gave her a chair. Next the witnesses were brought in. Oakley stiffened at the sight of them—the two French Canadians from the same camp on the trail. They and the woman must have traveled on an earlier boat. They confirmed the woman's story. She was screaming, they said, and the smaller of the two produced the cudgel he'd used to flatten Oakley.

"In one whack," he said.

Judge Thomas admonished the two that justice hung on the veracity of their words and asked them to swear to their testimony. After they did so and were returned to their holding room, the judge said to Oakley, "What do you have to say for yourself? Is it true that Miss Mayhew was in your camp? That you have met before?"

Zhampa had worked himself forward and Oakley caught his eye for the first time, but gave no sign of recognition. He said, "Yes. At a campsite, about a week ago."

"One of the witnesses said this woman turned you down for sex in the camp. Is that true?"

Oakley set his gaze far away from the room and blew air out his nose. "She turned a lot of men down for sex. . . . I wasn't one of them."

"You mean she accepted you?"

"No." The word dropped like a boulder in a pond.

"You were caught, beaten and tied last night in the presence of three people. How can we come to any other conclusion except that you are guilty?"

"I was out walking on the hillside. It's something I do. I don't like to be cooped up in buildings. Worse, a boat. And I was walking back through town very late, when I heard a woman screaming. I ran and found someone fighting with her in a doorway. I grabbed the man . . . and then I got hit, here." He tried to raise his hands to the side of his head. "I don't remember anything else."

"Did you get a look at the man?"

Oakley shook his head. "It was all shadow."

"You have no witness for your story?"

"No."

"You don't leave me much room here. Lake Clan justice is clear, and I'll have to . . ."

"Excuse me, Madame Judge," said Zhampa, "You can't sentence a man on the word of strangers."

The judge stopped and sought out the speaker in the crowd. "Who are you?" she asked when their eyes met.

"Zhampa DiOrio. I'm a doctor, traveling through. For the sake of justice, the woman should at least be examined."

"And you're an expert in such matters?"

Zhampa's mouth went dry. He was no gynecologist. The first child he delivered died and he had relied on midwives ever since.

"Yes," he said.

"Fine. I'll allow it. Miss Mayhew, please come to the side room." She beckoned Zhampa with her head. "Doctor?"

When they were inside, the judge commanded, "Remove your clothes."

"No, let's start with her other injuries."

The judge nodded.

"Come over to the window," he said. "We need the light."

"I don't want the whole town to see me," Bonnie protested.

"No worry of that," said the judge. "They're all in the pub."

The woman had friction burns on both wrists and welts and scrapes on her left shoulder.

"Does this hurt here?" Zhampa asked touching the base of her neck.

"Very much." She shied from his hand.

"Judge, there's no need to examine her personal . . . uh."

"Her genitals? Why not?"

"Look at these marks."

"Teeth marks. Did your assailant bite you, Bonnie?"

"I don't know. It all happened so fast."

"Have you seen the defendant's teeth, Judge?" said Zhampa, tapping his incisors.

Judge Thomas looked at Bonnie's neck and then at her memory of Oakley. She nodded, her face reddening. "Yes, yes. Thank you, Miss Mayhew. Please stay here."

Talk in the hall died as the judge and Zhampa reentered. Taking her seat, she called the marshal over and spoke in his ear. When he unbound Oakley, the crowd made vowels of confusion. "You are free to go, Mr. Oakley," she said. "We have new evidence." Then the marshal brought the witnesses back in.

When they stood before her, she said, "Bind them."

Hands flew in all directions; bodies heaved, but in that crowd there was no way for the two men to escape. They jerked at their restraints and bellowed, causing the judge to rise from her chair and to stand over them.

"I can tell the knivesman to take a lot or a little. The more trouble you make, the less generous I will be. Do you understand me?"

The men stilled. She sat again, throwing her braids over her shoulders, her aspect fierce. "In my experience, lies are necessitated by wrongdoing. By your own admission moments ago, a woman was raped last night." She looked from one to the other. "The truth now will save each of you a great loss. "Who is the rapist here?"

The men exploded with cries and pleas.

"Stop," yelled the judge. "Lie to me again and you'll both lose your tongues *and* your genitals."

The smaller man, Emil, whimpered and looked hard at his mate. The look was not returned.

"By telling the truth—right here, right now—the rapist will be spared his tongue. The accomplice will be spared his genitals."

Francis, the larger man, sat motionless, thinking. Emil's eyes were glued to him. Finally Francis addressed the judge. "I am the liar. It is right that you take my tongue."

The smaller man fought to his feet. "You bastard. You're a liar."

"Yes, I am," Francis said. "And I regret it."

The guard shoved Emil back onto the bench. "No," said Emil, "you're still lying. You are the rapist. And now you're a liar too. You sonofabitch."

"Listen to me, Emil," said Francis coolly. "Confess to the rape and save your tongue. Tell the truth for god's sake, for our sake."

"Judge," cried Emil, "I cannot tell the truth by telling a lie. He is the rapist. It was his idea."

"You little bastard. You'll ruin it for both of us."

"I've had enough," said the judge. "Take them outside."

People pushed out into the street toward a wooden block in the center of the square. When the prisoners were brought out, the judge waited for quiet.

"Today we do justice. A world that negotiates with liars is damaged beyond righting." Turning to the knivesman she said, "Take an inch of both their tongues and their cock prides."

"God. They do it right here?" Celeste said. She turned away, her hand instinctively on the handle of her knife, until she realized what she had done.

"No, Judge," cried Francis. "I confess now. I am the rapist and it was my idea. At least spare my tongue."

Emil breathed loudly in anticipation of the judge's reply. The judge turned away and then back. "So be it. Take an inch of this one's tongue," she said pointing to a cowering Emil. "But you, sir, have raped and lied and would have sold your friend. Take an inch of his tongue of two inches of his male part."

Whether in service of justice or crime, violence occurs quickly. The prisoners fought the sentence as anyone would, guilty or not. One at a time, Emil first, they were held down onto the cutting block by volunteers. Their tongues were seized and pulled long with pliers, and the sharpest of knives flashed with a skilled cook's cut. The prisoners garbled outrage and horror. Still, Francis had more to endure and the people of Parry Sound watched.

In May, they sailed on the *Sally Anne* and the *Headstrong*. They walked the narrows north of Sault Sainte Marie. They set off across Lake Superior. Zhampa saw patients in the mornings. When Celeste wasn't working, she eavesdropped on the women officers, learning their rhythm and patter. They noticed her and included her in their gatherings. She began to laugh from her belly for the first time since her mother died. The sound thrilled Zhampa, but made him realize his own lack of joy all through those years. He found himself near the bow on the *Pagan II*, reviewing memories from happier times. . . . Rinpo standing in the cabin doorway, welcoming him for his 'lesson' as he ran to escape a spring downpour. Discovering the goat kid and the kittens curled up together on his bed. Swimming underwater undetected and dumping his father Eric out of the canoe into the pond. Being hit in the back of his head with his mother Sumiko's snowball the morning after he came home too late from a night of carousing. Getting caught in Celeste's trap of string in the barn on his thirty-fifth birthday. Claire erupting into hysterics toward the end when she hadn't the strength to talk. Zhampa had laughed too, because her outbursts were so surprising in the deathwatch hours, and because, at the time, laughter felt so close to crying anyway, and because it was one of the last things they could share. Near the end his lady fell in tune with the irony of being. "It's all a miracle," she'd said, her eyes filling with ethereal light as the rest of her drained away.

He shook his head and the memories stopped. He listened to the sound of the waves and thought about taking his place in the flow of things.

Two days later, Celeste said to him, "You're relaxing."

"I'm trying," he said. "You can see it?"

She nodded.

The *Pagan II* had just slipped through a cluster of islands near the western end of Lake Superior. As evening approached, they stood by the rail. Fringes of rain trailed from clouds off to the south. High above, their tops were red and black. Water, gray-green into the distance.

"I didn't expect to be carried by the wind," he said. "Not until the ocean anyway."

She smiled. "I like sailing. I like it a lot."

"I saw you steering this morning."

"I had the boat in my hands." She trembled with excitement. "Zhampa, I love having women to talk to. Women who aren't Valley Folk. These women talk to me because of me. Not because of who you are."

"I know," he said. "They're impressive."

"Do you think it could all be this way?" she asked.

"The world?"

"Yes."

Zhampa thought a long while. "I don't know," he said. "If you ask me, greed always flourishes when peace comes. Not long ago we made a mess of the world, because money was more important than the climate."

The western sky slipped through the scarlet moment.

"I feel like I'm sailing away from my past," she said.

"Those three men?"

"Yes. They come up sometimes. But they can't hurt me."

"That's great," he said. But he was thinking about her question. He wondered if it wasn't somehow good for the world to have unraveled. And to have been purged by war. Then horrified, he shook himself from the thought. Stars began to appear. Out of their silence he asked her, "I wonder if you should stay here on the lakes."

"It wouldn't be a bad life," she said. "I could help people move safely."

"Yes."

"Do you think you can make it?"

"Alone? To Tibet?"

"Yeah."

"I don't think Rinpo would have set me to this if I couldn't."

"And you trust him?"

"I do. He knew the future. He wrote it down."

"He didn't know it enough to change it."

"Who'd listen to someone who said they knew?"

Celeste was quiet.

"It's a risk," he said. "But standing still is risky, too."

She nodded.

In the western Lake Superior port of New Thunder Bay, Celeste considered her options. The *Pagan II*'s first mate Stephanie had a sister who was looking for a crew for a local boat and Celeste sailed out with her on a day's shakedown cruise. The next day she walked outside the town into wilder land and settled by a muddy pond.

Zhampa thought too. He came to see that, if Celeste chose to live on the lakes, at least he would have satisfied Claire's request to take of her daughter. Then he turned his attention to the months ahead. Sailing the lakes had placed them well ahead of schedule. His best guess before leaving Vermont had been that they might get across the prairies and camp at the foot of the Rockies before winter. But now he wondered if a full crossing to the coast were possible that year. His maps showed the mountain range to be narrowest in northern British Columbia, but if they failed to cross, the winter in the northern latitudes would be harsh. In any case, the route from New Thunder Bay was clear for the first thirty days—due west. Having sailed, he, his companions and the cart were in good condition.

William started to talk again about leaving them. He wasn't going to Tibet. He would part company with them somewhere on this continent and each mile carried the tension of wondering if his next home was ahead of them or behind. Some of what the Lake Clan offered pleased him, but he never felt comfortable on boats. Ahead, some big cities would fall close to their path. He spoke of checking them out.

Oakley had had enough of 'lounging on boats,' he said. So they were all glad when Celeste announced that she would continue with them. She said that family and destiny were fused in her bones.

6

In the land west of New Thunder Bay, dry boots were a luxury. They traversed countless lowlands. They wound along lakeshores. With no signs to guide them, they lost their way. Blisters and boils plagued their feet and parasites attacked their intestines. Their bodies oozed fluids and they were rarely without pain. Only Oakley seemed unfazed by the skin coming off his feet in patches.

On a warm mid-June afternoon, they set up camp in a natural clearing by a lake. Stumps of large trees stuck up out of the water.

Zhampa said, "Looks like they've been getting a lot more rain here for a decade or so."

Oakley nodded. "Mother Nature's still trying to figure out what she's doing."

"I hope this doesn't mean there's drier lands ahead."

Celeste took William to find some herbs to salve their blisters and while they were gone, Barker wandered into their camp from the west, leading his horse along the shore of the lake.

"Rifles, Chief," Oakley said under his breath.

There were several, one well-polished in a saddle holster and at least two more barrels visible in the gear roll behind. The middle of the continent was still awash in ammunition, but Barker charmed them with good manners. He asked if they would mind if he rested a bit by their fire. His smile was warm, his speech slow and inflected with the prairie drawl. He had a cat-kind of body with blue and blond trimmings, a leaner version of Gabe, more seasoned. Barker was happy, he said, to find fellow travelers, was so sorry that they were heading in opposite directions and was full of information about the country ahead. He willingly offered to share his bounty of game—coyote that evening—and helped to create a mound of firewood. When the need arose, he was quick to root in his packs for a cooking fork.

"No," he said, "keep it. I've got another. I'm a scavenger, don't you know. I don't live here winters. You might call me a migratory bird. Move with the seasons. I set my mind to receive what the world offers and am happy to share. Yes, well, from Oklahoma, now that you ask. Down in the panhandle, Cherokee country. Well, where they got moved to. Got some native blood in me, don't you know. Oh, about a sixteenth. Just your regular American mongrel." To Zhampa he said, "You look like you've got your share in you. Am I right?"

"Yup. Some."

"What tribe?"

The question reminded Zhampa of his days in the Holistic Medicine Institute and he immediately made the connection—he'd studied in the prairie country, probably just a few hundred miles south of where they stood. His having native blood stirred racist sentiments in the school. He mused for a moment on his time there and on how the Unraveling shattered it. How, in his last semester, the peripheral melees with the Globalliance burst into direct frontal assaults with U.S. forces. His mother Sumiko argued that, unless his safety was threatened by living near a major metropolitan center, he should stay to finish his degrees.

"Don't worry about us," she said. "Vermont will be safe. There's not much here for anybody to get excited about."

He remembered being amazed at how she was calmly setting her world to battle stations; she'd been planning for years. Six weeks later, he was awakened by the dream in which she cradled the head of a man. It wasn't his father, but it was in the yard of the Hollow farm. He saw no cause of death, but his mother turned and looked at him dreaming in his bed. Her teeth were red, her mouth full of blood, her voice hoarse. "Get home. Now!"

"What tribe?" Barker asked again.

"Lakota."

"Ah! Lucky you. Noble people."

Zhampa shifted his weight on his feet.

"Not like where I come from," Barker continued. "The world is full of rascals south of here. Good you're taking this way over. Myself, I come up here to get away. You run into any yet?"

"Rascals? No, we're just walking through," Zhampa said. "We don't stir bees nests when we can pass by."

"That right?" he said. "You're smart. I figured you would be. Yes sir, it's true what they say about what goes around. But . . . sometimes a man wants the honey in the nest. Then he's got a puzzle, don't you know. I'd love to know how you handle that. Bet I could learn from a Lakota brave."

"Name is Zhampa," he said. "I'm just a man."

"What do you mean by rascals?" asked Oakley.

"Oh, yeah, rascals aplenty. The fighting still goes on down there. I was just a boy when the migration started, about fourteen, don't you know. We got swamped from the north. And of course, there was no way we could all get along. They were taking our land, the land God gave us. Death was common as sunrise down there. Hunger and guns is a bad combination. . . . I wonder who invented hunger," he said. His face brightened and he winked. "Here, let me split that for you. I ride more than walk, and y'all've done most of the work here." As he said this, he nearly pulled the ax from Zhampa's hand.

Celeste and William returned. Barker said he'd noticed that one of the packs was smaller. "Probably a woman," he confessed to thinking. He removed his hat and bowed, and was able to do so with the proper amount of self-deprecation to make them all be entertained.

In the morning, as they were readying to head their separate ways, he said, "I've got a gift for you," and went to his horse. He pulled his favorite rifle from its holster and carried it toward them in reverently outstretched hands. As Zhampa scrambled for words to politely refuse the gesture, Barker tipped the barrel up and trained it on the three men.

"Don't friggin' move." He was smiling. His voice was like honey. "Now Celeste, sweetheart, you're coming with me." Concentrating on the men, he waved a seductive hand toward the woman.

"Keep your eyes on me, Mr. Lakota," he said." I don't believe she'll be helped by you. Now very easy, I'm going to ask you to release your knives. Throw them over here. Gently, Mr. Oakley. Now I want y'all to stand over by that tree there and, gentlemen, place your hands over that low branch. That's right. And Celeste, would you take Mr. Oakley's rope coil there and cut me three pieces about four feet long."

"You're going to tie them up?" she said. Her voice was higher.

"Again gentlemen, keep focusing right on this barrel," Barker said. "Why, no. I have no intention of tying your friends. You will do the honors. Very tightly, please. Slip your knife out and cut me . . . "

"Let's not waste the rope," she said with such command that Barker was silent for an instant. "The stuff's hard to find. I got a better way to tie these bastards. I'm gonna make them wish they never had hands. Our honorable scout's been carrying bailing wire in his pack and it'll make a much tighter binding."

"Really, sweetheart, this is a delightful surprise. Most unexpected." He shot a quick glance at her. "And yes," he said, "bailing wire will do just nicely. Surprised you didn't let us know that yourself, Mr. Scout. I might have been inclined to go a little easier on you, don't you know."

He watched Celeste dump Oakley's pack, watched her bend down to gather the wire and the snips, and the sight of her contempt and aggression caused him to smile his first genuine smile. It was an unpleasant thing.

"I don't know how to get this across to you, Mr. Barker," she said, "but I've been dragged across this fucking swamp land by these sweet-looking assholes for work and for pleasure, and since I'm just the one, I've learned how to make them think I'm happy to be here." She punctuated her points by fiercely clipping the lengths of wire with the cutters.

Zhampa felt William shutting down next to him. He couldn't see Oakley but would have loved a few words with him knowing that they could probably rearrange the event into one with fewer losers. Barker was a psychopath and Celeste was flashing back, was all he could think. A dangerous condition, one he knew little about. But he didn't dare jeopardize her instinct for survival. He'd already failed her once.

"That right?" Barker said. "But 'sweet-looking' is a' awfully charitable way to talk about such a group of woeful souls. Perhaps as you tighten their hands around that limb you'd like to cut on them a little bit. Start with your honorable Mr. Oakley. He gets on my nerves."

One at a time, Celeste wrapped their hands on the tree limb so tight that they felt her venom.

"I'm not a cutter," she said over her shoulder, "I'll leave that to you if you want."

She took a fistful of William's hair. "This is for the last time," she bellowed and raised her knee into his gut. He vomited and cussed her. "I like to hurt men another way," she said, looking right through to Zhampa's retinas and spitting at him. "Some way they'll never forget."

"How's that?" Barker's eyes were on her now, absorbed like an owl seduced by a rustle in the grass.

Celeste walked over to the Oklahoman and pushed the barrel of the gun away as if it were a branch blocking her path. She said, "Best way to get even with that sorry pack of pricks is for you to take me right here in front of them," and with an assurance that made him flinch, she put her palm on his crotch and left it there.

"I'm a gentleman, mostly," he said. "I . . . ah . . . don't know about 'taking you' right here. I mean I do want to take you. Been thinking about it since the minute I saw your red hair."

Unchecked, Celeste slid her hand onto his belly, ripped open his belt with one stroke and pulled herself in close. The barrel of the rifle became drowsy as she popped the top button on his pants, her other hand behind his back, caressing, pulling up on the shirt. Barker tried to lead her over into the tall grass, but she said, "You don't know how it will hurt them to see me with you." She nuzzled into his neck, popping more buttons. And when he became jelly all over, she complimented him on his looks and on the sound of his voice. The rifle thudded softly in the dirt and he put his hands on her, stopping at the knife between her breasts. Slipping it out and tossing it away, he said, "We won't be needing that."

"Absolutely not," she said. "Nor you yours." And he laughed as his hit the ground. He freed her pants and sent them down as she tugged off her jersey. Then she dropped his pants, and went straight down with them to squatting, pulling one leg at a time past his dutifully lifted feet, one hand always holding his erection, right and then left, and right-handed she pushed her pants down to her boots and the hand returned with the sharp blade she'd hidden there, and in one clean stroke she separated him from his pleasure, like harvesting celery.

Barker wailed and went down. He rolled and kept checking through the blood that the thing had really happened, whining, cussing, squeezing the stump. Celeste, up, her pants up, too, looked down at him with an air of victory wound tight with fury. She snatched the rifle from the ground and picked up what he had lost, useless now. Not knowing what to do with it, she took the moment to watch him watching her and in the breathless silence of his worry, she spitted, "Your dancin' days are done," and threw the piece of it at him. She bent again, gathered the knives, then marched toward her mates, who stood wide-eyed, their bound hands as useless as paws, and finally, as if answering the question about her previous escape— the question asked a thousand times behind her back in The Valley—she growled, "Now you know," and passing them by, she went to the lake to wash her knife.

"Zhampa, don't let him die," she implored. "I don't want to repeat that part."

Complying, they made Barker as comfortable as he would allow and bound his feet and one hand and they stayed at the site. Zhampa tended the wound the best he could with cleaning and a few stitches—a procedure none of them enjoyed—and after spewing his whole tank of venom and humiliation, Barker settled into whimpering. In fact, no one talked much over a mumble for the rest of the day. They tended the fire and a front came over promising rain. Toward evening Barker babbled remorse, calling himself misunderstood and confessing to many 'mistakes' that preceded that day's. He avoided eye contact with Celeste, even though she was Zhampa's assistant through much of his duties. The times that their eyes did meet, a sound like rocks being crushed rolled in his throat. As for Oakley, he wore his military face, shifting from one spot to another around the campsite. Finally he took off to fish down the lake, returning late with a fat trout, already dressed, but still he had no words. William shrank, too, becoming as submissive as Barker, even though Celeste went to him and apologized for having used him so badly. His nodding was exaggerated, but he rarely looked at her. She spent most of her time on the edge of the clearing talking to herself. Zhampa overheard her say, "I'm a good person. I *am* a good person. I was just born in a time when goodness doesn't matter."

Zhampa's hands shook. They'd all seen that when he was working the needle through the flesh. He had struggled with the impulse to use the needle as a weapon. Afterward, he sought relief in the simplicity of sitting on a boulder a few steps out into the lake, staring at the sand, at the stones and at the action of the waves. He regretted having agreed to let her come on the journey and that she hadn't chosen to stay with the Lake Clan.

"Why does atrocity keep hounding her?" he asked himself. "Why can't I see it coming?" As the day progressed, he fell into his old logic that crimes against Celeste were retribution for his own crime. Out of hearing on long a walk, he ranted. "You chose the wrong man, Rinpo. She was just getting free. But because I wasn't paying attention, she had to go back into her nightmare." And in the silence that came as the answer, he realized how strong Celeste had become, and his head spun trying to cope with an unfamiliar hierarchy.

That night he couldn't sleep. He wandered by the lake in the dark, swinging at the mosquitoes. And his depression might have lasted a long time, if Gabe hadn't ridden Mercedes into camp the next afternoon. Celeste gave a shriek, practically pulled him off his horse and hugged him. Even Oakley broke into a twisted grin.

"I've been tracking you for weeks," the hunter said. "Hey, William, thanks for having a heavy right foot. Makes you like set of road markers. And this cart of yours, Zhampa, a hunter's best friend."

William examined his foot.

It was a testament to their integrity how long it took for Gabe to learn the nature of Barker's invalidity. "We had a little trouble that had to be resolved with unfortunate consequences for Mr. Barker," was how Zhampa put it.

On the other hand, Gabe's story flowed fast. He'd managed to get into Rochester. "Saw more houses than there was trees," he said. "Places where coming over a hill, all I could see was walls and roofs rolling with the land. Most every one of 'em had been picked clean or burned, but I did find these close-up glasses and they was a help, after I figured out how to use them. I got so as I could be my own scout, keeping away from gangs."

William drew closer.

"I had two close calls with gang people. First ran into a pair of scouts, Younger 'n me," he said. "They never saw me, though I think they heard Mercedes from a ways off. They came looking but we hid. And later, I got chased by a group of six or seven, and me and Mercedes had to outrun 'em. First time I ever heard a gun go off. It sounds like two stones clacking together. Nothing more than that, but one of the bullets just missed my head, like a sudden wind and whistle. Gone just like that," he said snapping his fingers. "Kind of exciting being the one who's hunted. I hightailed it out of there, rode until I got back into the country some. And I got to thinking my idea was pretty stupid."

He went east back around the lake to see if he could meet up with them on the other side. He crossed the big river in a raft. "Costed me three deer," he said, "Mercedes swam. I just kept clucking him and calling him. Then I met Michael. He had guns and didn't like the looks of me, he said, but after I explained who I was, I got a Lake Clan pass and took the overland route. He made me show him how to shoot a bow. That's how I got my pass.

"He told me about Annabelle shooting Coco. Weird about women being captains and judges and stuff, huh? I think I was about five days behind you the whole way. I tried to catch you at the Narrows. Then at the end of Superior I really pushed and could tell that I was closing yesterday, though I didn't think I'd find you just resting."

He looked at Barker again trying to imagine what had happened. Toward evening, he heard Barker cuss 'that bitch' under his breath, as his fever came on. When Zhampa took the headlamp to gather yarrow to knock Barker's fever down, Gabe and William kept the patient covered close to the fire. They entertained him when he was lucid. They held him down when he wasn't. When they rose to help him pee, Gabe learned all he wanted to know.

The next morning Celeste and Oakley took off to find an intersection that Barker had told them about before things got bad. It turned out he had told them the truth and they checked the road to see if they could get back on the route they had planned to take. At the end of the next day, Barker's fever was gone and his wound held dry. Confident he would survive, they planned their departure for the following morning, but they weren't sure what to do with him. He wasn't ready to ride; he would have to stay put for a while. And they didn't want to leave the rifles with him and be shot in the back. Yet without his weapons he'd be defenseless and unable to hunt.

In the end, they took his rifles, telling him that when he was well enough, he could travel west to a shack Oakley and Celeste had found. There would be a map inside telling him where they had hidden them. And if they ever saw him again, they . . . well, they hoped he'd learned his lesson. They left him three fish—two alive in a bucket—and wood stacked next to where he lay so he could tend the fire.

7

They traveled prone lands of juvenile spruce, growing thick in the old lumber tracts, the machete blade marking irregular measure to the squeeze and suck of their boots in the muskeg, bull-heading forward then circling back with curses when their way was blocked by bogs or granite-rimmed ponds and swatting—too late—at insects feasting on their blood. For days they wasted no words on each other. In camp, Celeste used gestures around the fire, and the curl of her shoulders told Zhampa she was dredging old questions. Knowing he wouldn't violate her ruminations, she fell naturally into walking close to him in the rear, though he usually waved her forward, so he could knead his self-condemnation without interference. William performed his chores stiffly and Oakley took to carving delicate things, then crushing them underfoot as they neared completion. Having no audience for tales of his adventures, Gabe looked after his horse, lingering with him in open ground, sometimes for hours while he grazed, then riding late into camp with meat or fowl to eat.

Finally, on a down slope, Zhampa let the weight of the cart push him up even with Celeste. "I just want you to know," he said, "I would have done it myself and never looked back."

She thought a while. "Then why, when you didn't do it, does it trouble you?"

"Because it happened to you."

"After the first seconds, you know, it wasn't fear. Something took hold of me, Zhampa. When I realized I wasn't his first victim, I decided I should be his last."

"After your abduction, I spent years preparing myself for it if it ever happened again. But Celeste, I've never stared into the barrel of a gun before. . . . I froze."

She shook her head as if to discourage a fly from landing. "Using the knife didn't occur to me until the last minute. I was just trying to string him on somehow. I even thought he might . . ." She stopped. "Then I remembered Oakley's trial. That judge's decision will make everybody there think twice about being evil."

The others were waiting for them at the shore of a lake.

"Damn. It's probably Red Tail Lake," Zhampa said, slapping his map. "This thing is useless. We were supposed to pass it to the north." Water stretched in both directions around islands and promontories. A blue and green world. "I don't know where we are on this shoreline," he said, waving his hands in disgust. "Somebody else decide which way to go."

Oakley kicked a stone, then another. Finally Gabe said, "Okay. Let's go north."

The road was paved and wound past specters of grand houses. The next morning when it turned unexpectedly east away from the water, they stuck to the shore on a gravel trail and entered an ancient forest. Off the track to relieve herself, Celeste spied two canoes on the water. Single occupants worked together, casting a net and hauling it in, emptying it of animated dots, then moving on. An hour later the fishermen abruptly hauled their net and paddled north in quick strokes.

"We've spooked 'em, Chief."

"Pay attention," Zhampa said. "If we run into people, don't do anything stupid."

In the afternoon Gabe raised his right hand to signal Zhampa and they stopped. After a moment of listening, Zhampa asked his hunter what he saw. Gabe mimed pulling back a bowstring.

"We're just passing through," Zhampa said to the trees. "We mean no harm to anyone." He waited again. "If you're there, show yourselves."

A dozen figures, men and women clad in skins stepped out from behind trees, carrying handmade bows with arrows notched, the strings not pulled taut.

Zhampa held his hands by his sides, palms forward. "We're unarmed."

Gabe said, "I have a bow, Zhampa."

"Except for his bow."

A man older than Zhampa stepped forward. His eyes were sad and his graying hair was pulled back. He carried only a staff, delicately carved and adorned with dyed wrappings, feathers and a gold band. "Where are you going?" he said to Zhampa.

"To the Pacific."

The man glanced at the other travelers. "Are you lost?"

"A little. We're somewhere along the old Canadian south border land, but I'm not sure of our exact location."

"What's your business?"

Zhampa puckered his lips. Finally he said, "Returning sacred objects."

The man nodded. "How far have you come?"

"Like a crow? Over a thousand miles. From a place called Vermont."

"I know where it is. Are you native?"

"Some."

The man looked up. "What tribe?"

"Lakota. One quarter. My mother's father."

"You look more than that."

"My mother's mother was Japanese."

"How about him?" he asked, pointing his chin toward Oakley.

"Scout," Oakley said.

The man with the staff nodded again. "What about you?" He pushed his chin toward Gabe. "What's the bow for?"

"I'm their hunter."

The man eyed the horse. "Nice animal." He looked at Celeste and the knife between her breasts. "And you?"

"I'm the cutter," she said.

The man pointed to two women and said, "They're cutters, too."

There was silence for a while. William shifted. "I'm a city man," he said. "Kind of a guest."

"Yes, you are." A smile tinged the man's cheek. "Guns?" he asked Zhampa.

"Don't carry any. Can't deliver sacred things with weapons on board. We just have knives and his bow to survive off the land."

Gabe looked off toward the lake.

After studying the ground, the man looked up. "Come with us."

They walked in silence for most of an hour and at length came to a cove with a camp on the far shore. The man with the staff swept an arc with his hand to tell them to walk around. Then his group launched four canoes and paddled across with hardly a sound.

As Zhampa's band approached the camp, smoke of grass and tinder greeted them. A score of canoes were pulled up on the shore. By the water, drying racks. Beyond, thatched domes with south facing openings big enough for a man to walk through. Children playing by the water stared at the oddity of a man pulling a cart like a horse. Then like swallows on the wing, they herded themselves into one creature with scurrying legs, coming close to watch Zhampa slip out of his harness. When he did, they jerked back with one motion, and he smiled for the first time in weeks.

A pubescent boy gestured that they drop their packs and told Zhampa that a hut had been prepared for him to rest. The boy led him up the bank above the fire pits and motioned him to enter. Zhampa glanced back, then ducked in. Soon he was dozing on a fresh bed of ferns and pine needles, waking later to the smell of fish cooking and yellow light cutting flat-ways through the trees. Seeing him stir, a young woman standing outside his door asked if he would sit in council with Elk Runner.

"Do you mean now?" he said.

"Yes, if you're ready." She led him through the camp, traversing obstacles with no excess motion. Only once did she turn back to see that he was behind her. Women by the fires lifted their heads as he passed and he saw Gabe sitting with the sharpening stones out, surrounded by children and a cache of knives. The path up the hill was well worn, winding through the trunks of trees tinged red with the time of day. His guide circled a stone face, then bent low and vanished into the underbrush, which was the door of a lodge, woven into the forest itself. Zhampa followed into utter darkness. Hands led him to sit. He heard the sawing of a fire bow, the crumbling of tinder, and a gentle blowing of breath. A leaf smoldered then burst into flame. Soon a bright fire lit the lodge. Faces in the light. Men and women.

To his left, the man who had spoken for the others in the forest lifted a wooden shaft, ornamented with polished metal, stones and ribbons, shiny with the touch of hands. "I am Elk Runner, chief of the We People. This talking stick allows us and strangers to speak the truth." He passed the object to the man beside him. "I am Broken Bow. Men and women must listen to each other before acting." And the talking stick went around the gathering, each person speaking a few words. When the old woman to Zhampa's right passed it to him, it felt impossibly heavy; a thousand voices emanated from the wood and traveled up his arms; his mind jumped with questions. But all eyes were on the fire. Then he heard words coming from the wood. "The living are entrusted with the gifts of those who have died.

We must protect and deliver them." He gazed a moment at the talking stick as if looking into a well.

Then Elk Runner lifted it and laid it on a finely woven cloth. Next, he lit a twig and, with deliberation, sucked the flame into the bowl of a long pipe. He sniffed the tobacco and smiled. As the pipe went around, each person drew from it. When it came to Zhampa, he inhaled too hard, and fell into a gagging cough. The laughter that arose was not bitter and Elk Runner caught the pipe before it hit the ground.

Again Elk Runner picked up the talking stick. He prayed to his family lineage, to heroes fallen in battles and to heroes fallen in alcohol. The woman who led Zhampa to the lodge spoke of the nobility of women. The old woman Wing in Sky said, "I stand on the border of the two worlds. Soon I'll deliver your prayers personally to our ancestors." Then she sang a long dirge in her native tongue. When it was Zhampa's time to speak, he sat still a long time, regretting that he didn't carry his grandfather's Lakota tradition. He thought of his mother. "I'm growing old pulling a wagon of anger," he began. He spoke of his father's death and of how his life had been cursed ever since. When he stopped, there were nods.

Elk Runner said, "You have sacred objects. What objects?"

Zhampa thought, shrugged and replied by pulling his shirt off. He withdrew the keela, the knife scepter, from its sheath. Its blade was silver, triangular in section with concave surfaces, cast with snakes, script and jewels. The gold handle was topped with the head of a horse. Its eyes were rubies.

"Does the horse have a name?" asked Two Stars.

"Hiyagriva."

"Big name," said Elk Runner.

"Enlightened horse," Zhampa said.

As the keela was passed around, they imitated Zhampa, holding it like a dagger, piercing lust, hatred and ignorance with one stroke, cheerful in the task of pretending to rid the world of small-mindedness. The heft and shape of the dorjay intrigued them, and when it came to the hand of Wing in Sky, the fire shrank with a sizzle and the air in the lodge pulsed with blue light. Wing in Sky cried out that it was too heavy to hold and begged for someone to take it. Finally she dumped it into Kicks the River's lap. The blue light vanished and the fire blazed again.

Out of a long silence Elk Runner said, "Zhampa, deliver your objects. We'll watch from here." Then Broken Bow sang a song of ending, keeping rhythm on a skin drum.

That evening, the travelers sat at the fires of various families. Zhampa sat with Elk Runner and Broken Bow.

"In the old days," Elk Runner said, "native life wasn't idyllic. Sometimes we starved. We fought with other tribes over hunting land. We fought over females. But," he raised a finger in the air, "we were in touch with the land."

"What about now?" Zhampa said. "How do you handle squabbles and aggression?"

"We sit in council until the problem is talked through. And until everyone lets go of his point of view."

"Hard to do with millions of people," said Zhampa.

"That's the point. Humans are tribal. We have to talk face to face."

"What'll you do when you're threatened by another tribe?" asked Zhampa.

"We'll welcome them. Make peace with them," said Broken Bow. "But if they can't make peace, we'll kill them. Or we die at their hands."

Zhampa considered if the Valley Folk were a tribe. "How's that different from the way things have always been?"

Broken Bow brooded. "Probably isn't," he said. "But we have . . . "

A howl of voices rose from the lower ground. High pitched arguing and scolding rolled up the hill, coming faster than those who were running with it. The young men of the village swept up William, Oakley, Gabe and Celeste and dragged them to Elk Runner's fire. A young man held a pistol out to Broken Bow and Elk Runner.

"They're liars," he screamed. "They have guns."

"Where'd this come from?" Elk Runner demanded, keeping one eye on Zhampa.

"The little ones found it in his pack," said the young man pointing to Gabe.

Zhampa felt Broken Bow move behind him. Something large was in his hand.

"You knew about this?" Elk Runner said, waving the pistol in Zhampa's face.

"No, I didn't. He was under orders never to carry one."

"You lied to us," Elk Runner said to Gabe. "What kind of a warrior are you?"

"You're right," Gabe said so all could hear. "I *am* to blame. It was my father's. It is the only thing of his I have. But I've never found bullets that fit it." His voice dropped. "I thought it was going to help us someday."

"Our code has been broken," Elk Runner said. He walked up and down, planting the walking stick as if killing rattlesnakes. Minutes passed. Gradually his strokes lost their force. Whispers and pointing drifted into stares.

"The hunter is my responsibility," Zhampa said. "I'll bear the punishment."

Elk Runner stopped and took Zhampa's measure. Then he nodded. "I believe you," he said. "Any other guns?"

Zhampa looked at each of his companions. They shook their heads. "No," he said.

"Any other secrets?"

"No," he said at last.

"All right," Elk Runner said, "everyone back to your fires."

"No," said Zhampa. "Let's do one thing right now." And they followed him down to the cove. "Throw it," he said. Gabe did. Silently the pistol looped high in the night and splashed into the lapis mirror of the lake.

As on any day the local birds greeted the morning with song, each according to its schedule and purpose. The first rays of sun penetrated the cool night, upsetting the air, creating ripples on the water and hissing in the trees. The sound of waves from the larger lake filtered into the cove and Zhampa awoke to the pine scent of his bier. He admired the thatch over his head. Celeste lay nearby, softly breathing, curled with her right arm under her cheek. He wondered if she should cut her hair again. And wondered if she would ever become a mother. And if he'd be alive to help her. He listened for the sounds of the native children, for infants straining to find a nipple and for the cooing of suckling. He listened for the whispers of adults and for early morning giggling. He strained to hear, and hearing nothing he sat bolt upright. The shore of the lake was clear; the We People were gone.

The thatch houses were empty. The racks by the fires had been picked clean of pots, fabrics and skins. The axes by the wood piles, the bundles and blankets that were everywhere the evening before, the whittled toys—all were gone with the canoes. He wanted to cry out to his hosts and to wake his companions but seeing the senselessness of both, he slipped on his boots and wandered toward the water.

It was as if the We People had lifted their footprints as they left. The grass under their canoes was already springing up. They had been gone for hours. The morning was sullied by their absence. "It must be the gun," he thought. "No, the lie." He walked toward the beach, but felt pulled up the trail to the lodge. By the door flap, a broken arrow fastened a piece of birch bark to a soft log. A note was written in charcoal: "We've gone to another camp. Please don't look for us. We're not the same as you. Below is a map that will help you around the lake. Good luck on your delivery. ER"

Zhampa reached for the scepters and sighed when he felt them. And in that moment, he realized how separate he was from them, how he had been traveling without feeling them, without thinking about his mission. Elk Runner's request to see them was a message. Where had his mind been? And he heard again Rinpo's voice, rising one syllable at a time from the text he had left with his things in the cave, where Zhampa would find it if he ever ventured there.

It had taken more than twenty years for him to go up and visit the cave. He'd relied on a list of excuses: that he was busy with survival and with the politics of The Valley; then that he was busy with Claire's illness; then that he'd worked to keep the seeds flowing in the North Country. But underneath, guilt over abandoning his boyhood promise to Rinpo kept him from making the climb. However, one Indian summer morning, he took his stone hammer and his bar to the sheep pasture. While rebuilding the stone wall, something caused him to gaze up at the mountain. He studied all the surfaces, but he couldn't find the cave opening; the vines had completely taken over. He marveled at the power of nature. What would be left of Rinpo's Jewel of Refuge?

Carrying a hatchet, he took the trail up through stands of hemlock and black cherry. Twice he lost his way. When he found the ledge that led across the stone face of the Scallop, he had to fight through wild growth, and at the cave entrance he chopped the vines down. The stone wall he had helped build as a lad still supported the woodwork his father Eric had made. Though the door was heavy with age, it swung inward on its hinges. Musty air fled. From within, he heard the distinct dripping of water into the rock basin collector and beamed in recognition. Sunlight burned a trapezoidal hole in the darkness and there in the light sat Rinpo's little meditation table, laid out and ready for his next practice. As always, the ritual implements and texts were covered with the heavy brocade cloth, its color hidden in dust.

He entered and rested on the stone outcropping on the back wall, his eyes adjusting to the darkness. How small the space really was and how seductive the lines of the hills beyond. The shrine table still held the bowls. The candlesticks stood empty. He lifted the picture of Rinpo's teacher, dusted it with his sleeve and held it in the light. The rugged face of a Tibetan mountain lama looked back at him. On the seat of the meditation box was a pile of wasting fabric with a silver pelt on top. He thought, "A fox found its way in, curled up and died. Amazing."

The sun swung across the autumn sky and when the light from the door sat squarely over the table, he lifted the edge of the brocade. The underside glistened with silver and gold thread and dust flickered in the light rays. The string of the rosary and the skins from the ritual hand drum had crumbled. Next to the cup that held the ceremonial fluid sat a large copper box ornamented with Rinpo's lineage seals. Zhampa had never seen it before. Something altered the light and he looked up to see a sparrow on the doorsill. She peeped twice, did a little scuffling dance and then flew an exploratory tour of the inside of the cave. For a moment she lighted on the box, breathing hard. Then she flew off.

Zhampa nodded and popped the lid free with his thumbs. On top lay an envelope marked with ink brush strokes. Some Tibetan word. He stared at it long enough for a memory to groan awake. Yes, the characters Zham and Pa. His name. The hair on his neck rose. Feeling he might not be alone, he looked around the room. There was no one, and he shook his head to clear it. He looked more closely at the fox pelt on the seat in Rinpo's meditation box. It was not a skin, but a shock of long gray hair. Human hair, bundled in the yogi fashion, lying like a carelessly tossed wig. He tried to remember what his father had said in his message announcing Rinpo's death. But thirty-five years had passed. There had been no funeral; he would have come home for that. But what had happened to the body? Had his father carried it out? He didn't know. He bent down and lifted the hair, inadvertently catching his fingers on some of the fabric underneath. Out of the folds of it, things fell and rattled on the floor. Groping, he found a thin object, curled like a delicate seashell. When he examined it in the light, his heart sank. It was a human fingernail. He groped again and found four others and a ring. Rinpo's ring. Overcome, he squatted on the stoop breathing heavily. Rinpo had died there. His body had disintegrated there. He imagined beetles and wood rats taking the flesh and the bones. And he grieved. He grieved for Rinpo, for his childhood, for his parents, for Claire, and for the world that had swirled into madness.

Later with hands that felt light and unsteady, he worked loose the flap of the envelope. The letter was in English. He read:

My Auspiciously Born,

When you find this, the last part of your life will have begun. The traumas will have descended and you will have prevailed. You may stay as you are or you may use your life to greater benefit. However, if you are truly my son, I ask that you abandon your post in the Hills like Women Lying Down. There is nothing more for you to do here. I ask you to dig into your past. The keys we buried there will open the passage through which you will walk until you can no more.

Chokyi Lodro Ngawang Selpo Rinpoche
"Rinpo"

From that day, Zhampa immersed himself in the contents of Rinpo's box. Both the letter and another short document, The Command, were written in English, followed by the same texts written in Tibetan. There was also a long Tibetan text, a Tibetan-English dictionary, a hand drawn map, a diary from another century and the scepters. All had outlasted Rinpo's bones.

Comparing the English and Tibetan of the letter and The Command, and drawing on memory, he called back the language that Rinpo had taught him in the afternoons after their walks and lessons. He labored the whole winter, translating, nights and days jumbling together in his passion. His thumbs thinned the dictionary pages. Gradually the sounds of the letters came back to his ear; brush strokes appeared on paper. He felt Rinpo's hand guiding his again. Occasionally he heard the old monk's approval replaying in his head. And the letters wound into words, and the words into a charge of a lifetime.

By that first solstice, he had become fluent enough to recite The Command in Tibetan.

The Command

Your life is not about you, Zhampa. Don't be seduced by fleeting things! Your seventy years is an eye-blink. It is cottonwood dander in the breeze. Be clear about what is important. Power and pleasure have no lasting potency. The earth is fragile and no cause outweighs the continuity of its inhabitants—countless species arising, suffering, and dissolving. Only selfless action is worthy. So lean into events. Apply yourself for the good of all. Take the long view. Make choices thinking seven generations.

This is the darkest hour of a Dark Age. Man's legacy is weighed in damage done. How unfortunate! This century is lost, Zhampa. Your culture nursed too long at the nipple of self-interest and will not survive. But don't waste time weeping; many cultures have perished from the same. Once again the hope of a fresh beginning lies in the Himalayas. The ancient cauldron of wisdom was shattered in the last century; the teachings were dispersed. I choose you to help heal what has been broken. Join the others. Return the pieces.

This small box holds three treasures. Twelve hundred years ago Padmasambhava forged this dorjay in the molten fissure deep in the mountain where the Potala now stands. It is pure wisdom in physical form. The keela belonged to Lord Mikyo. Its three blades subdue lust, hatred, and ignorance with one stroke. Handed down for centuries, these scepters were given to me to smuggle out of Tibet for safe keeping during the Chinese occupation. The text is the Song of the Great Seal, the fruit of my retreat years here in the Hills Like Women Lying Down. This instruction on building enlightened society came to me whole from the timeless voices of teachers gone into the sphere of enlightenment. It is an elixir that will bring peace to the next age. Learn the text. Carry it on your person and in your heart.

Take the scepters home, Zhampa. Take them to the far side of the world, back to Tibet where they were forged. Though they have little value here, in the hand of an Enlightened One, their power is beyond concept. Take them to the monastery at the base of the Naked Red Lady Mountain. They will be expecting you and will know what to do. Take your place in the flow of things. Think beyond your valley. Do this for the welfare of all beings and for those who will come in the Next Age.

Then below in a failing hand, he had written:

The scepters are safe from idle hands. But be careful. Protect them. If others learn of their power, they will become corrupted trying to take possession of them . . . And as you travel, keep to the north whenever possible.

It took two more years for Zhampa to translate the long text, *The Song of the Great Seal.* And as part of his labor he received the detailed instructions on the various meditations Rinpo had imparted to him when he was a boy.

Zhampa stood outside the lodge holding Elk Runner's map, but he saw only the one Rinpo had drawn—a puny thing of China and Tibet with a rough route sketched to the drawing of a monastery on a steep mountainside. By it, Rinpo had written *Naked Red Lady Mountain.* Zhampa fretted about its inaccuracy. Even being careful, he could miss it by hundreds of miles. For the first time on the journey, he unwrapped *The Song of the Great Seal* that was fitted neatly into the pockets he had sewn for it in the sash he wore around his waist. He spent a long time in the early light reading the Tibetan, and his fear that he might have forgotten how vanished. Then he read his own translation in English and he was moved by Rinpo's vision of the new age. Chapters on how to take care of one's mind and heart, one's family, one's community and the earth. How to resolve conflicts, and how to lead. How to stay married. How to live with respect. He tried to visualize the Naked Red Lady Mountain and saw himself arriving triumphant, delivering the scepters and imagined the rejoicing they would ignite. "How sorely they must be needed," he thought. "They've been gone for almost a hundred years."

The calls of his fellow travelers interrupted his contemplations. Rewrapping the text in the sash, he cinched it up again as part of him. He vowed to begin committing it to memory. When he returned to the camp, the others were agitated enough to not notice that something had shifted within him.

8

Two days on, they came to the old east-west Canadian highway and, hoping that the worst was behind them, they abandoned their principle of staying on back roads. Though the forest pushed right to the traveled lanes and grass had overrun the asphalt, it was still the excellent basis of a road. In truth, it would remain a raised thread on the land, unaltered by the elements, and its discovery in a future era would cause that distant people to ponder what forces had brought about the vanishing of the prior civilization.

After some days, as clusters of buildings looming out from the undergrowth told of their approach to the old capital city, William proposed that he and Gabe scout it out. But Zhampa ignored the idea. He led them south and around the city on smaller roads. Two days later the prairie appeared, not with nuance, but like a property boundary. During a meal of hushed voices beside a waggling creek, they contemplated walking under months of uninterrupted sky. Finally William said, "I'm not going out there."

"You going back to the city?" Gabe said.

"It's a safer bet than crossing that. No trees. No buildings. I don't like it."

After a minute, Zhampa said. "I guess it's the best thing for you, William. There's time before winter for you to figure out what's there and to get settled."

William smiled with no happiness and no one spoke for some time. Then Oakley spied rain approaching. "Let's go back to that little shack with the saggy porch," he said. "Spend the night. Reorganize. Say goodbye. It's only a couple of miles."

The common space had a rusted kitchen to one side, a table and a handful of chairs, no two alike. The room beyond was empty. Out of the rain, they focused on separating William's load from theirs. And everything was laid out in little piles when Barker walked in. His footstep on the porch froze them long enough for him to be inside the door before they moved. Celeste exhaled a short vowel and Zhampa took a step back, his heart jumping. Gabe made a move for his bow, then realized he'd left it on the porch. But Barker carried no rifle. He had nothing in his hands at all and he had regained his pleasant composure. He held up his hand as if to swear off his first forty-one years.

"No," he said. "No, it's not what you think. I'm not the man you met. I've been thinking and I've had what they call . . . what the preachers used to call . . . an epiffery. An epiffery," he said again to make sure it was right. He drew a chair up to the table sitting with his back to the door. "Yep! I'm a changed man." He punctuated his point with a head bob, and slapped his hands on the table. "A man can always learn," he said. "Even coyotes can be trained. This is an important moment for a longtime sinner. Please sit with me. I got some confessing to do." When they hesitated, he beckoned again, seductive. "Come on."

Zhampa glanced at Oakley for ideas, but his scout stood with his chin jutted out, his shoulders lifted and his fingers working his palms.

If Barker sensed their hesitation, he dismissed it with a shrug. "My life took a huge turn back by that lake. A lesson I'll never forget." He looked Celeste in the eye. "You did what you had to," he said, his voice sincere. "And sometimes drastic measures are necessary. Believe me, I know. I respect that. More so in a woman. These men are lucky to have you." His smile mixed with resignation. "Just 'cause I was complaining mightily three weeks back, don't think I couldn't see your compassion after you did what you did." He waved both hands again to gather them to the table. "You'll be happy to know I've sworn off rifles. I found them, thank you, and got rid of them in trade. Made out beautifully."

Oakley let out a held breath and put a hand on his belly. Zhampa tilted his head at the transformation. Barker took the time to look each of them in the eye and, to Celeste, he turned his right hand up in capitulation. Then that same hand made a large arc through the waistband at his back and returned with a sleek handgun, which he pointed at her.

"So," said Barker in the same easy voice, "it'd be a shame if you didn't sit down to hear me out."

"Sidewinder," Oakley said under his breath.

Barker turned his head enough to let him know he'd heard. He smiled his old smile. "Sit. Down."

They pulled up chairs, Zhampa and William to Barker's right, Oakley and Gabe to his left. Celeste sat at the other end of the table, staring at the gun barrel.

"Hands palm down on the table where I can see 'em. And if there's a complaint—the tiniest peep—this trigger goes." The hands came out.

"So you're probably asking yourself, 'How'd an Oklahoman mongrel come up with a pistol out in the boonies?'" He wagged his head as if just elected chief. "That's my trade, don't you know. And next, you might have doubts about it being loaded. Well, eight rounds in the clip. At this range, no survivors." He raised the barrel and twitched his finger. The wallboard behind Celeste exploded. "Excuse me. Seven rounds. Let's see. Five idiot Yankees. That gives me two extra."

In Barker's phrases, Zhampa read the man; in the pauses he thought. He thought of wandering the North Country looking for Celeste, and of the wisdom of revenge. He thought of Barker's mutilation, regretting it hadn't been enough. He felt Celeste falling but dared not look at her. He concentrated on the threat. The grin. The stink of the man. His catlike movements. And the arrogance. He heard William's multi-tonal wheezing on his right, a counterweight to the cavernous silence. He heard the shuffle of a foot under the table like a great stone being dragged over broken glass. A trickle of sweat ran in his armpit. The blinking of his lids passed like whole nighttimes, opening to reveal a new day, and blink after blink, the same bad situation. His heart beat in his ears like the DiOrio grandfather clock, that ticked all his days until they left the Hills like Women Lying Down—a turning forward, a click-stop; a turning forward, a click stop— measuring the narrowing of his options. Like swimming against the current above a waterfall. He settled on one point. Save her. He would kill. Or die in the process. And he knew that in doing so, he'd be linked to Barker forever. He thought of the dorjay and regretted that he would fail to deliver it.

"Stand up," Barker said to Celeste. He licked his lips.

But she didn't move.

"Yes," said Zhampa to himself, cheering her defiance. Then panicking, "No, get up," he urged telepathically. "Don't be sitting down."

"You deaf?" Barker said, his voice rising. "I said 'Stand up.'"

And she did stand. Like a drugged person.

"All I want is even-even, don't you know," he said, reasonably, looking at Celeste. "If I leave here, you're gonna be crippled like I am."

Zhampa glanced at Gabe and Oakley. They had no solution. Barker spat on the table. "William," he said, "you do the honors on your little slut friend, 'cause, I can't hold the pistol and make things right at the same time. Drop her trousers," he said, "and cut her clit to the bone."

William looked aghast at the gunman.

"She'd sacrifice you like *that*," Barker said, snapping the fingers of his free hand. "Get up and get even. Use that vicious little cutter inside her boot."

William stood but weaved as with a fever.

"Oakley," Zhampa said. "Tourniquet." Barker's eyes flickered, almost drawn to him. "Look at me, you bastard," he screamed inside his head. "Look at me one instant."

"Tourniquet," Oakley said. "You got it."

Barker wrinkled his brow and mouthed the word. Still not understanding, when he turned to look at Oakley, Zhampa pinned the forearm of his gun hand to the table with his left hand and leapt to his feet with such speed that his chair shot across the room. Barker wheeled his head to assess the pressure on his wrist and, bewildered, he followed the chair as it hit the wall. Zhampa's right hand disappeared behind his head, his long black hair whirling like a dumped bucket of crows, and out of the chaos of it flew a silver arching blur. There was thunder on the table, a gunshot and human cries.

Zhampa and Barker struggled with the arm as it gushed blood in four huge bursts. The hand, with the pistol still in it, lay on the table. Oakley snatched Barker's free arm out of the air and yelled, "Take it, Gabe. Take it," and when Gabe did, Oakley piped, "Tourniquet coming, Chief." He sprang toward his gear.

Seeing William and Celeste had both fallen to the floor, Zhampa cast away the machete and swung his right fist across the bridge of Barker's nose. The Oklahoman shivered and went limp. As soon as Oakley had three turns on Barker's elbow artery, Zhampa went to the wounded. William was trying to push himself up, but his shoulder was spastic. Celeste lay unconscious underneath him.

"Easy, William," Zhampa said. "Roll. Roll here."

William lay back with a sharp cry. Trying to get close, Zhampa slipped and fell to his knees. Celeste's right breast and the floor were covered with blood. Gently he palpated her and unable to find an entrance wound, he panicked and lifted her clothes. Underneath, her skin was white and smooth. The blood was outside, all William's and Barker's.

They tied Barker to his chair and while Gabe put pressure on William's shoulder, Zhampa paced on the porch, thinking about the rest of his life and the consequences he'd carried for killing Curtis. When he came in, he was set to save Barker's lying, violent life. He pulled the sewing bag, the scalpel and the pliers. When they set a new tourniquet in Barker's armpit, the bleeding slowed to a dribble. Zhampa tied off the arteries and pulled out pieces of shattered bone with the pliers. Then he stretched the skin of Barker's wrist tight over the stump and stitched it. Over the hours, the worst of the bleeding stopped.

William's wound was in the meat behind his armpit. His courage gave way to fainting, which allowed the cut to be made and the metal to be removed. Worried about infection in both patients, Zhampa used the last of his wood alcohol and Celeste applied poultices. Through the night Barker alternated his groans with curses and in the morning he cried that they were chopping him to pieces.

"It's crueler than meeting my maker." He begged for death to take him, and said if he hadn't been bound, he would do it himself.

Oakley encouraged him. "Do the thing then. Make the world a better place."

Waiting for the flesh to congeal. Gabe hunted and, working smoothly with Oakley, butchered and dried a store of meat for the prairie. He staked out Mercedes and Barker's horse Bob to graze on the rich prairie grass. Barker had lied. His three rifles were in his tent roll, and when Gabe suggested that they take them and the horse as compensation for the trouble, Zhampa agreed.

They lost over a week's time dealing with Barker's second diminishment, though no one regretted the days with William, who finally left to seek his destiny in the city.

Wounded and with no horse to ride, Barker wouldn't follow them. All the same, as they made ready to leave him, Oakley said, "Next time it'll be something serious." When they had traveled almost out of hearing range, they heard him screaming and turned to see him shaking his stump at them until succumbing to the pain of it. He hobbled into the house. When Gabe opened his mouth to run him down, Zhampa said, "Knock it off. There are no winners here."

Barker's horse paid for his association by hauling everybody's load. He pulled the cart with Celeste's pack tied on. Gabe and Oakley's packs were ganged together into panniers across his haunches. Freed from their burdens, they made good time across the first stretch of prairie.

And now they were armed. They had three rifles with over eighty rounds and almost two hundred rounds for the handgun. Four days out on the old road to Regina, Gabe convinced Zhampa to let him use some of the ammunition for target practice. They set up some sticks, but to Gabe's consternation, he was not a natural shot; the recoil bewildered him. Oakley watched from a distance, then came over and held out his hand for the pistol.

"First," he said to Gabe, "plant your feet. Be connected with the earth. The steadiness of the barrel comes from the ground. Second, Relax. Make the weapon part of your body. Third, Don't look at it when aiming. You don't look at your finger when you point, do you? Fourth, squeeze it like you're making juice of a potato." He wheeled to the targets, squeezing three times in as many seconds. The sticks flew. He slapped the gun back into Gabe's hand and turning to Zhampa said, "Third best shot in the marines firearms course." He paused. "It's been a while." Then he returned to where he had been.

Zhampa burst out laughing and the rumble in his body made him laugh even more. Having not heard that sound for a decade, Celeste, too, began to laugh. Oakley turned back wearing a boyish look and started to bubble-spit through his cobra opening, which brought on hysterics in the others. Though it was at his expense, Gabe joined in, too. Hooting, they all hung on each other until one by one they fell to the ground in no hurry for the fit to pass. And they camped right there. The next day Gabe learned to shoot.

The road improved and signs of war decreased. The broad sky and thick prairie grass spread before them, lush and waiting. "There's nobody left,"

Celeste said as they passed yet another abandoned farm, perfect in every other way. "Where did they go?"

Zhampa shook his head.

Another day in the distance, a herd of buffalo. Through the field glasses, Celeste saw magic, Gabe and Oakley saw meat. "New score," Zhampa said. "Nature, five hundred. Man, one."

Ten days after the gun practice, the horses halted, batting their ears. Some kind of thunder. Oakley turned. "A motor, Chief, coming this way. They must've seen the horses." And he made for cover with one of the rifles. A hundred yards off, two human heads skimmed the top of the grass, then stopped, motor idling. One man held up binoculars, conferred with his friend and waved. Zhampa waved back.

"Get ready for the past," he said to Celeste and Gabe. "And hold the horses. They're going to hate this." To Oakley he said, "I'm going to meet these guys. Whatever happens, protect these two kids." With the machete, he cut his way through chest high grass to a fair-skinned youth in a military outfit, standing next to a platform vehicle with wheels almost as big as he was. After they spoke, he climbed aboard and the engine roared. As the machine approached, the horses stamped their feet and flared their nostrils.

"Cut the engine, okay?" said Zhampa climbing down. "These are my companions, Gabe and Celeste. That's my friend Oakley over there, fiddling with the gear. This is LG Tanner—Lieutenant of God Arrod Tanner, right? And Lieutenant of God Luke Wilhelm. "

"Walking to the ocean, are you?" said LG Tanner bowing to Celeste. "Praise God. Bless you all. The main farm at Seradipa is about thirty miles from here. You're welcome to stay with us a while. But I warn you," he said. "You may never want to leave. I've offered to take you and your father there today, if you care to travel with us. Of course, I understand if you don't. He says you've never been in a vehicle."

Celeste turned her body to the side, and, the back of her hand on her mouth, looked sidelong at the two men. Zhampa knew she was tamping down a smile. Then she came and shook their hands. When Gabe came forward, he focused on the pistols in their smart leather holsters.

"Is it safe?" Celeste asked.

"It's loud," said Zhampa. "But it's not as bad when you're on it. What do you call that thing?"

"That's a prairie creeper," Tanner said. "Very safe. I ride 'em all the time."

"Prairie creeper," Zhampa repeated. "But, if we ride, Gabe and Oakley, you'll have to walk in behind us. You okay with that? They say we're pretty much on course to be going right by their place anyway. They got a community farm up there. How many people did you say?"

Wilhelm answered. "I think in the three enclaves we're at three hundred and ninety-four."

"Uh, uh. Three hundred and ninety-six," Tanner said. "Woman in the Thirty-to-Forty had twins, day before yesterday."

"Praise Jesus," said Wilhelm.

"Actually we're out here looking for someone," Tanner said, his tone more business. "Didn't come home two days ago. You can imagine that's pretty worrisome."

"Out hunting?" Gabe asked.

"No, we grow our own. You'll see."

"Zhampa says you haven't seen any sign of people over this way," Tanner said, his voice rising.

"No, we've been wondering if anybody lived out here," Gabe said.

"Yes, sir," said Wilhelm. "Lot's of people live here. By the grace of God."

9

Over even ground, the creeper had a top speed of fifteen miles an hour. A type of methane tractor, it was geared for power. Panels salvaged from old automobiles ringed the deck to form a waist-high rail. Lieutenant of God Luke Wilhelm's any little twist of the steering wheel caused the huge front tires to squirm in the soil. While stopped at the ford of a creek, he explained that after the Wrath of God—as he called the Unraveling—the first Seradipans collected as many vehicles as they could find fuel to drive or tow and stockpiled them near Enclave One. Using the parts, they had been creating any machine they needed.

In the afternoon, they rode through miles of pastures and carefully tended fields. On the crest of a long prairie slope, Celeste gasped at the sight of the compound.

Tanner leaned into her ear. "Father John says that if buildings are set on the land properly, just seeing them allows the Elixir of God to enter the soul. He says that our work is a gift to humankind. What do you think, Miss Celeste?" He offered Seradipa with a theatrical drag of his hand.

Celeste's eyes followed the cuff link on his khaki uniform and then scanned him again. He was blond, clean-shaven, with the pink still in his cheeks. A strong chin and an easy smile. His boots were new and spit-polished. His sidearm, his broad brim hat and the little brass button on his left collar were all stamped with SPD. He had green eyes and a melodious voice.

"Very beautiful," she said.

"Over to the left is the old farm complex—the original buildings," Tanner said. "And you can see the new main house for Father John on that rise behind. Great view from up there. Those smaller houses by the pond are for the Council of Elders. It's hard to see from here, but there are three new barns, just the roofs showing. The big building in the center of things is our new sanctuary. It's being completed this week. Father John had us burn the old one. Said it was impure and that fire was God's cleanser. The school for the little ones there, and the machine shop. That blue building houses the kitchens. Those low ones are the barracks. They're the heart of the community, as Father John says. 'Without the workers what are we?'"

Zhampa counted eight low buildings made of sloping concrete walls set into the hill, the ends of their rafters almost touching their neighbors.

"They look like old silage sloughs," Zhampa said.

"What?"

"The barracks."

"Yeah, I think they were," Tanner said, "but they've been quarters as long as I can remember. The tannery's there. That long building's the methane facility, and the generators are next to it. By the way, Mr. DiOrio, you might appreciate this. Our plan is to process our own oil someday soon. There are some old wells not far from here, and we're trying to get them running, but we haven't mastered all the mechanics yet. Father John says oil will give us more time for rest and praise."

In the common yards and down lanes, people were raking and painting. Several crews of carpenters were busy. Three young men wheeled carts loaded with debris. Beyond the school, lines of laundry flapped in the breeze.

"It's like a beehive," Celeste said.

"That's good," Tanner said. "It's a lot like that. We work in eight-hour shifts, clear around the clock." And responding to Zhampa's look, he said, "We're short on housing and the shifts allow us to share beds. But we're planning to build more housing soon."

"Families function that way?"

"We raise our children communally. Father John says that ownership of children is one of the roots of animosity. Mothers share in the care and schooling and in that way they learn how to love all the children. It's the root to greater love. Here our women are mothers to everyone."

Wilhelm guided the creeper along the dirt tracks through the compound. The glances they got varied, as if some residents hoped the strangers were someone else, and others were happy they weren't.

"I spent my first ten years in this one here," said Tanner pointing as they passed the row of barracks.

"And now?" Celeste asked.

"I'm in one of the ones for men. The Twenty-to-Thirty. It's down on the end."

Celeste looked where he pointed.

"When my hitch on the Perimeter Detail is up, I hope to get moved to the ILO. That stands for Interior Law and Order. Luke and I both do, 'cause that's usually where the council elders are drafted from."

"You have crime here?" Zhampa said. "Hard to imagine."

"It's rare, really. Only when someone gets confused, you know, forgets the essential points. Then the ILO is called upon for his safety. We all see it as a helping role."

"What's the Council?" Celeste asked, "And what's it mean to be drafted?"

"To be of service. Father John says God wants us to dedicate our lives to the community as a way to show our gratitude to Him. The good thing is that Councilors have their own rooms in one of the old main houses. It's quieter up there."

The prairie creeper backfired three times as Luke cut the throttle. People nearby covered their ears. Zhampa smiled and put his arm around Celeste. She leaned into him for a moment, then busied herself with her clothes and ran her fingers through her hair. Wilhelm guided them into the yard of the Seradipa Garage and killed the engine. There were seven bays.

A man with grease up to his elbows came alongside. "She run all right?" he asked.

"Yep," said Wilhelm. "No problem. This one's a rock. Good ol' Number Six."

Two men in the green outfits of the ILO strode over to meet them. The first one asked, "Any sign?"

"Not a thing," Tanner said. "But we ran into this group. From the east. All the way from a place called Vermont. They say they're going to the ocean."

"Whoa!" said the second man. "The Pacific? Praise be to God. On foot? What inspires that?"

"Got to renew some old connections," said Zhampa, stepping down. His legs buzzed from the ride.

"Welcome to Seradipa. I'm Day Officer Markell of the ILO. My partner, Officer Keeps. Must be a very important connection for you to go all that way."

Zhampa nodded.

"What kind of traffic have you met on the road? Uneventful I hope."

"Really quiet lately," Zhampa said reflecting. "Beautiful country. So great to see the buffalo. Well, now that I think of it, we did run into a sorry rascal some weeks back."

Officer Keeps glanced quickly at Markell, who shook his head. "That's good, I mean about the quiet," Markell said. "We hardly get many folk up here anymore. I don't think we've seen more than a dozen parties since last fall."

Celeste's eyes fixed on some intensity inside the garage. Zhampa turned and saw bare bulbs hanging. "You have electricity," he said.

"Yes," said Wilhelm climbing down. "We're on generators; they run the whole place. Someone'll give you a tour, I'm sure. Wish we could, but Tanner and I have to debrief our patrol."

As the four men left, Keeps nudged Tanner and spoke into his ear.

"Oh yeah," Tanner said loud enough to hear, "she'll be a beautiful piece when she's cleaned up."

Halfway through their tour, Zhampa became restless. They'd seen the machine shop, the school, and the weaving shed. They had toured the kitchen and had eaten good food with butter. They'd marveled at the methane facility. But during the explanation of the lights in the barracks coming on an hour before the next shift was due at work, he began to wish he were with Gabe and Oakley. The idea of sleeping in a dorm full of men—the Forty-to-Fifty—depressed him. Four months out, he'd become used to infinity overhead. Seeing the herd of seven hundred cows, he longed for his own barns. But technology and the division of labor mesmerized Celeste; men did the hard work and taught the high school. Women gardened, cooked and made boots and clothes on electric machines. And in the machine shop they made pots and pans and all manner of metal goods.

"You're doing a lot of building," Zhampa said. "Where's the lumber coming from?"

"We're dismantling the farms all across this part of Saskatchewan," their guide said. "Taking them down piece by piece," He introduced himself as Joseph. The sunburst badge sewn on his blue jumpsuit said, "Construction Detail."

"Using the prairie creepers?"

"Yeah. They haul flatbed trailers. We remill everything over at Enclave Number One. It's about a dozen miles from here."

"I wondered where all the prairie creepers were."

"Actually most of them are on perimeter duty. But we have three for transport of lumber and whatever we find out there. The two new creepers are almost finished. They'll have twice the range of the current ones, about six hundred miles."

"That's thirty days of our walking. So Enclave Number One is as big as this one?"

"Used to be the main complex and people still work there, but at night only a few men stay over."

"Joseph," said Celeste, "do you want to be want to be part of the council, too?"

Joseph made a sour face. "No chance of that," he said.

"If you joined the SPD, couldn't you get drafted like Tanner and Wilhelm?"

Joseph worked his jaw muscles. "I praise God," he said, "but I don't lick my honey off a sharp knife."

After dinner Zhampa and Celeste and all residents under the Council level were divided by gender to attend Bible study and just before the lights went out in the Forty-to-Fifty, an ILO poked his head in the door. "It's been a beautiful shift, by the grace of God," he announced, "and tomorrow is a new dawn. Let us praise Him now and first thing upon waking."

Mouths moved following the prayer: " . . . And God bless those who walk among us who carry the word. God bless Father John. God bless those whose time has come. And may false prophets find their way back to the fold."

Celeste didn't sleep well in the women's Twenty-to-Thirty that first night. In the few minutes she had after breakfast, she told Zhampa that the door kept opening and closing, but in the pitch black, her drowsy mind couldn't make out who was using it. When the first shift whistle blew, she was taken off to the boot shop, which began her scheming to have new footwear made for herself and her companions. She learned how to lay out patterns on cowhide and how to operate the mechanical shears. In the middle of the morning, Tanner came by to make sure she was being taken care of. She reddened with his attention and afterwards, she felt the eyes of two young co-workers. Susan, the head of the shop, and Cloe, a sweet mother of six, who moved like a great river, looked at her, too, but with wistful and sweet expressions. It was all very confusing. Before they were separated for Bible study, she told Zhampa that she was looking forward to getting some guidance on things happening there.

Zhampa hung barn doors with a building crew. When Gabe and Oakley didn't show up that evening, four Council Elders interviewed him, asking questions about his journey and his faith. He felt spared by the arrival of Wilhelm, who gave his recollection of finding Zhampa's band. One elder groused about Tanner's unavailability, but in the end, they dismissed Zhampa and Wilhelm with salutations for a pleasant night.

The next morning Zhampa had less than a minute with Celeste as she passed by on an errand. Her face radiated and she said that wonderful things were happening and promised to fill him in before dinner. Late that afternoon Oakley and Gabe walked through the main square, accompanied by an ILO detail. Zhampa jogged over to greet them.

"Where've you been? Everything okay?" he asked.

"Broke a wheel on the wagon," Oakley said. "Had to spend most of a day putting the spare on."

Zhampa knew there was no spare wheel; he and Oakley had discussed the risk before setting out. Oakley was telling him to play along with his story. "Yeah," he said. "I wondered if that was what happened. Did you find the tools you needed all right?"

"Took a while. You buried them in the bottom of the gear."

"I'm ready for my ride on the creeper," said Gabe.

"Impatience," Oakley said dragging out the first syllable. "We got to get the horses to the barn first. Talk to you at dinner, Chief?"

"Well, maybe at the end of Bible study."

"Whatever," said Oakley. "I know my bible pretty good already."

"You're gonna learn a little more here in Seradipa."

"Things aren't what they seem here, Chief," Oakley began when the two men walked through the stubble of a hay field after twilight. Away from the lights and the humming. Gabe had taken off in a creeper after the meal; Oakley said he'd seen an SPD pull him out of the dinner hall.

"That was Wilhelm. Probably a good thing. I can't imagine how Gabe'll take to Bible study." He smiled and shook his head.

"They're looking for somebody. Somebody special." Oakley said.

"So I gather."

"We ran into the guy."

"Really?" Zhampa paused to consider. "What's his story?"

"It's hard to keep it straight. He says he used to run this place."

"What?"

"His name's Thomas. He's a mouthful of religion," Oakley said.

"What'd he do?"

"He says he's been under house arrest for three years. Got away two months ago. Says his protégé led a revolt. Locked him up and turned this place into a . . . a cocktail of wine and arsenic."

"Wilhelm and Tanner said they were looking for somebody who didn't come home two days before. Remember?"

Oakley nodded. "Probably just covering up."

"Is the protégé's name Father John by any chance?"

"John. Yeah," Oakley said. "Don't know about the 'Father' part. Thomas got hot when he talked about it. He says John's rewriting history."

"You know, I'm getting the sense that Father John's ill. Nobody sees him around."

"Not according to Thomas. He says the guy's an operator. Says 'Absence creates myth and myth is power.'"

"You mean he's staying out of sight for the effect."

"That's what I gather. They were friends for a while. Worked together. But they disagree on faith—what it is and how to hold it. It's an ugly business now, Chief."

"An old drama."

"One that's about to boil over is my guess. As far as Christians go, Thomas seems to be the real deal. He joked that his only mistake was he turned the other cheek. Says this John fellow stirred up the girls. Took the young men on trips. Foraging days became training missions." Oakley slapped his hands twice like they were covered with flour. "Quick coup d'etat," he said, "and now John's rebuilding paradise."

"It's more like an armed camp, these boy soldiers and all. Makes my flesh crawl."

"I got eyes, Chief."

"Where's Thomas now?"

"Can't say. He's on the move. East of here maybe. We split up yesterday. He said we might see him again, depending on how things work out. He's got friends inside here. Asked me to carry a message to the mechanics. But they're in a tricky spot, these people. If they don't go along, they might join the Fifty-Fives early."

"What are the Fifty-Fives?"

"Haven't heard?"

"No," said Zhampa.

"Anybody over fifty-five is done contributing. Diminishing returns on their labor. At fifty, they're sent to Enclave Number Three. And—here's the kicker—at fifty-five they're offered back to the Lord. John's idea. Thomas thinks it was just a plan to get rid of him."

"They're killed?"

"I think they're left out on the prairie. In late fall."

Zhampa reflected; there were no old people in Seradipa. "How old is Thomas?"

"Close to sixty, I guess."

"So why's he alive?" Zhampa asked

"Too big a fish, maybe. Besides, it's hard to kill your teacher."

Zhampa rubbed his mouth.

"John's a mechanical engineer. Religion's a tool to him. But you know the funny thing?" Oakley said with a sarcastic smile. "By keeping Thomas alive and absent, his power's stronger than ever. Seems John still has things to learn."

Zhampa looked at the horizon and dreamed of pulling the cart.

"We've walked into a cat fight, Chief. We got to get out of here."

"I'm ready. But I'm worried about Celeste. I hardly see her and something's cooking. Maybe Gabe will be a problem, too. Did you see his eyes?"

"Like a bobcat's. There's a lot here to turn the head of a young man. The mechanical world, Chief, it's a powerful drug. And there's sex, too. Seems John has his gospels sort of blended with the physical."

"Huh?"

"The way Thomas tells it, sex is the reward for loyalty. The young bucks have the run of the place."

"But they're teaching purity."

Oakley shrugged.

Zhampa halted. He looked at the stars coming on. Saturn was heading for the horizon. He began connecting dots. . . . The barracks. The age categories. The door to the Twenty-to-Thirty swinging all night on its hinges. The generosity of the mothers. "Our women are mothers to everyone," Tanner had said. "Oakley, I don't think the mothers here know who the fathers of their children are."

"That's a lot of pressure, Chief."

"God, what a mess. I hope Celeste can handle herself."

"If she understands what's happening."

"She's probably out of her depth. And Gabe's definitely going to be a sucker for all of it."

"I'll bet he hasn't been laid back to back ever."

"If we don't get him out of here, we may lose him."

"Worse than that. If his lips get loose about who we met out there, some folk in Seradipa may pay the price."

"We're not safe either, if he talks."

"They have creepers, Oak. We got to walk out of here nice and easy. We got to get free without causing suspicion."

"I think it's getting time for you to start figuring out how to run that dorjay."

Zhampa laughed a gallows laugh. "Well, I could put a hell of a dent on somebody's skull with it. Strange, isn't it? I'm carrying a tool of incredible power and don't know how to open it."

"Are you trying?"

"No," he said, Coco's death flashing in his mind. "Rinpo didn't tell me I should go be a sorcerer's apprentice."

"Ol' Rinpo's not here anymore to tell you what or what not to do. Mister, I don't think that dorjay's going to save the world all by itself."

They turned to go back. The Northern Lights rippled the heavens. A warm breeze floated from the south.

"By the way," said Oakley, "I gave the rifles to Thomas. Figured he could use 'em."

"You're taking sides, aren't you? I don't know how smart that is."

"You'd have done the same. That there is genuine man. Have they asked you about guns?"

"No," Zhampa said. "I think they have so many they aren't worried. And the kids that carry them are true-blue Father John. But, Oakley, didn't the guys on the creeper see our rifles? What happens if they come to take them?"

"Shit. I didn't think of that."

"Here we go again."

They walked a while.

"Chief," said Oakley finally, "you know, if I had my way, I'd go back to be with the We People."

"I know. I think about them too. They weren't perfect, but they were on to something. And that old woman in the council got the dorjay to glow." Then he added, "You're free to go if you want," but immediately regretted making the offer.

Oakley said, "You don't have to worry about it, Chief. I owe you one."

In the middle of the next morning, two ILO came to Zhampa's carpentry site and summoned him to the new farmhouse. He worried that Gabe's absence from Bible study had run them afoul of the system. Or maybe he had blown Thomas's cover. On the way past the garage, he looked in to make some contact with Oakley, who was working there. His scout gave a simple wave.

They led Zhampa to a pleasant room overlooking the ponds on the far side of the hill from the main complex. He sat on a grand couch and recognized two of the three men seated across from him as Elders from the late night meeting. The third man sat slouched, filling a wingback chair. His chest decals outweighed those of the other two. After tea was poured and clover honey offered, the man said, "I am Robert Logan, Adjutant General of the Council of Elders. Allow me to come straight to the point. LG Tanner tells us that you're a healer."

Zhampa returned his look but said nothing.

"What kinds of things do you do?"

"I had training in various disciplines, but it was years ago. There are many things I can't do." He thought of Barker's hand. "Are you sick or injured?"

"Seems that young lady you brought—your stepdaughter—has been singing your praises. She says you're a walking hospital."

Zhampa chuckled politely.

"I presume you are aware," Logan said leaning forward with a pallid smile, "that she is hooking LG Tanner."

Zhampa pursed his lips. "I haven't had a chance to speak with her," he said finally, "or hardly to see her at all in three days. And actually I resent that."

"I understand," Logan said. "Seradipa's a world unto itself. And many people who come here get caught up in the excitement of the transformation of the spirit. For others, perhaps like yourself, it takes some getting used to."

Zhampa took a sip of tea to hide clenching his jaw. "She can take care of herself," he said. "Truth is I'm more worried about LG Tanner. You don't know her like I do. But we ran into you by chance. We're on a long trip, and now that the other members of my party have arrived, we're getting ready to leave."

"We know your plans. And we understand, of course."

"We will be heading west tomorrow after breakfast."

"That'll be unfortunate. You haven't had enough chance to see all that we can offer."

"I'll be fifty in two years." The words just flew out.

The other two elders shifted in their chairs, but Logan was cool. He replied that he'd heard the cockamamie story of the Fifty-Fives and assured Zhampa that he, Logan, was fifty-seven and still quite comfortable in Seradipa. "Perhaps you'd care to stop by to see my quarters before lunch, or maybe after. We can talk about these things."

"If there's time, I'll look you up after we pack our gear."

"That will be something to look forward to. . . . Mr. DiOrio, we're not all that bad. You've been comfortably cared for during your stay? And well fed?"

Zhampa nodded.

"And we know, for instance, that your Celeste is making boots for your party while she's here. Actually we're happy to share our bounty. After all, it is the gift of God. And please feel welcome to replenish your foodstuffs from the kitchen before you leave." Logan gave a charitable nod to his two junior councilors. "But today, we are interested in you for your abilities as a doctor."

Zhampa felt the pinch of jaws. "I'll be happy to help, but I'm not a doctor."

"You are not underestimating yourself just a little?"

"There are some things that I am good at. Diagnosis and pain management."

"You can adjust bones and joints, correct?"

"Most of the time, yes."

"That's good. All we ask is that you treat Father John. He's wrenched his back and wants to be able to address the congregation on Sabbath, day after tomorrow. We're hoping that you will be able to stay that long. In fact, we insist." The elders chuckled as if at a previous joke.

'Stay inside the system,' Zhampa counseled himself. And he nodded his assent.

"Good. It's settled then. Father John would like to be treated directly."

An ILO officer showed him to a room, prepared with a treatment table, two chairs and a desk. When Zhampa told the officer that he needed to get his supplies, the ILO motioned him to the window. His cart sat outside the door on a covered porch. Zhampa feared violation, but Logan appeared in the doorway.

"We haven't touched your things," he said. "We respect all our guests here."

"I'm sorry. I'll be glad to help. And I didn't know about the boots. Thank you."

"Please wait here. I'll go get Father John."

Throughout the main compound, crews of all capacity focused on the preparations for the first full Sabbath gathering to be held in the new sanctuary. Seating arrangements were fine-tuned. Grounds were swept. The kitchens whirled in high gear preparing special delicacies. The carpentry crews worked with urgency. The choir rehearsed and the children drilled in their banner parade and pageantry. The laundry team took on several more women in the ironing room.

Late in the evening, Zhampa was ushered into Logan's outer office and found Oakley and Gabe waiting for him with a sergeant and a corporal from the ILO.

"Day after tomorrow," said Oakley, "they're going to transport us by creeper to the western perimeter."

"That's great." Zhampa looked for confirmation to the ILO officers; the sergeant had heard this, and said so.

Oakley continued. "And since they say you'll be busy here through the Sabbath Celebration, we need to make sure we have what we need from the stores and that you have your cart and gear together and ready to go."

"And I'm heading out early tomorrow on Mercedes," said Gabe, "because he can't keep up with a creeper and I want to make sure we meet up out there where they drop you off. Do you know which direction we're going exactly?"

"What about Barker's horse?" Zhampa said. "Are you leaving him here? Shouldn't we take him along?"

"I'm planning to lead him. It's real nice having two."

"Well, we're heading west northwest toward Unity and Macklin. Are the roads in decent shape?" he asked the sergeant.

The sergeant shrugged. "I've never been that far out."

"Okay," said Gabe. "I'll take Coco's packs and the tarp and enough food for about four days, in case we miss each other." His voice was leaping with excitement.

"And Chief, I'll take your cart down to the garage before we leave." Oakley pursed his lips. "Any chance you can have it ready by tomorrow evening? We leave early in the morning."

"Sure I'll take a medicine kit with me to the celebration in case Father John needs anything."

"Zhampa," said Gabe looking straight at him, "I'm going to need the bailing wire in your pack to get out of here."

Zhampa knew that Oakley carried the wire. "Okay," he said, looking hard at the hunter, "but my pack is still in the Forty-to-Fifty."

"Can I just go in there and get it. If so, I'll go now."

The ILO looked at each other and the sergeant said to the corporal, "No, why don't you get it for them?"

"Now?" said the corporal

"Yes, please. That way we can finish this meeting early and I can get home to my evening duties."

After the corporal left, Gabe turned to the sergeant. "Can I get more tea?"

"No, no, I'll get it for you."

When the sergeant slipped out the door and walked down the hall, Gabe grinned. In a low voice, Oakley said, "We're leaving sooner than we're telling you, Chief. You got to get free before the show is over."

"Why? You just said we'll be clear to leave in the morning. They've asked me to stay in case Father John needs a twist. Apparently he puts on quite a show. Leaps around the stage when the Spirit of God enters his body."

Oakley pouted his lips and shook his head. "*We* have permission to go day after tomorrow. Gabe, Celeste and me. But they aren't going to let *you* go at all."

Zhampa raised his eyebrows and in the silence they all listened for footsteps returning. "How do you know?"

"Luke Wilhelm is working for Thomas," said Gabe with a seriousness that was new to Zhampa. "The mechanics and one of the Elders, too. I'm leaving tomorrow morning. They're leaving after the show starts, and a bunch of others."

"Others? Walking in the dark?" asked Zhampa with a snort.

"No. On creepers."

"Creepers? You've heard how loud they are. They'll be on us before we reach the horizon. I don't like this."

"They've worked it out, Chief. Got to trust us on this one."

"We've got to run the perimeter, too, Oakley. Think of that. Nothing a couple of little suck-up SPD boys wouldn't like better than to catch us on the run."

"Chief, these people have been waiting for a chance like this for a long time. Their stars are lining up. Gabe here has a part to play early on." Oakley glanced at the hunter; he became sad and his lips rattled as he blew out. "And the celebration is a perfect diversion, one they're handing to us.

If we don't go now, we may be stuck here for years waiting for this Spirit of God to find a crack into our brains. Me, Chief, I'm going to the ocean. And I'm going tomorrow night."

The sound of footsteps coming back from the kitchen caused Oakley to lean forward. "Bring your cart down with you to the main square before the Sabbath Celebration," he whispered. "Leave it in the garage yard. Get back there yourself, ready to go, two hours after sunset and don't be seen."

10

In the bustle of the Sabbath morning, Gabe slipped out of Seradipa without attracting attention. He was worth watching. Rarely would the Seradipans see a creature that was not of their world and so gifted at his calling. The hunter. His clothes moved on his body like a hide, smoothed from the miles, colored like the land. And schooled by the distances behind him, he walked with no wasted energy. In the barn beyond the methane complex, he had packed the two animals with provisions from the kitchen stores. He'd added another canteen and a coil of rope. With the new boots that Celeste had made for him on his feet, his quiver slung over his back and, mounted on Mercedes, he looked like a prince off to war. He had his instructions. "Be seen heading west outside the perimeter and then disappear." The SPD was informed of his departure, of course, and the mechanics noted his timing.

Oakley also rose early and organized his pack in the Forty-to-Fifty. The few items of clothing thrown on top and the buckles undone signaled he was planning to spend another night.

Celeste hadn't consummated her attraction to Tanner until that night just past, though on several nights previously, he'd walked her through the Seradipan mating ritual. That morning she was among the last to leave her bunk in the Women's Twenty-to-Thirty. She puttered in the bathhouse and came late enough to breakfast to find only dregs of chicory coffee and some cold corn meal shrinking in the corners of a pot in the washtub line.

In a distant part of the compound, Zhampa fretted. How was he to show up at the garage at the appointed hour with his gear and the cart without being seen? His duties that morning left little time to think. After Father John's treatment, a stream of elders and ILO officers presented him with a wide range of conditions, from jammed fingers and sciatica to insomnia and parasites. They came in groups, each getting treated and carrying on their meetings and debriefings, as if he couldn't hear.

"So is there anything we can do with the lighting if Father J isn't up to his charismatic best tonight?"

"The children will be ready to come out at any moment with a ribbon parade and I'll check with the choir masters. They're old hands at this."

"All he really has to do is give the Fire of Faith speech to keep them inspired until harvest time. The man always comes through in the clutch."

"Maybe so, but there were a few hairy moments during the Easter Service when I thought he wasn't going to be able to continue. Thanks to God for the Holy Elixir. He seems to lift up when he's got a couple of capfuls down."

"Amen to that."

"Praise God."

"We've got another problem with Craven having his Fiftieth later this month. He's too well liked to just be sent to Number Three."

"Yeah, I think we may have to have another revelation from on high and extend the age."

"But we have the Thomas problem to resolve first, otherwise they might be asking for the return of the old ways."

"The Perimeter Detail is still finding signs and they're doubling patrols. It's just a matter of time."

Those patrols circled Serdipa clockwise and their efficient schedule protected the Seradipans from outside threats. Oakley learned that a typical shift left the compound heading west out to a distance of more than fifteen miles, the exact mileage determined sometimes by orders and sometimes by the pilot, if he were acting on appropriate signs. The patrol would proceed around the horizon, returning some seven hours later, unless they discovered something on their route that required investigation or a swift return to the compound for further instructions. Occasionally they stopped at Enclave One, which was thirteen miles north of the compound or traveled out thirty miles to check on the Over-Fifties in Enclave Three.

Gabe walked Mercedes and Bob west-northwest and waited in a creek bed until he heard the noontime creeper approaching from the south. He made sure that his backsides were seen heading off beyond the reach of Seradipa before he turned north, scribing an arc parallel to the usual creeper course. When he estimated that he was ten miles north of Enclave Number One, he headed south until he came upon the cluster of cottonwoods he sought. He unloaded the horses and set them to graze. Alone for the first time in weeks, he settled in the shade and ate some pork ribs. Two hours before sunset he hobbled both animals, then took off south on foot armed with his bow, the coil of rope, a canteen and a blanket.

Celeste spent that same dinner hour alone; she had no appetite. Tanner had mumbled a stiff farewell just before his eight p.m. patrol with Wilhelm. If she were leaving first thing in the morning, he said, he would still be asleep and would miss her departure. Oakley found her watching frogs by a small pond beyond the first set of pasture fences.

"You going to be ready to leave soon?" he asked.

"You're ripping me away from the first good place we've found," she said. There was a whip in her voice.

"It's not all bad, Celeste." He regarded her for a moment. "I'm sure Zhampa will understand, if you want to stay. We'll be leaving tonight, around eleven, if you'd like to say goodbye. We're meeting behind the garage. Just remember that no one knows, so be smart if you come. If you don't, I'll tell him I saw you."

"Eleven?" she said.

"Change in plans. An hour after full dark. Keep it confidential." As he walked away neither of them looked toward the other.

Around noon of the Sabbath day, Zhampa treated Father John with a stomach tonic and felt his patient's lower back spasm release under his hands. Afterwards, he lay down on the treatment table and slept until an ILO aide brought him a plate of dinner.

"Mussels?" Zhampa said. "Fresh water mussels? You have everything here."

"Yes, Sir," said the aide. "We have a special breeding pond. They're reserved for the elders and Father John."

"Ever had one?"

"Ah, I shouldn't say, Sir, but yes, I sneaked one once."

"Have another."

The aide slurped one down and smiled. Then he turned to Zhampa and said in a low voice, "I am here to help you leave, Sir. If you pack your cart the way you want it, I'll see it gets downtown."

"When?"

"Tonight, Sir." And he winked. "I'm working with Wilhelm."

"The cart's out on the porch. Give me five minutes."

He tied up the few open satchels and slipped the machete back into its sheath. He felt a blood-rush of excitement, knowing he was soon to be back on the road.

Backstage in the new sanctuary that evening, Zhampa wondered how he could possibly get to the garage at eleven if the show lasted until midnight; two ILO aides and the newly appointed Elder Fritz never left his side. Beyond, the hall was filled with singing and the pageantry of various performances of children and women. At ten o'clock a dramatic history play of Seradipa started with a blacked out theater and twenty men beating wildly on percussion instruments, symbolizing—the audience was reminded—the Wrath of God. In a short scene, Thomas was portrayed as a well-meaning man with small vision, whose flimsy project survived by the arrival of Father John.

For the first hour and a half of the evening, Father John sat in the wings, musing, tapping his fingers to the music and sipping on a golden liqueur. Twenty minutes before he was to go on, he paced—rather unsteadily, Zhampa noticed—and gestured, silently reciting his oration.

Two minutes into Father John's performance, Zhampa's two ILO escorts left to join the audience. Elder Fritz seized his elbow, ushered him away from the stage and opening the backstage door, he said, "Lean on me. I'll get you there."

"He's taken a bit ill, I'm afraid," Fritz said when they passed the lone ILO in front of the sanctuary. "I'm taking him for a walk. If the air doesn't bring him around, we'll head back to find his treatment cart. By the way, son, Father John's speaking. I'm sure no one will mind if you slip inside."

"Yes, Sir. Thank you, Sir."

"Jesus loves you, son."

They walked slowly under clouds that hid the close-to-full moon. As always, the mechanics were working on two of the creepers, preparing the fleet for the next day's patrols.

"Are we taking them?" Zhampa asked.

Fritz shook his head and kept walking. On the backside of the garage the doors to the bays for the new creepers were open.

"In here," he said. "Climb up and Godspeed."

"Will you be all right?" Zhampa asked him. "The guards have seen you with me."

"Not everyone gets to freedom." He shoved out his lips in resignation. "Things will fall apart here in time. Then there will be new possibilities. But Thomas must get through now." Fritz shook his hand and pushed him toward the gangway. At the top Oakley pulled him up. Celeste and the rest of their gear were stowed alongside the left rail. The girl was numb. He went to her and sat down. When he touched her, she didn't turn to him; nor did she pull away. They waited.

Inside the church, a single beam of light shown down on Father John, whose voice filled the air with passion and promise. Not a soul dared look away. The spotlight faded to black. As symbol of the spirit of God passing amongst the Seradipans, Father John lit the candle of the New Gospel and, with it, ignited candles held by Elders, who moved through the crowd as the drums and cymbals created a rousing din.

The noise reverberated throughout the compound, and at that sign, a number of bodies rode the shadows from all directions, mounted the gangways and settled into the two vehicles. Two men sprinted from the generating facility and arrived breathless. Both mechanics appeared and took up pilot positions. The super creeper engines fired, but the expected roar was tempered by their newly fashioned mufflers. The machines jolted into gear and, without their lights, rolled out from their berths, following the tracks countless patrols had carved ahead of them to the west. After they had gone three hundred yards, the mechanics broke into broad smiles and a hushed cheer rose among the passengers.

Earlier that evening, using the place of the setting sun as his right-hand guidance, Gabe trotted like a wolf through shoulder-high grass back inside the patrol perimeter. In the last of the daylight, he found the compound and the mill of Enclave One quiet and stole through piles of used lumber to the house where the guards slept. He leaned his ear against the outside wall and counted four distinct voices. He listened for some minutes. Finally the one they called Eben said clearly, "I got to hit the outhouse. Don't drink all the beer before I get back." As Eben's friends laughed, Gabe sprinted across the yard to the outhouse, pulled back the little door and slipped inside. When he heard footsteps, he stood on the shelf that was the seat and hooked his fingers between the slats of the roof deck, pulling his body up into the peak where the darkness was thorough.

The door opened. Unaware, the man lowered his pants and sat. He didn't suffer long. He made only a short sound as Gabe's powerful legs wrapped around his windpipe. After, Gabe looked at the face to remember it, then removed the man's pistol belt and buckled it around his waist. He checked the gun's load, slid it back into the holster and patted it. He left the body as it was and closed the door. Again pressing his ear against the wall of the guardhouse, he heard the men gradually stumble onto the concern of missing their mate.

"I'll check for him," said one in an annoyed tone.

"I'll come with you," said a second.

"Not me," said the last, with a great burp, "I'll be right here topping myself off."

Realizing the difficulty of taking two at once, Gabe melted into the dark and assessed their strengths as they called from the porch. "Eben, Eben. You out there?" He heard them reassure each other before they split up to cover the area.

He caught the weaker one on the far side of a lumber pile. Caught him by lying down face-up in the weeds. "Waiting is good," Wicas taught him early on. "Sometimes track. Sometimes wait." The man who had been annoyed at Eben's disappearance would surely have become more so, if he'd had time to understand what happened next. Seeing Gabe's crumpled shape, he bent down to get a closer look. Wicas's knife thrust upwards through the soft spot where the tongue attaches to the lower jaw, pierced the roof of the mouth and entered the brain. Gabe finished the job with a swift rotation of the knife handle. The guard managed only one guttural groan before sucking a cupful of blood into his lungs. Though his pistol was in his hand, he couldn't think to fire it. Exhilarated, Gabe stood up, his legs astride his victim. He looked at the body in the moonlight, a man hardly older than himself, and he searched vainly for the words to one nagging question. And he might have stood there a long time, if the roar of a creeper approaching from the west hadn't distracted him. He was stunned by how close it was.

"If I'm going to be a warrior," he thought, "I'll have to think less."

Lights bobbing on the prairie caused the shadows of the mill buildings to leap against each other as in an earthquake. The two remaining guards gathered on the porch of the house. They expressed relief as the creeper came close. They slipped their weapons back into their holsters as the engine quit and the pilot dismounted.

"Great timing," called out the first. "We're having a strange night for the first time in my service."

"What do you mean?"

Gabe recognized Wilhelm's voice.

"Two of us have lifted off the face of the earth in the last half hour."

Wilhelm asked, "Are you sure it's not a miracle?"

The guards became quiet to consider the possibility.

"I mean, how do you know?" Luke said, walking closer. "What are the signs?"

"It's simple. They've gone out and not returned."

"Well, I haven't seen anything. Just swinging by to check on you. Had a feeling about tonight, you know. Don't worry. It can't be Thomas. He's out here somewhere, but he's an old man."

"Well, who, then?"

"Just me," came Gabe's hoarse whisper.

Luke jumped with the others. In the light spilling from the house door, they could clearly see the barrels of two Seradipan guns trained on them not five feet away.

"One at a time. Put your guns down on the deck. You first," he said to Luke.

They obeyed.

"Who are you?" one of the guards asked.

"A warrior," said Gabe. He directed Luke to tie the two guards with his rope and bind their feet together on the floor of the main room. Then Luke picked up his gun and led Gabe to the creeper. Tanner was inside bound and gagged. He stiffened and squirmed when he saw Gabe.

"He doesn't understand," said Luke. "Maybe Celeste will get through to him. Let's haul the wagons out."

The stealth crew in Seradipa had moved with simple and devastating effect. When the spotlight faded out and the Spirit of the New Gospel moved through the crowd to the cacophony of rattling and drums, the operators of the power generating plant scuttled the generators by pouring acid down the air intakes. They would not run again for many days. Father John and the others expected the lights to rise, but they learned yet again the lesson about relying on expectations. Seeing no need to blow the methane tanks, Thomas gave orders that they be spared. He wanted time, not death and destruction. There were four creepers not on patrol. Over the evening the mechanics ground their distributor shafts out of shape and slipped them back into the engine blocks; those motors would turn over but wouldn't fire. Father John, the true engineer, would think to check the shafts eventually; the mechanics gambled they would be out of range before he thought to do so.

The only other obstacle that could have hindered their progress would have been running into one of the four patrol creepers on duty. But as Luke piloted the last one out of Seradipa, the others, in their clockwise tour had already passed by the northern escape route that Thomas had planned. It would be another two hours before the next patrol even came in to Seradipa. It would need to be refueled and armed. Then they would need to catch the escapees. A race was a possibility, but the size difference of the fuel tanks meant that the patrol creeper would have been able to chase for, at most, 150 miles if they planned to make it back to Seradipa. Thomas was willing to take the chance, knowing that they would have a thirty-mile head start. Perhaps Father John would just let the super creepers go. In any case, it would be morning before the damage to the Seradipan systems could even be assessed.

Thomas wasn't restricted by thoughts of returning. The vehicles had a six hundred-mile range and he was intent on starting a new community in the foothills of the Rockies. First, the pilots headed to the mill to collect four salvage wagons, two for each creeper, to carry their gear. They pulled into the mill yard close to midnight and found the wagons, loaded with all the tools that Luke and Gabe could gather. Things like flourmills, scythes and shovels. Buckets and masonry hammers. A hand pump and a wheel harrow. From there they drove to Enclave Number Three where the Over-Fifties were waiting on the porches. Luke and Gabe drove the patrol creeper north with a fifth trailer to collect the horses.

Through the night, the travelers clung to the heaving decks of the creepers and spoke few words. They peered forward into the short blaze of the headlights and aft scanning for any sign of a pursuing party. Of the Vermont band, only Oakley slept, his head bouncing against the rail. The sight of his friend's repose comforted Zhampa, who rode with his arm around Celeste. She leaned into him, her mind drifting from the possibilities she had lost, to feeling slightly ill with the creeper's motion and to imagining the scene with Tanner.

"He was defiant until the end," said Luke.

"It looked as if he wanted to talk," Gabe explained as they switched the trailers so Mercedes and Bob could ride behind the quieter super creeper. "So we took his gag out. But I tell you, he didn't say "Praise God" once."

Luke concurred by wincing. "He was married to the New Gospel and wouldn't leave it," he said. "Denounced me and Thomas as heretics and said we'd be found and burned, just like in the old days."

In all they said, Celeste heard nothing to suggest that she was on Tanner's mind as they left him tied with the others at Enclave One. Around her in the dark, a sea of faces took on personal qualities as the dawn approached. So intent were they, she noticed, that when one head turned to a new direction, the others followed, like her flock of geese in the Hollow. Scattered among them were several lucky families who knew their true paternity. The mechanics each brought a lady. One ILO officer held two pregnant women close to him. A young woman who clutched a boy child, turned out to be Luke's mate.

The lead creeper was similarly loaded. Beside its pilot stood a weary man, the eldest among them, slightly stooped, yet swept with elegance. His eyes focused beyond the beam of the headlights. A delicate grin mounted the purse of his lips and his long gray hair gave him a slightly androgynous look. Now and then he spoke in low tones to his pilot and at the loading of the Over-Fifties, he had briefly squeezed Zhampa's hand.

"Companions in travel," he had said. Zhampa felt washed in peace.

When the terrain presented obstacles ahead, the vehicles consorted side by side. Often it was Luke in the center creeper who made the recommendations.

"He's Thomas' son, you know," said an elderly lady into Zhampa's ear.

"Why would Father John ever let him be in the SPD?"

"John, the *engineer*," she corrected. "He never knew who the father was. The mother, she's over there," said the lady flicking her finger toward a matronly woman. "It was a secret love and the child was born before John came. She guarded his lineage for more than two decades. Luke only learned himself two years ago. Thomas was supposed to be celibate, you see, but he loved Melissa. It was she who helped him realize the fullness of God." After a pause, she said, "It's nice to think they can spend their golden years together and in the open."

Twice the convoy halted for five minutes, once after sunup and again at noon. Without grumbling, all re-embarked in order to make their goal of one hundred and seventy-five miles before dark. Finally as the sun turned cool and red, they came to a river bend blanketed by trees. Luke determined that they would be well hidden. In the twilight, sixty-seven grateful bodies lay down for sleep.

At dawn, as Luke and Gabe joined the camp from their sentry post, wisps of river fog flowed down the same course as the water. The escapees spent their first hour of freedom lying on their backs looking through the cover of leaves at the bluing sky.

Thinking of the River Jordan, Thomas soaked his feet in the water. He contemplated that his life, like Jesus' before him, might hold only a few short years to convey what he had learned. An hour later he stood with his back to the water and gave his Sermon of Freedom, as he called it. To Celeste's ears it was full of obtuse references. People around her sat, squatted or stood to hear Thomas speak of their new opportunity to pursue the Kingdom of God, "No longer through intermediaries," he said, "but through our own efforts. We're free now from the fear that bound us, that cut off our ability to love God. We're free from the perversion of the true words of Jesus the prophet, Jesus the lover, Jesus the teacher, Jesus the carrier of God's way. For the rest of our lives we can seek the Holy Spirit within. We can examine ourselves to find the beginning, and to find what was before the beginning. Now we're able to go through the troubles into astonishment, and then to know that we are none other than God ourselves, by finding the God that is inseparable from ourselves."

When Thomas spoke of ecstasy and of the power of Holy Spirit, it seemed to Zhampa to be a description of a mind running wild with dreams and visions, with voices and suppositions. But the people around him were rapt and weeping.

"We're hoping to head west-northwest," said Zhampa to Thomas as they sat by the river after the late morning meal. "I assume you're going to a particular place?"

"We're shooting for Fox Creek. I spent my boyhood summers there."

"That's a good direction for us," said Zhampa. "But we're a burden to you, aren't we?"

Thomas shook his head. "We couldn't have escaped without you." When Zhampa raised his eyebrows, Thomas said, "Listen. First your men carried a message to Luke that I needed to meet him. That Tanner boy threatened our every move, and his preoccupation with your daughter made it possible for Luke to take the creeper to come find me. We finalized the escape plan that night. You treating John distracted the hierarchy just enough. It was the Grace of God in every way. " He paused and rubbed his face. "Your hunter opened the Mill."

"He murdered two men," said Zhampa, his voice heavy.

Thomas went quiet for long time. Then he said, "We're in that boy's debt."

It was Gabe who discovered the defect in their escape plan. The patrol creeper needed to be abandoned in less than fifteen travel hours for lack of fuel. Its goods and inhabitants would have to be shifted into the two larger vehicles. The horse trailer would be too much for an overloaded creeper to pull; it would have to be left behind.

"I'm not leaving Mercedes in this stupid grassland, Zhampa. I'm going to ride him out."

Zhampa didn't look at Gabe for more than a glance. "Yeah," he said.

"Well, if you're going to roll on then with this band of patsies, I guess I'm on my own."

"Talk to Luke," snapped Oakley.

'Yes," Celeste said, "talk to him."

"What for? I'm not leaving my horse. He's not like a dog, you know."

The remark made Zhampa hold his breath. Softly he said, "Let's see what makes sense after another sunrise."

The land turned more rolling that afternoon. And the first herald of winter blew in with a gray massif of clouds. Everyone's mood changed from the giddiness of being beyond the reach of tyranny to other worries. At the next stop, Zhampa gave Gabe his blessing to ride Mercedes where he would. He gave him one of the compasses and landmarks such as Thomas could remember, in case he wanted to follow them to Fox Creek.

"I might show up," Gabe said with a cavalier look. "But maybe it's time for me to find my own way. These people are going into an early winter. Follow them and you'll not all make it over the mountains, if they're as high as you say. We should be going south to get to the coast before the snow. Have you thought of that?" he said turning to face Zhampa down.

"Every - single - day." Zhampa said, staring back. But it was he who first looked away.

Luke had a third idea. He bartered for Bob. In exchange, he offered food for the trip over the mountains and any tools Zhampa's band needed to take. The horse would be critical in helping the community get started. Would Gabe bring Bob to Fox Creek? And when the third vehicle was left on the upside of a grassy slope and the two remaining creepers headed off, all eyes were on the warrior wondering if he would follow through.

Before climbing back on board, Celeste had hugged him, long enough for him to have to pull her arms off from around his neck. Oakley gave a military, "Good luck." He bit the inside of his cheek. Zhampa's goodbye surprised himself. Just a long laugh that broke to the surface from deep inside. And it made everyone else laugh, too. He'd known the rascal since he was five. And he suddenly realized if this boy was ready to take on the world, he, Zhampa was getting old. Gabe would never be hungry; that was clear. And now he could kill. From the deck of the creeper, he watched the figure of the hunter shrink into the horizon.

11

Fox Creek was not as Thomas remembered. The fields around the village had been taken by residential subdivision—long-deserted when they arrived—and the once-free river oozed thick with erosion in a concrete chase. Thomas shook his head. Though the fuel tanks were close to empty, they would not settle there. He gathered his people and reminded them of the Israelites. "We'll trust in God to show us our new home," he said. "And we'll walk if we have to."

Celeste pulled Zhampa and Oakley aside and argued that the three of them should stay in town until Gabe got there. Oakley was certain they'd seen the last of him and Zhampa was becoming intent on crossing the mountains while the weather was still warm. But in case Gabe did arrive, he pinned a neckerchief to a pole at the main intersection using a stick carved in the shape of a crude arrow. It pointed west-southwest toward a fold in the foothills where Thomas said the Lord was calling them to go.

"Don't worry, Red," he said. "He can track us over sheer rock if he wants to."

Further west, rolling land replaced the prairie. Water ran in the creek beds. Trees grew in the hollows. The Seradipans looked in wonder at the new environment. The party camped at the base of foothills of the Rockies where a stream cut through two abandoned dairy farms. Conifers thrived on the slopes behind.

"We'll never use methane again," Thomas said looking at the barns, "but maybe we'll find some cows. I think ten will be plenty."

Thomas and Luke spent the night walking the land. At the Morning Prayer gathering, Thomas proclaimed the place worthy of the Lord's work. Clear weather confirmed his choice. For a few days the Vermonters prepared for their climb to the coast. As Zhampa had decided to pull the cart, they picked though their gear to lighten their load. They parted with the last of the seed and two of Barker's rifles. In return, they got salt pork, ten pounds of beef jerky, dried oats, wheat, beans, a container of salt and a large block of cheese.

Any hope they might have had about the hunter arriving was dashed by Zhampa's dream of Gabe riding south and not responding to his name being called. So they set off with the foothills on their left, looking for a way into the mountains. The smoke of homestead fires rose on the hillsides and they passed through two villages. In the second of these, a young mother told them that there was a main road into the mountains half a day's journey farther on.

"Not a lot of activity, though," she said. "People don't often pass through to the ocean and there's more game down here from what they tell me." They thanked her and headed to the abandoned town at the junction of the road to the provincial glacier park. Walking the grade west through a long alluvial valley, Zhampa shook his head at the size of the mountains.

On the second day, they walked along a brown river, musical with tumbling stones. That evening Oakley brooded by the fire.

"Something's up with the river, Chief."

"What you got?"

Celeste stopped her chores to listen.

"No fish. Not a bite."

"Water's dirty here, Oak. Too much silt, you think?"

"No eagles or hawks either."

With the noise of the river close at hand, they hadn't noticed that the woods had no hum; no squirrels chattering, no chipmunks scrambling away with paranoid peeps, no small birds darting in the lower branches.

"No buzzards," Oakley added. "Don't like it."

For the next three days it rained, and though they looked hard, no one saw a creature bigger than an earthworm.

"Maybe it's time we take to eating 'em," Oakley said with a sarcastic lick of his lips. "They were one my staples back in The Valley when things were tough."

"Okay," Zhampa said. "Show us how. I'm worried about higher up."

Celeste furrowed her brow.

"Don't be a weeny," Oakley said to her. "The French ate snails. Worms go good with greens. Dry-fry is best."

Over the next days, higher peaks came into view and the tributaries of the river disappeared into steep canyons; what was left beside them ran fast and loud until it too vanished into a side valley. The road climbed in long switchbacks. Zhampa rested often. The temperature dropped. They spoke less. Oakley tightened his belt another hole and Zhampa lightened the cart again. More trees lay blown down across the road.

"Should we leave the wagon?" Celeste asked.

He shook his head. "There'll be a downhill at some point."

Celeste saw him first. A figure not much larger than a fleck down where they had started that morning's climb. Her excitement turned into a whoop.

"It's Gabe," she cried. "And Mercedes. I knew he'd come."

Zhampa visualized the horse pulling the cart. He whistled through his fingers, but Gabe was too far down to hear. Giddy, Celeste waited while the two men went ahead to make camp.

"What are you living on?" were Gabe's first words when he reached her.

"Little of everything. Mostly beans lately," she said. "And Zhampa and I are finding stuff."

"Beans? That's a miserable mouthful. They just make you fart."

She laughed and for an instant forgot her hunger.

"You didn't tell him what we're eating?" Oakley asked when the conversation was rerun in the camp.

"How's Mercedes?" Zhampa interrupted.

"A little grumpy," Gabe said. "Not much grass up here."

"Do you think he'll like 'em?" Oakley whispered into Celeste's ear. She swatted him, only half-playful.

"We'll reach the pass soon," Zhampa said. "A couple more days of this long draw. Hope we don't hit snow. What do you think, Oakley? Maybe 120 miles since leaving Thomas?"

Oakley shrugged and nodded.

"You found them, I guess?" Zhampa said to Gabe.

"Course. Bob'll be happy there, but they'll work him hard."

Above the tree line, the wind howled. Ahead everything disappeared into white. On the pass they rested in the old tourist center. A river of blue ice hung on the opposing peak.

"What'd they do here?" Oakley asked. "Watch the glacier?"

Zhampa snickered. "Watched it shrink."

Oakley soured his lips and nodded. "Seems it's growing again. See the blue ice?"

When a sign still on its post pointed right to the Skyline Glacier Drive, Oakley said "Let's take the other road, Chief. Get out of this altitude."

They descended into the trees again, but there was still no game. Mercedes' ribs were showing. Gabe worried. Celeste noticed. "Those two are connected by a string," she said to herself.

Moving north and west on Forest Service roads, they crossed two interior ranges. The mornings were cool and they awoke to huge views with fog settled in the low grounds. Before the sun struck, every needle and leaf was thick with dew. Their fire snapped and the smoke ascended straight. But it was as the young mother in the foothills had told them; nobody was passing through. Whenever they saw a farm in the low ground, they made for it. Each one was abandoned, with no signs of looting.

Their luck changed briefly when they came upon a small flock of snow geese in a pond. Gabe caught one with his bolo, but the others hammered the water and were gone. That night Celeste taught Gabe how to write his name. He carved the letters into a camp log and ran his fingers over them saying the word.

They climbed once more on a rutted road, and halfway up a bad stretch, Mercedes refused to pull the cart. He jerked his head away from Gabe's hand. He pranced and cried, so Zhampa harnessed himself to it again. Frosts became more frequent and cold shortened their sleep. When the sun shone, the thawed soil became slick. They all fell. Conversation turned to body parts. When Oakley tore open his knee, he met Zhampa's instructions to keep it clean with a bold laugh.

Zhampa tasted plants that looked familiar, trying to identify ones they could eat. One day when he felt nauseous and his head seemed a long way from his feet, Celeste caught him taking some of the Vermont medicine. "You're not feeling well?" she asked.

He made a face of indecision. "I'm experimenting."

"But you're not well," she said.

He nodded. "Keep it quiet."

In late September they rested on a pass. To the west a shoulder dropped below them into a high valley. Beyond was a long ridge with a cliff face and in the distance, a lake. It was jewel-like, as if aqua-colored glass had fallen from the blower's pipe into that wooded valley and cooled there—long, snake-shaped with a bay on the far end. As the eastern slopes of the lake were steep, the road circled south around the long ridge. Imagining a place to rest and fish, they headed down under an opaque sky. Over the years, water had covered the macadam surface with stones and these rolled under their feet. When Oakley fell on his knee again, he swore. The horse, too, clearly strained with every step. Gabe was patient with him; he didn't push. At times he and the horse fell a mile behind the others.

Early the next morning at a fork in the road, they came upon an emaciated man sitting on a boulder. His beard was thick with gray curls, and his eyes glowed.

"What a blessed sight you are," he said. "How are you doing for provisions?"

"Very little left," said Zhampa. "We were hoping the lake had fish."

"It does. It does to be sure," said the man, looking from one to the other, "but they're small. We've eaten the big ones." He smiled. "You've come a long way. It shows in your step. Come rest by the lake. It's a humble camp, but it's warm and dry. We'll shake out the pantry. Get you back in shape to travel."

"How far?" asked Gabe. "And if we go, can we head straight down or do we have to come back this way?"

"It's three miles and yes, you can. My name is MacComber. Saw you coming down this morning. Pretty horse you got there. Lucky."

"We wouldn't be here without him," Gabe said.

"Is there game around here?" Oakley asked.

"Yes, but I'm better at fishing." So they followed MacComber up the road, which climbed, then descended around the last of the mountain, he, chatting all the while. And from what they heard, they were prepared to meet MacComber's companions but not for their appearance. Jeb was a lumbering mast of a man with huge, bony hands and heavy brow bones. He watched every move with flat eyes and, if his smile came at all, it came late. Between the men was a woman they both called Wife, who answered 'hmm' and 'no' and who walked without a sound.

Jeb and Wife were in the midst of a great cleaning, she scrubbing the floors with a worn out bristle brush, he sweeping and straightening. The house, a log home in a mature stand of evergreens, was set back from the bay they had seen from the pass. From the porch, one could see patches of lake water through the branches. Pristine woods came down to the far shores; rockslides scarred them from above.

"It was built by the Forest Service to house a ranger," MacComber said.

"Damn," said Gabe, slapping his thigh after a quick tour of the place, "I didn't think to ask if there was any open ground for Mercedes. There's only an hour's worth of grazing down by the edge of the water."

"No problem," said MacComber. "There's a great meadow down below. I'll take you there after you rest." He worked with Wife and Jeb making preparations as if for a feast, though there was only a string of perch from the lake.

Finally, Gabe said, "MacComber, that stew of yours is just going to make us all hungrier. Take me down to the meadow, so Mercedes can eat. And point me to where you saw that big buck you were talking about."

"Gladly. Change our fate, I beg you. Me, I confess I haven't killed anything large for a long time. I can't help myself. I make a racket coming through the woods."

"Perfect. Let's work together. You can drive him to me."

Celeste felt drawn to Wife; the woman listened with distracted strokes to all that was said, miming sadness in every gesture. Her gray eyes lingered on no one. When the men were out for a moment, Celeste asked her if she were okay. Wife twisted her mouth into a smile.

"Hmm," she said.

"We never expected to find folk so far up in the mountains."

Wife shrugged and busied herself with a rag.

"How long have you lived here? I bet the winters are tough."

"Longtime," Wife said. "Things is slim now. In the past we had better luck living off the lake and the gifts of travelers."

"Are there many? We haven't seen a soul for weeks."

"None since midsummer," Wife said.

"Sorry we have nothing to give you," Celeste said.

Wife turned her back and shrugged.

Toward dark, MacComber returned, beaming.

"Your hunter sends this gift for our dinner," he said dumping a large cut of meat from a cloth wrap. "He bagged us a porcupine. Shot it right out of a tree," he said with a laugh. "And the horse is grazing. Seems like he'll only stop long enough to drink."

"Is he on his way?" Zhampa asked.

"He said to tell you he's staying out. Might not be back 'til morning. He's tracking that big buck. He said 'There's meat in our future,'" To Jeb and Wife he said, "So generous. Said he'd split the kill with us." And spreading his arms wide, he said to his guests, "You can rest as long as you need to and then head to the ocean with dried venison to see you there. I think it's only three weeks more now if you can beat the snow."

"You've been there?" asked Oakley.

"Well, no. I'm from up north. That's what folks passing through have said."

The meat was boiled in the base of a stew. Zhampa contributed wild artichoke tubers. Celeste collected the last of the season's wild raspberry leaves for tea. When the six of them sat, MacComber said a rough blessing to the sound of fat sputtering in the lamps. No sooner had Oakley bitten down on a piece of the meat, then he jumped across the table, bad knee and all, and knocked MacComber backwards off his chair. His left hand held MacComber's scrawny neck and his knife flashed in his right.

Wife squealed. Jeb bolted out the door.

"It's not porcupine, you sonofabitch."

"Oakley, off of him," yelled Zhampa.

"Not porcupine, Chief," he said spitting gravy, his eyes locked on MacComber's.

Wife fell to the floor and cowered by the wood stove making rabid sounds. Celeste whipped out her own blade and grabbed the woman by her hair. "Shut up," she yelled. "Shut up."

MacComber lay gasping but worked one hand to his chin in a gesture of prayer.

"Where's Gabe?" Oakley shouted.

"He's out hunting, like I told you. We'll go down when it's light. You'll see."

"Then why did Jeb take off?"

"You scared him. You scared us all."

"Chief, we'll check out his story in the morning, but they spend the night here. Under guard."

Zhampa was too tired to confront his friend. After a minute, he nodded. And as they bound MacComber and Wife, Zhampa asked, "You got any guns?"

MacComber shook his head.

"Gabe's got one of the Seradipan pistols," Celeste said.

"Where's our rifle?"

"In the corner, Chief."

"Let's assume Jeb's armed anyway," said Zhampa, finishing a gag on MacComber.

"It's his country, Chief. We're at a disadvantage."

"But we've got his friends," said Celeste.

Zhampa made a face. "Would you give a shit about these two?"

Oakley spat, Wife squirmed and Celeste went still. Zhampa took Barker's pistol and handed the second Seradipan gun to Oakley. "Guess we're gonna have another tough night," he said.

"I'll take the first shift, Chief."

Zhampa sat up leaning into his pack. Celeste lay near him, but no one slept. Finally when the night was darkest, MacComber snored. After, as Wife's wheezing became regular, Zhampa felt Celeste go limp. He awoke to MacComber's coughing fit. The moon was up, casting a pale light through the conifers. Oakley was gone and he didn't return until long after the fire was out.

"Jeb's not nearby," he told Zhampa. "We'll have to track him first thing."

Celeste awoke at the sound of his voice. "I hope Gabe finds him first rather than the other way around," she said.

"Gabe can handle himself," Oakley said.

In the morning they found the little fishing skiff gone from the shore. Zhampa rolled MacComber over with his foot.

"Where'd he go?" Zhampa asked. "I said, 'Where'd he go?' Answer me, godammit." When he kicked MacComber in the stomach, Celeste threw herself between them and ripped free MacComber's gag. She shot Zhampa a look of fury.

MacComber coughed and choked. Finally, he said, "We have a fishing camp up the lake. It's not more than a lean-to. Hard to get to by land. Maybe he's up there."

Feeling it was only right, Celeste removed Wife's gag and as she did, MacComber said, "Whatever you say, make sure you tell them the truth."

Wife shuddered. She took a few careful breaths, looked quickly at MacComber and said, "I don't know either. He's a good man. He's done good by me." Then she cried without tears.

Later, Celeste took Barker's pistol and walked Wife to pee on the edge of the clearing.

"Do you have anything to tell me?" she asked.

Wife shook her head.

"What's going on here?"

"Just some people living the best they can. Stuck up in these cold ass mountains."

"Are you here against your will?"

Wife rolled her eyes." Where've you been?" she said. "Every woman lives against her will."

MacComber and Wife were gagged again and tied to trees. Oakley hunkered down nearby in case Jeb returned. Zhampa and Celeste followed Mercedes' tracks down the path that ran west along the creek that drained the lake. Zhampa carried Barker's pistol, his finger on the trigger. His free hand was in Celeste's. The trail was easy to follow until it crossed an outcropping of ledge; they picked it up again on the other side. Farther on, they came to a place where the horse had stood a long time before being led away. Clear Seradipan footprints headed up another trail.

Zhampa sighed with relief. "We've made a mistake. Looks like MacComber told the truth about Gabe going up the mountain."

"We've been behaving like animals," Celeste said. "It's the hunger."

"Let's get Mercedes and Gabe and get out of here."

Ahead off the trail a row of A-frame racks blended into the jack pines. Shapes hanging in the air. The ground a carpet of gray sticks. Underneath the frames, a pile like a night robe tossed on the floor. Had it not been for steam rising from it, they might have passed by. Zhampa recognized that an animal had been butchered and skinned and turned to investigate. He was about to call Gabe with congratulations—for the pieces of the buck were large and would feed them all for a week, maybe two—when he glanced at the robe pile. Along with the innards still slippery with life lay the unmistakable hide of the horse.

Celeste pulled free of his hand and ran thirty paces to a little building of undersized logs, with the corner notches crudely whittled, the roof topped with rough shakes. No windows. Zhampa watched her cock her head, then, bewitched, move to the one door. Voices screamed in his head. They were being watched. "Warn her," he thought. "Tell her 'no.'" But when he opened his mouth, he found no air to breathe. As she entered the building, Zhampa wheeled and, in a crouch, scrambled to the base of a large tree. There he knelt and checked the load in the pistol. And only then did he hear his own voice. Only then did he realize that he was screaming. He watched her hand reach from inside to grab the doorframe and watched it pull her body free as if from a pit of slime. Her head appeared and what she had to say erupted as projectile vomiting. She dropped to her knees and crawled a few steps, her fingers tearing the rotting forest floor. She howled like a lioness. "Gabe."

Then Zhampa saw in the gray stick litter years of bones cracked for their marrow. And he, too, was drawn by the building. He moved to and through the door and smelled the must of the smoke house and the flesh of his hunter, his warrior, hanging on hooks from the cross ties of the roof and he saw the pile of clothes with the Seradipan boots beside. The light was dim and he did not look long, only to see the thighs, skinned. Later in tortured nights, shapes would loom up in his dream consciousness, like rolls of butcher paper stacked on a shelf—calves and forearms—unfinished work for another macabre day. And the eyes of a crushed skull would stare up through the water in the fire-blackened kettle behind the door, waiting to be boiled and scoured as delicacy by beings that had lost their way.

In the minute he spent inside the little building west of the jewel lake, the world lost its color. He and Celeste made their way back to the stream where they sat without speaking. Finally as they rose to leave, Zhampa held a finger in the air to ask her to wait. He ran back to the smokehouse, returning with Gabe's pistol and belt. Back at the log camp, Wife was throwing her head from side to side, babbling muffled lines into her gag.

MacComber slumped forward on his binding. As Oakley appeared from his hiding place, Zhampa lifted Gabe's belt. The scout nodded, thrust out his jaw and turned away.

But Jeb's being loose allowed no time to grieve.

"Let's be miles from here by dark," Oakley said.

Zhampa stayed with the prisoners while the others prepared their gear. They debated whether to carry some of Mercedes' meat, with each of them taking both sides of the argument. At last they agreed that the horse had always given his body for them and that his meat should be taken, regarded as sacred and eaten with reverence. But they had neither heart for gathering Gabe's body parts nor the ability to think of a fitting ceremony for him—which they came to regret.

Not until the cart was packed did they look to their prisoners.

"We can't leave them like that, can we?" Celeste asked.

Oakley dismissed her question with a blast of air.

"Jeb will come back," Zhampa said.

"He won't," pleaded Wife. "He won't. He's a shadow man. Probably miles from here already."

"We can't leave them," pressed Celeste.

"Give me half an hour with this asshole, Chief," and without waiting for response, he freed MacComber and led him, hands tied, down his own trail.

"Don't leave me," Wife begged, looking only at Celeste. "I'll be eaten by coyotes before morning. They'll come for me on the strings of stars. At least cut me free."

When Celeste pled the case that Wife would die one way or another if they left her, Zhampa agreed to let her come.

Oakley returned alone.

"Did you kill him?" Zhampa said.

"No," he said. He smiled as if biting a bullet. "I took stones from the creek and broke all of his fingers. Then I bound his feet and locked him in the smokehouse. He'll have plenty of time to think."

So it was that four travelers came to the jewel lake and four travelers left heading down the western slopes on the first rise of the Rockies. There the warrior was taken from this life in the way that he had lived—by craft, by violence and by hand.

The road wound out of the mountains and they drove themselves hard along it. Wife's physical strength impressed them, but there was no peace with her around. She walked apart, reciting her side of conversations with MacComber. At times she would shake her head violently, stamp her foot and contort her lips, speaking with him in a hoarse whisper through the door of the smokehouse.

They joined up with another river.

"No reason to waste time fishing," Wife chided. "God's poisoned the earth." Then to MacComber she whined, "What's to become of us?" and protested his answer, "No, no. It's not as you say."

She was right about the fish and they saw no signs of game. As the river widened with tributaries, they came to broad valleys with farms full of empty corrals.

Once out of the hills, the slope of all that land turned dramatically south; Zhampa guessed it was part of the watershed that fed Vancouver some five hundred miles away. So they left the river and to the west the land opened into a high rolling plateau. The walking would be easier. But across the old main highway to the towns of Rupert and George, they entered a forest of Douglas fir and spruce, standing dead as far as they could see. Only the aspens were healthy.

"What do you think it is?" Zhampa asked.

Oakley took his knife to the bark. "Bugs," he said.

"All these trees?"

"Might make things worse for us."

"It can't get worse than now," said Wife.

"I doubt we'll find game in a dead forest, Chief."

They took a rest day to mull their direction over. Oakley returned to camp in the evening with a pair of ducks.

"Shot 'em both with the pistol," he said. "And I came across a family of natives heading south for the winter."

"What are they eating?" Zhampa asked.

"Dried fish. They said if we get out of this watershed into the coastal one, we'll be okay."

"How far?"

"If we head straight across on the old logging roads, five days, maybe six."

"What'd they say about the trees?"

Oakley shrugged. "Didn't ask them. But listen, there's logging roads all through the plateau. We'll have to follow our instinct, but at least we won't have to bushwhack."

The next day they found a beautiful unpaved road going due west. And Wife began to walk alongside them. They spent more than a day traversing a large burn. After two more days, they found live trees again and toward evening Wife spied a raccoon, slowed by a thick roll of fat. When Oakley dispatched it, Wife showed her prowess with a knife. Beyond in a great water valley filled with aspen, they found an active beaver colony. The two men cut a wide breech in the dam and when the moon rose, Oakley shot a three-year-old male who came out to do repairs. Having eaten well, their energy revived.

They passed three great rock mountains with glaciers and climbed a long ridge to the height of land. Heading down a steep slope on one of the last days of Indian summer, they first heard and then came to a river crashing through a gorge. In the boil of water Celeste thought she saw an eye open and close.

Wife yelled, "Fish" and threw down her pack. She moved so quickly over the ledges, for a minute Zhampa thought she was intent on offering herself to the river. But she stopped at the edge and stamped her foot. "No net. We need a net."

Sleek bodies jumped upstream in the white froth.

"What is it?" asked Celeste.

"Salmon," Oakley said. "They're going home."

"Home?"

"They were born up there," he said pointing. "They swim the oceans, get fat, then they go home."

"Why?"

"To spawn in the same pool they were born in."

"Really?" she said, looking at the water. "God, did you see that one jump?" Then she shook her head, "But they can't get up this part. The falls are huge."

"Some will."

She thrust out her lips and shook her head in disagreement.

Zhampa saw a huge salmon with a white stripe rise and disappear at the base of the falls. To him as well, it seemed more than any of the fish could manage. Was it the excessive rain that swelled the river? "What a tragedy," he thought, "to live so long and travel so far just to die near the end of their journey." The four of them stood, unable to look away. Blinded in the aerated river, salmon launched themselves in chaotic fashion, sometimes straight into the sides of the gorge, hitting hard and falling back.

Picking her way upstream, Celeste discovered part of the river had come free up above and, after working its way over the ledges, was returning to the main current there; she peered over. Below, where the waters met, a green pool rotated slowly in the bottom of a cylindrical core. In it were many fish, swirling, resting, some dying. She called the others and when they had gathered, a fish jumped right up at them, slammed into the smooth stone and fell back.

They groaned. There was a loud smacking in the pool. The fish with the white stripe had joined the others. It poked its head out of the water and stared at Zhampa, or so Zhampa imagined. It circled twice and exploded up the little watercourse. But like the others, it crashed hard, short of the top of the ledges.

They moaned again, but the fish was unharmed and rejoined the circling mass. Then it disappeared in the depths.

"Big fish," Wife said.

The surface of the pool ripped white and the sleek body tinged with scarlet shot up to their head level and landed hard at Zhampa's feet. It flopped a few times and then lay still.

"He's breathing," Celeste said. "Can't you help him?"

Zhampa put his hands on the body, but they slipped off. The fish didn't flinch with the touch.

"Get him into the water," she said. But it was Oakley who responded. With one hand clamped in front of the tail, he eased the fingers of his other hand under the flesh behind the head. He carried it to the side stream and laid it in the five inches of water, but save for the feeble working of its mouth, the fish didn't move. Oakley gave Zhampa a fatalistic look.

"Looks like that one escaped a bear," Wife said. "A claw made a stripe. Lucky fish."

"It's like he offered himself to you, Chief."

"Then let's eat him," Wife said. And as Celeste turned to annihilate the woman with a look, the fish gave three flicks of its mighty body, powered through the shallows and vanished into the smooth water above the falls.

The river itself was an invitation. It flowed north and somewhere downstream it connected to the sea, but first it would thread through two big towns and it would take them way out of their way. Now that they had fish enough to carry, Zhampa was determined to go west. "I don't want to risk a violent population," he said. "We're liable to run into all kinds of folks up there."

"I know, Chief."

When Wife said, "My people is from up there. They're tougher than me," Celeste agreed with the plan to continue straight to the sea. With each rain, the snow line dropped lower on the hills behind them. Near the end of October on a coastal mountain pass, they caught a glimpse of a gray ribbon to the southwest. A stroke of ocean.

Celeste grabbed Zhampa's arm. "We've done it."

Oakley nodded as if it was something he had expected at that hour. Even Wife brightened at the prospect. But in the valley below, their road turned ninety degrees and headed north. Zhampa checked the map and guessed that it would loop into the old coastal town. It would take them a hundred miles farther toward the pole, and then another hundred out over a long glacial delta region into the thick of the Inside Passage islands.

"I'm going straight up and over to the water," Zhampa said. "We are running out of time. We can make it in a day or two. Three at the most."

Again they consolidated their gear and Zhampa released the harness to the wagon for the last time. They took the cutting tools, the weapons and the fire bows. They broke the whetstones in half. They took the rope, the canteens and the last piece of Gabe's tarp for cover.

Wife refused to go with them. "I still have relatives up the road, I think. And you're going to die up there. My payment to you is done."

12

Seven chevrons of geese flew overhead the morning they started the climb over the coastal range. The day was warmer than any in the previous weeks and even Oakley spoke with anticipation about seeing the ocean. Celeste imagined it as some vast magic, like discovering a new color in the spectrum. Zhampa smiled at her prattling. When they reached the ridge in mid-afternoon, they saw not water but another range that blocked their view beyond. Their frustration was mitigated by the valley below having escaped development. They wouldn't have to avoid people or deal with the depression of another place in ruins. But they might have taken it as a sign. Old logging roads provided a web of trails down through third-growth woods and they camped between ridgelines under graying skies. A whiff of salt rode the air and they slept, optimistic that the next day would bring them to the water.

The temperature dropped through the morning and snow began to fall before they reached any steep ground on the mountainside. Cold wind cut visibility. At midday in the shelter of pines, they lit a fire and discussed options.

"We should push on before the snow traps us in between ranges, Chief."

Zhampa nodded inside his hood. "Are you up for it, Red?"

"Yes," she said, but her mouth was tight.

In the middle of the steepest grade, the snow turned to rain, soaking them to the skin. They stumbled up the slick ground. When the wind circled to the north, the rain turned to sleet and then back to snow.

"I've had enough of this, Oakley. Next viable sheltered spot, we're stopping."

But the mountain got stingy with accommodations and dark was falling before a big enough place appeared—an ideal seam in a stone face close to the ground with a weather-twisted pine as a windbreak. A fire blazed in thirty minutes. Blinded by the weather, they didn't know they had climbed over the shoulder of a coastal mountain and were close to clearing the southern ridge.

The next morning, as snow kept them hunkered down, Oakley said "I can't go."

"Huh?"

"I can't go, Chief. I know it's my turn, but I can't."

Never had his partner used the word 'can't.' He must have misheard. But Oakley's body was slack with failure. The man was no match for the simple task of gathering wood.

"Are you sick?" Zhampa asked. Celeste roused herself from her hunger doze and listened with incredulity.

"No." It was clear that the news was worse. Groaning, he slid his knife down the in-seam of his left pant leg from the knee to the ankle and rolled the fabric away. His flesh was a mangled mass—brown and purple—the knee swollen to twice its size, the skin stretched to the point of tearing. Celeste gasped.

Oakley hid his surprise in a snicker of disgust. "Thought it was just a bruise, Chief."

Zhampa clenched his jaw. "You should have checked it."

Celeste crawled to the front of the seam, packed a pot full of snow and placed it on the cooking rocks. Next, she laid snow directly on the knee. Oakley yelped at the first touch.

She gave him a look. "Suck it up," she said. Her hands turned pink, then white, carrying snow. As she bathed the skin with a sliver of soap, the pressure of her strokes milked pus from multiple lacerations. Later, when Oakley was hanging his head, she said, "Listen. No one is carrying you off this hill. You're going down on this leg or not at all."

At this Oakley made a move, but she held him down. "Plenty of time for heroics later."

Zhampa lanced the pockets of pus. "You waited too long," he said quietly. "Looks like the infection has involved the joint." Then he ruminated. "We're going to be here quite a while," he said. "I've got to go hunting."

Celeste looked at him in disbelief. He was abandoning a lifelong promise.

He shrugged. "We don't have any options. I got to do it." He took Barker's rifle with ten rounds and headed down the west side of the shoulder into a world of blowing snow, all the hunting stories he'd ever heard pouring through his mind.

"Steady," he said to himself, "Imagine you're a deer or a raccoon. Where would you go? Where do you eat? What time of day? Gabe, help me. Remind me."

In a gully on the down slope, water trickled under the snow and he followed it into denser tree cover. Finally he found some sign. Deer tracks. "Or are they mountain goat? Hard to tell with the snow blown in them. Look. Pawing by a pool in the rivulet to drink. Up this high, it's got to be a buck, home in his favorite haunts. Should I track him or wait? Track him, my ass! He'd keep pushing ahead of me. I'd never see him." He felt for the breeze. "Wait for him. Get downwind. Find a hidden spot. In the drift there, by those boulders. Dig a snow cave."

He scooped himself a cocoon and squirmed inside. Out of the wind in his fatigue, he dozed. He dreamed of his mother with that man in her arms. An old dream. Claire used to tell him he was trying to change it.

In that first winter of the Unraveling, the Valley Folk formed a militia to defend themselves. When the green-uniformed Globalliance forces swept through the country from the north, they stripped farms and homes and killed the owner of the store. Dressed in camouflage and armed with hunting rifles and false hope, the Valley militia lost many men to the high-tech force, which had no intention of occupying Vermont. They streaked toward bigger prizes in the south, leaving hunger and desperation in their wake. Those stiff Valley men—in their shock and resentment—dragged out their old scapegoat. It was time to see if the rumors about the DiOrio granary were true. And maybe the old man had a stash of gasoline somewhere.

"Why," they wondered, "should those pacifist flatlanders live safe up in the Hollow while we're down here where the real fight is?" A band of twenty set out at three in the morning.

Sumiko DiOrio had gone early to the barn to collect eggs and, in the first daylight, the dark shapes of the posse slinking up the road stood out against the snow. She dropped her basket and ran to the house, screaming Eric's name. The Valley men took up positions around the buildings.

Eric DiOrio's heart had mellowed with the decades and at seventy-two, he had little to fear. So after a short fussing argument with his wife, he slipped on his boots—but not his shirt—and his great winter barn coat, and the bear skin hat with the frayed lining and walked out into the rose light that bounced off the snow in that bowl of land. His eyes were sensitive from being in the darkened house and from his many years, so he was mostly blind when he held up his massive hand and bellowed "Hello." The word was still echoing between the buildings when a lone shot brought him to his knees. He didn't recognize the shooter. He hadn't seen the lad for years, the son of his neighbor over the hill to the north, who was one of the classmates who had bullied Zhampa when they were six in the village school.

But Sumiko heard Wicas yell as he ripped the rifle out of the young man's hands. "Godammit, Curtis, we're not here to kill him."

She tore into the barnyard with a blistering stream of profanity. She kneeled and raised her husband's torso onto her lap holding his head upright to remind him how to avoid dying. When it was clear she had failed, she screamed out her son's name. Through her caterwaul, the older men conferred behind the barn. Some argued that, because Sumiko had witnessed their crime, they had to kill her. They would say they'd found the DiOrios slaughtered in their yard. But in the end, some fragile decency kept them from compounding their stupidity. Instead they stole three hens and a goat and walked back down the Hollow road.

The disaster in the barnyard of the Hollow farm resounded that same day in Zhampa's dream state in North Dakota. Both he and Sumiko tried for three days to reach each other by phone. Finally, they shared a short conversation and her message was clear, though much of the detail was lost on account of her delivery.

Zhampa left school immediately. First he drove his car on the smallest roads he could find, siphoning gas as he went. In the farmland west of Chicago he collided with a truck and fought with its driver. He drove away in the truck until a tire came off the rim. From that point, his memory of the journey was of a tornado, a black, swirling energy, indiscriminately consuming things and spitting them out. In three weeks of driving, walking, hitching, never stopping, hardly sleeping, hiding in the mass of humanity that choked the roads looking for safety, he traveled fourteen hundred miles in midwinter back to the Hills like Women Lying Down.

When he stood at last in his own dooryard, he found his mother keeping the fires going but not eating. After dragging Eric's body to the barn, she'd left everything untended. A prize sheep had gotten stuck in a fence and died, and the hens had pecked each other in their house. The weakest of them lay dead and devoured. The cold had preserved Eric's body enough for Zhampa to have a final conversation with him—thirty minutes of confession and anguish. And everything that Zhampa could divine from the quizzical look frozen on the corpse's face commanded him to pluck 'An eye for an eye.'

Learning that his old tormentor Curtis had shot his father, Zhampa grabbed a pipe wrench and took a back route to the neighboring farm. Over the open ground near the house, he moved behind stone walls and slithered into swales. He watched the comings and goings from a pine thicket. Curtis returned from the barn. Later, carrying baskets, his mother and sister departed down the road.

"That leaves just one miserable soul," Zhampa thought.

He crawled to the rear door in the gray haze that substitutes for daylight in New England winter. Then disgusted with his cowardice, he stood and entered as if the house were his own.

"Sally, is that you?" a voice said from a room beyond the kitchen. It was flat, uninterested in its own question. Without hurry Zhampa walked into the parlor and found Curtis bent over the pieces of some mechanical thing in his lap. The pipe wrench hit the floor and Curtis raised his head in time to see Zhampa's hands wrap around his throat.

In one motion he swung Curtis' neck to the Oriental rug and drove his knee into Curtis' chest. The farm boy made no sound but flopped like a weasel in a trap until Zhampa broke his left cheekbone with his right fist. The eyes rolled back and Zhampa landed two more blows, but when he was pulling back for another, he clearly heard the voice say, "I did not train you for this. I did not raise you for this."

For a full minute he balanced above the body, then seeing the life flow out of it, he rose and left. For years, Zhampa had carried that indignant voice, wondering what he was trained for. He had always presumed the voice was Eric's, but long after Claire was gone, on that Indian summer day rebuilding stone walls, he heard the voice clearly again. And at that moment, he looked up at the mountain to see Rinpo's cave.

Zhampa's snow cocoon collapsed and he awoke sputtering, his head jumbled with thoughts of guilt and hunting. A cold front had cleared the sky and the late afternoon sun lit every ice-caked surface the color of gold. Forgetting the cold and the ache in his stomach, he crossed the slope looking for a clear view to the west to see if there were more ranges to cross. The ocean was there, maybe five miles down. Deep, indigo blue, dotted with islands, green and black. To see more, he climbed a tree. North, in the distance, a glacier spilled into a fiord. But he saw no structures. He would have to build something to cover them for the next five months. Glassy-eyed, he pondered survival as the sun went down and twilight came. Finally, the cramping in his feet reminded him of Celeste and Oakley. He hadn't hunted at all. Yet as he descended, he heard the yip of coyotes in the distance and, much closer, the sound of a large animal, roaring. He stopped. A mountain lion? A bear? Something that could climb? The cry was powerful, yes, but emotional. Hoarse exhalations. He stood frozen on a lower branch, his senses open. Banging through the brush out of sight, crossing above him, the beast cried like a cow stuck in a burning barn.

Then he knew. "I have to take this animal."

He dropped the last few feet to the ground, checked the rifle and moved uphill. In fifty yards he found the tracks of a deer. Walking, not running.

"Can a deer bellow?" He flicked on his head lamp and thirty feet away, a nine-point buck lay in the snow, head bobbing, breath steaming. Numbly it turned and looked into the light; it didn't freeze the way the Hollow deer used to when the family car would catch them on the roads at night. Tongue out. It tried to rise but merely rotated its body in the place where it had dropped.

They assessed each other, then the buck turned its magnificent head away, as if escape was the same as looking in the direction of freedom. Or as if to say, "If you are going to shoot me, just do it." Zhampa listened for the coyotes. Their yips were fading in the distance. He raised the rifle; he was too close to miss. The buck kicked its hind legs to rise and a swatch of blood on its hind quarters glistened in the light.

"Ah! They caught him and he kicked his way out. It's not decent to take him now."

The buck exhaled a groan and dropped to the ground, its head waving unsteadily. Zhampa lowered the gun and stepped closer. A mass of innards lay flopped outside its belly.

"What a heart you have," Zhampa said.

Unflattered, the buck laid its head down as if to sleep. Zhampa knelt, took off his gloves and placed his hands on the heaving body, tentatively at first, then as a doctor to a patient. The iris of the eye was pure black. It looked at him sidelong, helpless, confused to see a being so close. One last time it raised its head, but the futility of it was clear to them both, so Zhampa cradled it and the antlers—shushing, coaxing, stroking. The eye took on profound simplicity. The breathing slowed. The impulse to flee was snapped clean off. The head became heavy and the body jiggled a little under his hands as its soul lifted. For a long moment, Zhampa didn't breathe. Fresh from the dream of his mother, he was Sumiko in the barnyard.

"Thank you," he said.

Then he turned the animal head down on the slope and, with his knife, finished what the coyotes had begun. With the exception of the liver and heart, he left the organ parts steaming in the snow.

When he had done the best he knew to do, he shouldered the carcass— about a hundred pounds, he guessed—and carried it home.

They had food but no mobility. For lack of topical ointments or antibiotics, they fought Oakley's infection the old-fashioned way: with boiled cloth compresses, lancing, a poultice of pine bark, and hope. From his place in the back of the seam, the scout instructed Zhampa on skinning and cutting the flesh and they ate venison stew and pieces roasted on sticks.

On the fourth day, snow fell and Oakley ran a fever. Quiet settled on the travelers.

"If we don't move, we'll die," Zhampa whispered to Celeste.

"He's in no condition . . . "

"I know."

"If we could build him a sled . . . "

"I've been thinking about it, too. But it's not straight downhill to the coast. We've got some uphill, too, from what I could see."

"I'll be lighter if you cut off my leg," Oakley said without opening his eyes. His cheeks lifted in a weak grin.

"You with us, old man?"

"Hanging on every word, Chief."

"Can you travel?"

"Can you pull?"

Zhampa stared into the fire for a full five minutes. Finally, he said, "We'll leave in the morning, snow or no snow. Red, cook up the rest of that meat. We'll take every scrap we can carry. I'm going to build us a sled." He grabbed the bow saw and the hatchet and headed down the slope.

The next morning, sun broke on a foot of new snow. They laid the old warrior head uphill on a litter of fir boughs that Zhampa had trimmed and woven together with bailing wire, butt ends bundled together pointing down the slope. Celeste held a length of deerskin strips tied to the uphill end of the boughs; she was to be the brake, if they slipped out of control. With the rope Zhampa harnessed himself to the downhill end, lifted it slightly, leaned forward and pulled.

The thing slid on top of the snow and over rocks. After two hundred yards, they cut Oakley a thick staff for him to help with the braking and maneuvering. But it was slow going; balancing momentum and friction was exhausting. They passed where the buck had died. Twice they had to unload Oakley and carry him and everything over rough terrain.

It shouldn't have happened when it did. Not right after the mid-afternoon rest. But rocks under the snow were slick with ice. Zhampa lost his footing and the litter lurched downhill. The butt ends caught him in the small of his back. He stiffened from the neck down, both his feet came out from under him and the litter picked up speed. The air was thick with hollering. When Zhampa got his legs heading downhill, he dug them deep into the snow to find a hold and they all heard his femur snap, and the swallow of air that went into his lungs.

On a sunny day just miles from the ocean's edge on a treed slope, Celeste became their leader. She got both men under the boughs of a clump of fir trees, and gave a hard pull on Zhampa's calf, which he begged her for through gritted teeth and which allowed the shattered ends of bone to not grind on each other with each of his breaths. She made a splint for the thigh with stiff limbs and wire from the litter. She set up the tarp and then built a fire pit and the fire to warm them. But she lay awake most of that night, listening to the fire taunt her about being alone in the world. At last, Zhampa's groans made her hitch on her pack. She took meat, a hatchet, a canteen, a poncho, a compass and a fire bow. They watched her go, saw her turn one last time to look as she headed into the trees. With that one snap of bone, Oakley became the more able-bodied of the two men. He fed the fire and treated his infection with compresses and the last of the soap. He hoped that Celeste would find some building to take over for the winter, that he would heal and become their hunter, that spring would come early and that Zhampa would walk again.

Zhampa took doses of boneset until the bottle was empty. He drank some needle tea in the afternoon, but he refused supper and began to talk in rambles after dark. Oakley couldn't get him under the tarp, so he covered him with the deer hide. Zhampa drifted in and out of delirium. He spoke to Rinpo. He helped Sumiko dig ginseng. He buried her under the oak tree. Claire appeared, too, suffocating in her tumor. She raised her arms, begging him to pull her free. He tried and fell over backwards when her hand ripped free from the wrist, whereupon she vanished. And clutching that last memento of her, he lay down with it next to his cheek, while several hooded warriors tied him into bed, but not for sleep. They broke his legs and pulled on them. They celebrated his agony. He cut their heads off with the dorjay, then lay panting for hours, unattended, desperate for water. Finally, the sheets were pulled back for some goddess to check him all over. She pinched and prodded and stroked him. She cooed. She stirred his sexuality, but he realized she was a slave trader, checking his use for fieldwork. He struggled to see her face. But in the candlelight on the slave dock, he got just one a look at the back of her head. When he pulled at his bindings, a voice whispered, "Rest."

Celeste followed a streambed, down into the thick, newer growth of trees. And at the top of a waterfall, the sunset reflecting off the ocean made her look up. She would be the first to reach the Pacific; it was not a half-mile down. Her exploration would begin the next day, so she camped on the height and lit a huge fire to fend off her loneliness. In the morning as she walked to the stony beach, she was observed by a party of three.

13

New Moon was the first of her people to notice the activity on the mainland. Three days after the storm that lashed her island with wind and rain, she saw smoke rising from the top of the mountain. When she saw a second fire on the Slope of Slides, she threw on her hooded robe and walked down to the village. She took Red Otter to the eastern shore lookout. Together they saw the roaring blaze above the beach.

"They're from away," New Moon said to her cousin, "or they wouldn't have come down the steepest slope on the whole coast."

"Raiders don't light fires," Red Otter pointed out.

"Row over tonight and investigate," she said. "And take Alison Feather Eye with you. You may need a water carrier."

Red Otter understood. New Moon played out events in the way of feeding the fathoming line on the harpoon when it caught the whale. It was right that she held the Lineage Lance, the symbol of the authority in the Mother Lineage of the Tlingit.

Straightaway, Red Otter roused his sister Alison Feather Eye and the others, some of the best rowers on the Inside Passage. They were to report back by midmorning of the second day. They wouldn't be armed for combat. Instead, they would rely on stealth and speed. They rowed over in the moonlight and landed in a cove up the coast. In the dirt Red Otter sketched the land around the beach.

"Stone Wolf," he said, "Go to the browsing ground here." Stone Wolf nodded. It was a favorite spot to find deer in the fall hunt.

"I'll hide at the base of the falls. Alison Feather Eye, stand on the lookout rocks. We'll gather there when we know what we're dealing with."

The one thing they weren't expecting was a lone woman with thousands of miles behind her. Distressed, Celeste abandoned the skills of walking in the woods and entering foreign country. She was looking for people, or a building, or a place for a winter camp. And she walked right past the Tlingit scouts.

But once on the rocky beach, she thought to mark the trees at the foot of the brook with her hatchet to help her remember the spot. She walked to the shore, mesmerized by the waves and by the sea birds, which eyed her, from a safe distance, hoping that this stranger signaled a change in their diet. Alison Feather Eye followed her thirty steps behind, carrying her knife laid across outstretched palms, so when Celeste saw the Tlingit woman, she realized that she was in no danger. By the end of that day other crews had carried Oakley and Zhampa down to the shore and had ferried them to their island.

"How's the chief?" Oakley asked before Celeste could say anything.

"He's conscious, finally," she said. "Still a little feverish."

The room was spare and clean. In the corner Oakley's pack gave off a rank smell. Out the window, a fir tree and the blue-gray of rough ocean water. Oakley lay in bed under a sealskin coverlet. His face shone clean; the minders of the clinic had been seeing to that. But his features were sunken. For the first time she saw him as old and it shocked her.

"How's the bed?" she asked.

"Miserable thing. Not enough rocks in here. Can't get used to it."

She tried to laugh. "The biggest problem is his bone. Having it heal right. He's worried."

Oakley nodded.

He and Zhampa lay in the Tlingit hospital, a small complex of buildings that had been offices of the Canadian Coast Guard before the Unraveling. After about five days, Oakley was up and around walking with a staff. But Zhampa had to lie virtually still for ten days. Celeste stayed in a traditional Tlingit home made of wood plank and soil. And she watched Alison Feather Eye's comfort of being on the earth. She had a song on her lips for every time of day and for every task. A song of waking, a song of fire-making, a song of water gathering, a song for food preparation, a song for wood, a song for company and a song for solitude. The faces of young Tlingit men lit up when they saw her, but Alison Feather Eye showed no interest in her effect on them.

One day the last boat of the hunting season came back from the mainland, rounded the point and entered the harbor. Alison Feather Eye put down her handiwork project, summoned Celeste, and walked to the docks. Four men jumped out.

"This is Turtle Man," she said to Celeste. "He's my husband."

Like many Tlingit men Celeste had met, Turtle Man moved like a deer in a meadow into which no predator had ever come. His grace made Celeste feel suddenly dizzy. She was still a traveler, ready to have stability taken away, always ready to reach for her knife.

"I want a home," she thought.

The deference Tlingit men gave to women was astonishing,

"Tlingit women are the water carriers," Alison Feather Eye said.

"What's that mean?"

"It doesn't refer to work—though we do carry the water. Water's the feminine element, the source of life. Men make the fires that keep us warm, but in the end it's the absence of water that signifies death."

"I don't follow."

"It's like this. If a man doesn't behave, the women around him refuse him water."

"You're not serious?" said Celeste.

"Completely."

"Well, he can get it from another woman or on his own, can't he?"

"Not from another woman. She would be breaking honor. Our society would fall apart. And sure, he can drink from a stream, but a man who isn't given water by a woman has no home to go to. He's alone in the world."

Celeste observed the men. They built, cut, lifted and worked in teams, just like the Valley men. They did the rowing and the harpooning. They made the weaponry and trained the boys in its use. And they did the killing when it was necessary.

"But everything they do, Celeste, is reviewed by the Women's Council of the Water Carriers. If they go fishing late in the year against the will of the Council, when they return—if they return—they may have no home to go to."

"But what if the women are wrong?"

"Women can be wrong, of course. But unless they haven't been respected for a long time, they generally choose wisely. Our men understand this. They know mothers see the long view."

Celeste could find no questions. Finally Alison Feather Eye asked, "So what do you think? How do you handle life?"

Celeste turned sharply. "I don't handle life, Alison Feather Eye. I just do what I do." She began pacing and slapping her thigh. "And what do I think?

I think I'm a lost woman. I'm twenty-six years old. I don't have a home. I don't know what men are. And I can't have a child, because I wouldn't know how to raise it." She stopped and held out her arms. "Do you think I'm too old to learn how to carry water? It seems simple, but obviously, it isn't."

"Come tomorrow afternoon," Alison Feather Eye said. "I'll introduce you to some of the Council."

"They've given her the name Red Cloud," said Oakley.

"I get the Red part," Zhampa said. "What's the Cloud?"

"She said, 'It carries water in a hidden way.' Oh! 'And it has no sharp edges.'"

Zhampa laughed. "No sharp edges? Be sure to tell that to our old friend Barker."

Oakley had mostly recovered, except that he had a limp. His face was softer. He started talking in longer sentences. Zhampa attributed this to his being taken into the widow Three Cries' bed. He spent his days with the men in the long hut, repairing and building boats for the coming season.

Snow lay thick on the ground when Zhampa made his first trip out of the hospital. Two weeks later, he was placed in the home of a couple with two married daughters. There were ten of them, counting the three little children. Zhampa slept in the bed of a son who had disappeared on the mainland.

In time he sensed that the smiles coming from Silent Swan, the water carrier in his house, invited romance. He felt dazed. He didn't know what the Tlingit customs were. Was he obligated to respond? The notion struck him as impossible. But he decided, if cornered, he would tell her that she should not feel rejected. He would make her understand that when Claire died, he had laid his romantic yearning aside to engage other things: his granary, the seed deliveries, Celeste and finally becoming Rinpo's porter.

Still, Silent Swan's tiny smiles aroused thoughts that had long been asleep. And at that, his tenderness awoke and spoke to him in a whisper of sadness at the sight of snow clinging to a cluster of pine needles. He heard it in the sweep of the golden eagle's wings and saw it in the mists by the waterfalls that he discovered on his walks up behind the village. So when

Zhampa heard the sounds of lovemaking in his darkened house, he was moved. Soon other water carriers in the village seemed to smile in Silent Swan's way. It was confusing. Other men seemed oblivious to his situation. Oakley just shrugged and grinned.

Two weeks after the winter solstice, he and Oakley spent an evening in the whalers' lodge. Close to a hundred men rocked for hours, singing songs with abandon to commemorate the passing of a Tlingit man. Though the old language and the stories were foreign, the power of the community— their joy of being together—was impossible to miss. That night Zhampa realized his people hadn't sung together and he wondered if such traditions might have saved the world its fire and grief. He brooded on this until he remembered that what was done was done, and that now he was part of the renewal of things.

To return the scepters, they would need a seaworthy boat, better fishing gear, and different clothing. Unconsciously, he planned the next phase for two people. He saw Oakley navigating and trimming the sails and fishing to feed them. After all the cards were played, it would be Oakley who accompanied him to the Naked Red Lady Mountain. And Celeste would stay behind. Many days, Zhampa saw her only across the village. She was spending much of her time with the water carriers. Her talk was animated and her listening intense.

Zhampa had been on the island six weeks before he heard any hint of problems in the leadership.

"The Mother Water Carrier has lost her chief, Zhampa," Celeste told him as they sat outside on a rare warm day. Sun careened off the snow. The harbor was frozen. Beyond the ice, blue sea.

"What happened?"

"He drowned. In a whaling accident."

"Is there someone stepping forward? Another chief?"

"It's generally a hereditary lineage, unless the chief disgraces the Tlingit. The son marries the next Mother Water Carrier, who is chosen by the Council. And there *was* a son, but he drowned, too."

"What's the tradition for cases like this?"

"I don't know. The Mother Water Carrier is making the major decisions alone right now."

"Like a chieftainess? So you've met her?"

"No. She lives apart. Some place in the hills where she can see both sunrise and sunset."

"Always? The leaders always live separately?"

"I don't know. I'll ask Alison Feather Eye. She's becoming a good friend, Zhampa. And Turtle Man is . . . Well, I've never met men like they have here."

"I like it here, too. It'd be nice to stay, if I didn't have some place to go." He winked. "I don't know though, about living on an island. I'm partial to mountains myself."

Celeste's smile was complicated and he chose to let it be.

"Is he walking yet?" New Moon asked. "The one with the horsetail hair?"

"Yes, more and more," answered White Raccoon.

"So he is healed?"

"He has no limp. He is very strong already."

"Good. I want you to bring him here when the moon is dark. Trick him if you must."

White Raccoon understood and said she would.

To strengthen his legs, Zhampa began walking every day and in any weather. The mending had gone well; he felt no ill effect to his gait. He took to using Water Bear's snowshoes. Each day he scouted a different trail. He'd been up the hills to the east of the harbor and had looked down on the village. One day he made his way south along the shore, then cut up overland and came to a meadow with a sweeping view to the south; several islands dotted the distance. To his left, the slopes of the coastal range plunged to the water. He tried to imagine the route they had taken and nodded in honor of the folk who had carried him down. From there, he saw hills on the northern end of the island and resolved to climb them.

The next day he packed some venison jerky, a small box of rose hip jam, a flask and a compass. He borrowed Long Braid's backcountry gloves and skin hat and headed east, then north along the high ground. The sun emerged at midday, so he swept the snow off of a rock for a place to sit and he ate some of his food. He massaged his thigh; the muscle tone was returning and seeing the trail disappear into a lovely grove beyond, he cut himself a walking stick and continued on.

Away from the ocean, he heard in a fresh way the sibilants of wind in the conifers, the crunch of the snowshoes, his own voice yelping when a branch dumped a load of snow on him. He heard a brook under the snow, and in an open pool he filled his flask and drank. His chest felt like pure crystal. He trudged on, switching back, crossing the brook again, heading east up a steep slope where the trees grew huge. On the ridge he halted to catch his breath. A soft drum. A woman singing. Following the sound, he came to a clearing and on the far side, a lodge with bark clapboards sat concealed in a grove of Sequoia. Snow on the roof, icicles hanging. He glanced down the meadow and on both sides of the ridge of the island he saw the sea.

"The home of the Mother Water Carrier," he thought.

The singing stopped. He heard a door open and close. A woman in a hooded robe walked into the trees and returned with an armload of wood. Five trips she made. Shortly, sparks rode the wood smoke. She left again with two empty jugs and returned with them full. Back inside she sang once more, a funeral song, it seemed. In the gusts of wind, the syllables were lost.

He didn't notice when the singing stopped, or when he lost sensation in his feet. His thighbone throbbed with the cold and he chided himself. He checked the light to the west. It was late.

"It'll be faster," he said aloud, "to get back on the trail they use from here, than to go back the way I came." He circled away from the lodge to not be discovered and made toward the low ground. He found the trail the woman had packed getting water from the brook and the steppingstones across it. He set off at a good clip and nearly collided with a hooded figure coming up. Both stiffened and stopped—a few paces between them.

She was tall. In the shade of the hood, only her mouth was visible.

"I mistook you for Long Braid," she said after a moment. "You're wearing his hat."

"Yes, I'm a traveler. A guest in your village."

"Take it off, please," she said.

He did.

"You're the one they call 'Chief?'" she asked.

"Yes. Well, Oakley does. It's his way of telling me he doesn't want to make decisions."

"He had the infection? In his knee?"

"Yes. But he's healed now. Your doctors have treated us very well."

"I see you're healed, too. That's good. It was a bad break. I'm told your friend and the girl are settled in the village."

"I hardly see them."

The woman gathered her hood tighter across her chin. Her hand knew work. "I hear you're a healer," she said.

"Yes. Vertebrae and acupuncture. Herbs."

"They tell me you're good. Good with pain."

Zhampa acknowledged the remark without a yes or no.

"We have our own medicine. But it would be good to know your techniques." She took a step closer to him. Her face was younger than he expected.

"I'll be happy to treat your patients and to teach what I know," he said. "To repay you."

"You know who I am then?"

"You must be the Mother Water Carrier. I just learned of your losses. I'm sorry."

New Moon looked at his snowshoes.

"We plan to leave in the spring," he said, "but if you can think of someone for me to train, it would be the least I can do. We have four months, I think, before we can travel."

"We'll send you someone," she said walking by him toward her lodge. He watched her go and was looking in her direction when she hesitated and turned. "Come to the house, she said. "You're too far from the village to get there before dark." She walked quickly on and disappeared.

Zhampa's leg was tired and he was unable to keep up with her. Arriving at her back door, he thought it would be rude to enter that way, so he rounded the house to enter by the main door. Finding none, he retraced his steps and removed his snowshoes. Just as he raised his fist to knock, the door flew open. New Moon had removed her hooded shawl and her hair was tied up on her head. A broad and intricate necklace—one too elegant to have been wearing for chores—lay upon her clavicle. The flash of impatience in her eyes drew his attention, at which her look slipped into embarrassment. And in the transition, he caught a glimpse of the woman beneath the necklace.

"You're here early," she said.

"I am?"

"Yes, I'm not ready."

"When should I come back?"

She bit her lip. "In two days," she said.

"I'm sorry," he said. "I thought . . . " He turned, pulled on his hat and bent in the fading light to put the snowshoes back on.

She watched him from the open door and when he reached for his second snowshoe, she said, "No, no! Now is fine. Come in."

He undid his straps, stood, leaned the snowshoes against the wall of the house and looked past her into the lodge. The floor was stone. The chimney, too. Furniture of hand-carved wood. An embroidered hanging shielded a corner.

Stepping aside, she said again, "Come in." This time her voice was warm. He stamped his boots in the entry and she helped him with his coat. "You're cold," she said. "Go get warm."

In front of the fire, he shifted from foot to foot, then looked at her for permission to remove his boots. She nodded and picked up a piece of wood, tilting her head so he would know to move aside. She stirred the coals and placed a blackened pot on the little shelf inside the firebox. When she stood in the freshened flame, Zhampa saw her face was not yet creased by having to endure painful joints and irregular sleep. Her eyes were almost true black and her skin red, smooth except for a scar by her ear. She lit a tallow lamp and placed it on a low table nearby. Two bowls followed that.

They ate the meal of stew with few words between them, but when she rose to fix tea she said, "You must tell me of your travels. You've come from places no Tlingit will ever see."

Zhampa began at the beginning, at the DiOrio farm and, though he spoke of it simply, the emotion of remembering it painted a mural of the Hills like Women Lying Down and of the life before and after the Unraveling. He watched New Moon's face grow soft and he felt her like a bowl into which his stories were offered. She wanted to know all about the land around the Great Lakes and the various ways people and animals were surviving along his route. She clenched her jaw and said Celeste gave Barker what he deserved. She nodded in recognition at the life of the We people.

Zhampa awoke to the sound of kindling being split and thought himself in the Hollow. He drew a swollen hand across his face and blinked his eyes open. The scent of the wood and the light didn't fit. For an instant he felt sad. But the stories of the night before returned like the swelling of a stream after a rain. He couldn't recall falling asleep, or how he came to lie on the bench in the south window under a skin coverlet. He sat up.

"How did you rest?" she asked, looking over her shoulder. Her hair was down, long across her back.

"Like a stone in a well," he said. "When did I fall asleep?"

"The first time?" she said. "In the middle of a sentence." Her voice was buoyant like a girl's. "I'm sorry I kept you up so long."

"I remember. I was telling you about the We People."

She nodded. "Yes, you were telling me about the council. I want to hear more. But first we'll eat." With a dipper she filled a kettle. It sizzled on the fire ledge. They ate corn cake, kelp chips and tea. Then she left him to carry buckets from the spring.

"No. No," she said, when he volunteered for the job.

He walked outside into a clear morning and looked out over the meadow. Suddenly he realized they would worry about him in the village. When he rounded the house and came upon New Moon, she knew his thought. "They know you're here," she said, and when he looked at her quizzically, she added, "I saw another set of snowshoe tracks. They look like Little Tree's. So don't worry. Stay and finish your stories."

"I'll need to walk to strengthen my leg."

"There will be time later." She entered the house.

So he began his story again. She said she understood about him using the machete to protect Celeste and furrowed her brows during the Seradipa story. She winced when Gabe killed the guards.

"I wanted him to stay a hunter," she said.

"We all tried to keep him from crossing over. He was determined."

"Good hunters don't necessarily make good warriors. So what happened to him?"

He puckered his mouth. "We lost him."

He tried to explain Thomas and she covered her mouth with both hands at the cruelty by the Jewel Lake. When he finished, she asked "How far is it to Tibet? Are you halfway?"

"No."

She was silent a while. "Why are you going? Really?"

"The scepters belong there. And my teacher chose me."

"I envy you," she said. "We don't have teachers anymore."

In the afternoon, he walked up to the height of land. He stood there a long while between the continent and the sea.

New Moon cleaned the house and renewed the stew. For stories she told him about the Tlingit Diaspora and about the struggles when she was young. For one hundred and fifty years, the Tlingit lived scattered through the provinces working in menial positions. After the Unraveling, she found herself swept up in the migration returning to the Tlingit ancestral lands. There were years of hunger.

"We'd forgotten how to hunt our whales," she said. "And the pods were small in the beginning. Many men died trying to relearn our skills." She stared into the fire.

"If you want, I will listen to the story of your husband and your son."

New Moon jerked her head to face him. "What have you heard?"

"Just that they died at sea, whaling. I shouldn't have said anything."

"They didn't die together, you know. And my son wasn't whaling. . . . Our chief was harpooning and got caught in the fathoming line. He hit his head on the gunwale as he went over and was pulled under. It was quick."

Zhampa waited.

"Our son, the next chief of the Tlingit, rowed out to save a foundering boat in the Right Whale migration last May. The weather was bad, but he said that if he were to be chief someday, he should earn the position. He was the only one not to come home. He was still young."

"I'm sorry," Zhampa said.

They listened to the fire for a long time.

"I will soon enter the flower of my moon," she said, turning to him.

When Zhampa understood what she meant, he said, "I must go" and looked toward his boots.

"No," she said putting her hand on his knee. "No, you don't understand. I need your help. We're without a chief."

Zhampa pondered the kind of help she might need.

"We need a chief," she said again.

"I'm not a chief."

"Your friend says you are."

"I'm not a full blood," he said. "Just a quarter. Though right now I wish I were. I wish I could help you. Besides, I'm going to Tibet. Shouldn't you take someone from your people?"

New Moon pursed her lips, amused. "You don't understand," she said. "Why should you? In the Tlingit, the women choose the men. It's the Mother Water Carrier who gives the chief his power. If a chief fails in his duties, it's the Council of Water Carriers that removes him. No, you're not the chief of my people. That's not what I'm asking. When the chief dies, it falls to the son, if he is worthy." She nodded. "I no longer have a son. Our tradition demands that I seek a mate outside our community to keep our people vigorous."

She waited.

"We need a chief and the Council still wants me to keep the line. I need your help. They are willing to wait for me to have another son." She put her hand on his thigh.

Though he understood, he did not move.

"I'm only a quarter. And it's Lakota."

"You'll do," she said. And then softer, more confidently, she repeated, "You'll do."

In Zhampa's mind, the little house suddenly seemed large, the colors intense. He saw years fall from New Moon's face.

"But the truth is," she said, her eyes darting, "my moon flower isn't tonight. It's two days away."

He heard New Moon, but felt another presence as well. It was Claire. From somewhere in the shrouds of loss, Claire was finally letting him go. "I can wait," he said.

Then New Moon fidgeted. "You know women are a mystery, don't you? Our timing is never exact." The smile that spread through her was not for her people, but for herself.

"As long as we're telling the truth," he said, "I'm very rusty."

"I know. Your daughter Red Cloud told us you lost your water carrier."

"Have you met Celeste? Red Cloud? She says you haven't."

"When you all first came to the island, she didn't know one or another of us. And I asked to keep my identity secret. Listen, it was I who first saw your fires on the mainland. And I was looking there for a reason. For three nights in a row, I'd had a dream of a chief arriving over that mountain. I helped hold you down when your leg was set. Yes, I know you and you will do. You will do splendidly."

"Those were your hands?"

New Moon nodded. Then she put her finger to his lips. "Shh."

She stood and walked to her sleeping corner and slipped through the drapery. When she returned, she was wearing the necklace again. Zhampa smelled rosemary. She held out her hand, raised him up and had him stand by the drapery.

"This is a chief's bed," she said lifting the fabric. Candles fluttering on ledges cut into the walls encircled a round bed made of wood with the bark still on.

"It's the stump of a tree," Zhampa said. "A huge stump."

"A Sequoia. My husband carved it himself. He built the house around it. His courtship is here. The roots anchor me on the earth." She stepped into the circle and facing him, knelt on the fur skin coverlet. "Come," she said. "We have offerings to make."

He knelt facing her, knee to knee.

"As the father of a future chief, you must profess honor to the Water Carrier Lineage. You must know beyond doubt that you and all men are but a half of life. Without women, you're dried husks. Your intentions will fail. Speak now," she said, "and speak clearly."

He waited for the words to come. First he honored the chief who had built the bed. Then he spoke of his grandmothers, Chantelle Bouchet DiOrio and Nuni Kamiora Tanka, and of his mother Sumiko Tankha DiOrio. "I pray," he said, "that I may father a son who never goes against the wishes of women who hold the earth and carry the water."

He was about to say more when New Moon again put her finger to his lips.

"That was perfect. Now remove the necklace."

To fulfill the need of her people, Zhampa and New Moon took to bed as often as lovers half their ages. And though New Moon knew exactly when she ovulated and even felt a jolt as her egg was fertilized, she kept quiet and floated with the bliss of the man.

When she missed her menses, Zhampa asked, "What if you give birth to a girl?"

"She'll have beautiful genes," she answered. "And I'll tell her the story of her father, who traveled to the other end of the earth to help people who hadn't been born."

"But you'd still need a chief."

"Yes, but the chances are very good that it will be a boy."

"Fifty-fifty?"

"Yes," she said. "Very good odds."

And when spring came, Zhampa decided not to leave. Like all the Tlingit of the Inside Passage, he wanted to see if a new chief would be born. New Moon's abdomen swelled with the pumpkins. And when the constellation Virgo rode the mantle of the sun, she gave birth to a boy, whom all Tlingit came to know as Little Bridge.

In the second winter, Oakley sat Zhampa down and looked him dead in the eye. "I never felt like I belonged anywhere before," he said.

Zhampa nodded and let out a long breath. "Do you think I'm doing the right thing, Oakley? 'Cause sometimes I feel like a jackass carrying iron relics to some mountain in China."

"Hope so, Chief."

After they were quiet a while, Oakley said, "Thanks for letting me tag along."

Zhampa waited.

"I was pretty near crazy when I came to The Valley, you know."

"We came through some hard times, Oak."

"Well, now I know what crazy really is. You know, Barker, Seradipa, MacComber."

"There's plenty of crazy to go around. You'd think a good unraveling would make people smarten up."

Oakley ignored him. "Three Cries accepts me for what I am and for what I'm not. So I'm gonna stay still, Chief. I'm not going to go on with you. I'm going to stay here and help these people . . . 'til my eyes go. 'Til the rest of my teeth come out." He laughed and began to bubble-spit.

Zhampa nodded. He'd been wondering about his friend. Finally, he couldn't hold back a grin. "Then I suggest you stay out of saloons," he said. At which they both roared. It was how they began their goodbyes.

In their sixth season on the island, Zhampa said to Celeste, "I feel like an old onion."

Celeste wrinkled her forehead.

"You know," Zhampa said, "like the ones in the bottom of the basket at the end of winter, all sprouted green." He stretched out a measurement with his thumb and middle finger. "You pick it up and it's got roots right through the wicker weaving into the dirt."

"Yes," she said, still unsure of his meaning.

"It's going to be hard, Celeste. Hard to pull myself off this island. Do you feel that way, too?" he asked.

"Yes, we have lots of ties here. And it'll be really hard to leave Little Bridge. He's like my brother." It would have been the perfect time to tell him. She was soon to learn that the acceleration of events before setting off causes one missed moment to feed another.

In spring of the second year, when Little Bridge had begun to crawl and had shown affinity toward laughter and manual dexterity, New Moon took him down to the harbor to watch his father, Celeste and a young brave from the next island south climb into a sturdy trimaran that the islanders had built and honed into a sleek craft. The boat was stocked with dried meat and vegetables, water casks and extra sails, four hundred feet of handmade three-braid rope, trolling net, lances, a wealth of other survival gear and Tlingit gifts of silver jewelry, furs, ivory, soaps and oils with which to barter upon arrival. With the songs of the previous evening still echoing, the sailors bade farewell. Out on the edge of the harbor, the south wind caught the boat's sail and drove her around the point and out of sight heading north. Oakley and Three Cries returned to their lodge.

14

The first hours onboard the trimaran *Naga*, Celeste stood in the bow watching for humpback flukes and blows and chattering to the cormorants and red-necked grebes that the boat flushed out of the water. In the stern, Fire Hawk—the Indimo, as he referred to himself, because of his mixed heritage—stood with the tiller cocked in his armpit and his eyes on the waves, a great smile pulling at his face. He was heading north, back to the land of his mother's family on the Arm of Alaska. He hoped his old Poppop and aunts were still alive and that his boat-mates would need a rest before running the Aleutian chain. He longed to hear the drum songs of his youth again and to visit his mother's grave. Now that he was a man, he wanted her advice: which people should he live with and where should he find a wife?

When she died twelve years earlier, his father Yanu'uck took his young son to live with his own people in the Tlingit island clan. In that way the boy learned the traveling songs of both cultures and the waters along the first part of his passengers' crossing. A born sailor, the taste of salt water on his lips and the slicing sound of the boat in the water cheered him.

Oakley and the Tlingit builders had taken a regular twenty-six foot whale canoe and set a pair of spars crossways through her gunwales to outriggers carved to look like dolphins; the spirits of the sleek ocean mammals would bring them good luck. A super-deck was laid over the spars with enough space underneath for crates and bags and for the sailors to get out of the elements. Fresh water bladders, one on each side of the bilge, undulated like napping walruses. A firebox lined with tin metal and filled with sand dominated the open cockpit. Their main sail was a fine-weave linen, the product of hundreds of hours of Tlingit women, embroidered with the Lineage Lance, tip-down, as a sign of peace. Whalers from Kayak Island stopped rowing to stare at the boat.

"How does she handle?" Zhampa finally asked as the outgoing tide shot them between the islands in boiling channels.

"Nice," Fire Hawk said. "She's faster than the waves. Your old scout was smart." He tapped his temple.

In the northern archipelago, Fire Hawk sang new songs describing the landfalls and shoals. In the harbors where they stopped, Tlingit pushed forward to confirm the rumors that had spread north about the band from the other coast and to see the man who had conceived them a chief. They took on wood, potatoes and onions in Petersburg.

Beyond the protection of the islands, the sea below the glaciers glowed green for miles. A school of bottlenose dolphins escorted them through the morning, but when they left, Celeste became ill with the motion in the long swells. She vomited and was lethargic.

On the second day she said, "Zhampa, I think I'm pregnant."

"You sure?"

She nodded, lips together.

Zhampa didn't speak for a long while. He worried. He knew he was no midwife. But then he brightened. Celeste had found someone to love. He turned beaming and she told him the story of falling in love with Crane.

"You picked a good man. Guess I've been blind lately, huh?"

"Yes," she said. "Yes to both."

"Then what are you doing here?"

"It was a hard choice. In the beginning, Zhampa, I came because I didn't want to live without you. But now—I can't explain why—I feel this is my journey. I have something to accomplish independent of you."

He smiled to hear her. And over the course of the day, his jaw and lips worked—clenching, sucking, pouting—as consequences began to unfold. Beyond the risks of childbirth, traveling with an infant presented problems. And the older the child became, the slower they would have to go. Would it be possible to walk to the Naked Red Lady Mountain in one year? He didn't know. He started viewing their future in two frames—before and after birth. They would travel as her condition allowed until finding a place for her to go into labor and recover. Then they would carry on.

"I wish I'd kept the cart," he thought.

Fire Hawk had been thinking, too. And singing his songs. Since there were no harbors in the five hundred miles where the mountains plunged straight into the sea, he tacked on a long reach into the Gulf of Alaska. And tacked back three days later. The cliffs of Montague Island told him where he was.

Villages appeared along the coast. They saw smoke from fires and sheets flapping on drying lines.

"White people," said Fire Hawk.

"How do they survive?" Celeste asked.

The tillerman shrugged. "Fishing, I guess. Maybe some gardens. My people avoided them."

Zhampa scoured the shore with binoculars.

"Small boats in the harbors," he said. "A few burned buildings." He handed the glasses to Celeste. "Were there battles up here?"

Fire Hawk shrugged again. "Yes, but my people laid low."

In the afternoon a boat closed on them from the stern.

"No sails," Zhampa said.

"Gasoline," said Fire Hawk, "Haven't seen one since I sailed with my Poppop. What do you want to do?"

"Celeste, are you willing to get below and cover yourself with gear in the bow?"

She nodded. "You want the pistol?"

"No. You take it."

"Zhampa, let's raise the yellow pennant. Means we're passing through and we'll just keep to our course, so they don't get all sprung, if you know what I mean. Our story is we're going to see my people six days ahead."

"You think they'll be curious who I am?"

"If they're white, they'll think you're one of us."

The boat caught up with them in late afternoon. An old salmon seiner belching black smoke and sounding like a rockslide. Three heavy-set men, bearded, pistols in plain view. Zhampa waved. One waved back halfheartedly. A second eyed him through field glasses. Fire Hawk turned the *Naga* into the wind. She stopped, bobbing on the waves.

"What's your business?" said the man with the glasses.

"We're Tlingit from way down the coast," said Fire Hawk. "Heading to see my mother's people five hundred miles farther on. We're just passing through. We're flying yellow."

The three men conferred behind their hands. One gestured wildly.

The spokesman called over, "Yellow don't mean shit no more."

"It's been the sign of peace since I could walk." And while the men gestured and conferred some more, Fire Hawk yelled over, "So who are you?"

"We're Sounders, born and bred. This is our piece of the earth."

"Well, we're no threat to you. We'll be out of your waters by morning."

"How do you know where our waters are?" asked the one with the wild arms.

"Lately," said the spokesman, "we've had raiders come under the yellow pennant."

"In motor boats?"

"No. Under sail. Nobody has oil up here no more but us."

"Who's the old guy," asked the one who hadn't talked.

"I'm his uncle," Zhampa said.

"Why the spear on your sail?"

"It's the symbol of the Tlingit."

"Looks like a war sail to me."

"No, no," said Fire Hawk, "it's a whaling lance. And it's pointed down to show peace."

"Then you won't mind if we board you."

Fire Hawk looked to Zhampa, but he was already waving them on.

In the swells it took a full five minutes to get the boats safely close enough for the man with the field glasses to bound over onto the super-deck. He dropped into the cockpit, squatted and peered into the gloom under the deck. After thirty seconds he stood up.

"Where'd you say you was going?" he asked.

"To visit my people."

"And after that, we're heading all the way to Asia," Zhampa added.

"That's good. I hate liars. You're carrying too much stuff to be local. They're on a long trip, looks like," he called to his mates. "Bunch of handmade shit. We couldn't use it anyway."

Minutes later the boats pulled apart, though the pistols didn't find their holsters until they were heading for the widest part of the Sound.

They stopped for water on Kenai and caught a sea bass on the trolling line on the way to Kodiak. At the fish market in the protected harbor at Port Lions, tables were piled high with crab, bass, flounder and salmon. Fire

Hawk asked around the other boats for news along the Arm, but the only boat that wasn't local had come in direct from Dutch Harbor. Its captain said that he had no news from the villages on the Arm itself.

Headwinds through the Shelikof Strait frustrated Fire Hawk; he hated being so close to home and making such slow headway. But finally, after twenty-six days on board, they made landfall in the Indimo's territory.

"It's not like I remember," he said.

"Things always look different when you've been away a long time," Celeste said.

"We should be seeing boats."

"Maybe they disappeared in the Unraveling?" Zhampa said.

"No. I remember them," he said, sweeping his arm along the coast and then using it to cover his eyes. He handed the tiller to Zhampa and went to sit before the mast. Again and again he sang one particular song running his hand through the air as if over the contours of mountains. Eventually he fell silent and listened to wind worrying the mast stays and the edge of the sail. His face was sour when he came to eat. In the slackening winds of twilight, Zhampa guided the *Naga* around the point of land they had taken as a mark earlier in the afternoon.

"On the far side of this point," Fire Hawk said, "there should be a bay with a rock island in the middle and a quiet anchorage. Only about a half day sail from Poppop's village." Then suddenly he was up and hanging off the windward stay. "I recognize the rock slides there," he said excited. "Keep the island to port. Water's deeper on this side." Five minutes later, Zhampa turned the *Naga* into what was left of the wind and Fire Hawk threw the anchor off the bow.

In the morning he washed himself in the sea bucket and donned a tunic with a sealskin collar not in the Tlingit style. Later, as they rounded the Point of the Sun to enter his Poppop's fiord, Fire Hawk barely breathed. In a village of that size there would have been boats coming in with them from the day's fishing and women and boys hauling them above the reach of the tide. There would have been girls and little children carrying baskets of the catch up onto the cleaning tables. There would have been men barking orders and dogs imitating men. The air would have been filled with the smell of fish hanging on the racks. But their welcome was the creaking of metal roofing flopping in the breeze. On the sun-sides of buildings, clapboards curled, spitting their nails into the dirt. Doors yawned open. Not a word was said, but they all knew they would go ashore. Fire Hawk let the anchor fall into the blue waters and pulled the line to hook it fast in the crags below. They dropped the canoe from its hold over the stern and paddled to the old marina.

"The dock's still in good condition," he said. "But the water's higher than it used to be. About four feet." He led them directly to the cluster of Poppop's buildings to find them burned to the ground. As devastated as the place, he walked in the rubble, pointing to things that weren't there and describing their meaning. At last he found a smooth river stone that he had painted as a gift to his mother. He slipped it into his pocket. "Let's go," he said. And when they reentered the strait, he assumed his place before the mast and said nothing for a full day.

Days on down the Arm, the weather was cold, the land windswept, bare. Bluffs purple, grasses washed-out yellow, the water and the sky trading shades of gray. On one island, they found distant relations to Poppop's tribe, though none could shed any light on their fate. No, they said, they'd never heard of the Unraveling and sat wide-eyed to realize they were more alone on the earth than the day before.

The islands beyond were smaller, with steep cliffs and fabulous rookeries. They collected baskets of eggs and topped off the water bladders when the land offered a fresh source. Somewhere ahead, the island chain would give way to six hundred miles of pure sea.

On the summer solstice Fire Hawk said, "No one beyond here will know anything of the Tlingit." So they lowered the sail and clipped out the embroidered threads of the Lineage Lance.

That evening, Zhampa held a cup of water aloft. "I could be off by a couple hundred miles," he said, "but let's toast the longest day of the year and being halfway to Tibet."

"And," Fire Hawk said, "let's drink to being on top of the world, too, as far north as we'll go. It's all downhill from here."

Zhampa laughed. "You have no sense of mountains. Bet you've never been more that two hundred feet above sea level in your whole life. The base of the Naked Red Lady Mountain is probably ten thousand feet higher than where we are. So I correct you. It's all uphill from here." They laughed, drank more water and became light-headed.

Ten days later they came to a petite island, grass-covered with a modest cove. Two stone houses, not thirty feet apart, held the entire population, a small, Arctic people the color of storm clouds. Even the faces of the children were creased by the wind. They understood neither English nor Alutiiq.

"We're farther west than we think," Fire Hawk said.

Zhampa drew circles in the sand to show the islands they had passed and when he included their houses in his drawings, they were quick to understand. "Dom," they said pointing to the two buildings, nodding. "Dom." Big grins.

"They're speaking Russian," Zhampa said. "Da. Da," he said back. And the islanders raised a chorus of "Da, Da," almost dancing. He then drew another circle beyond their island and gave a grunting shrug to ask if there were more places to stop or navigate by.

One of the men took his staff and drew two tiny circles and then smoothed the sand beyond to show that it was open water.

"Okay," Zhampa said. "We'll head southwest as the wind will give it to us and hope to hit Kamchatka." The islanders let them fill their water bladders from the little spring uphill from the huts and on one of the trips to the *Naga*, Celeste thought to bring them the embroidery threads, which they grabbed for as if it were gold. In return, one of the men produced an uncut jade stone, the size of his fist and offered it to Fire Hawk.

"What else can we do for these people?" Zhampa asked.

"We have rope to spare," Fire Hawk said, and when he returned with one hundred feet of Tlingit manila, the islanders could hardly contain their excitement, each one handling it at the same time and testing its strength. Then an elderly woman removed a carved ivory talisman from around her neck and laid it around Celeste's. She placed her hand on Celeste's belly. Then all the women surrounded her, smiling, saying 'ah.'

"My God, Zhampa," Celeste said. "How do they know? I'm not showing."

Beyond the island of Dom, they lost their confidence about their heading. The map from the DiOrio atlas was weak regarding the curvature of the northern latitudes and their compasses began to swing wildly. Had there been a clear night, Fire Hawk could have navigated by the stars; but there were none. More islands appeared than the old man on Dom had drawn.

"I wonder if we've wandered into the Bering Sea," Zhampa said. "We better head south-southwest."

As the last of the land receded, Celeste tied herself before the mast with tail of the main halyard.

A week out from the island of Dom, a storm blew in from the north dragging steep swells. Even with her sail reefed, the *Naga* headed south at great speed. Still the waves outran her. Each one lifting her from the stern, hanging her bow-down above the trough, setting her to perch a second on the peak, the world black, howling, water in tantrum, and then slipping her down the back of the wave with her steerage gone.

In the daylight, Fire Hawk guided them through the rolls. Celeste and Zhampa quick bailed each time the bow lifted skyward and bilge water slopped over the rib skeleton into the cockpit. In the night they proceeded by feel of the boat alone, their voices to each other their only hopeful reference point. As the wind and rain diminished after dawn, one by one they fell asleep at their posts.

They had lost much of their firewood and the canoe had been ripped free. They threw over the dried fish and the herbs that had been ruined.

"Any guess about how far we've come?" Fire Hawk asked.

"I was going to ask you. Were we making over ten knots?"

"I tried to gauge it. Twelve. Maybe fifteen. I could be way off."

"Worst case," Zhampa said measuring his map with his fingers, "we could be five hundred miles south of where we last headed west. Twelve hundred miles from land."

15

They were at sea three more weeks. Once a sail appeared in the distance. But it vanished. They came, too, upon a huge hull, listing and lifeless. Five days later they tacked through a stream of flotsam—processed wood and garbage—giving them hope they were near land. But the days dragged on and their water ran low.

Before light one morning near the end of July, as the Naga drifted windless in a warm fog, Fire Hawk heard the scrape of waves on a shore.

"Red Cloud, Zhampa. Get up. Land."

Zhampa dragged himself from the hold and hobbled stiffly to the bow. Hanging on the forestay, he shook his head to clear it. He listened, then thrust his thumb in the air.

Celeste responded by dancing the first ten steps of The Sea Otter Comes to Dinner. But it was too soon for real celebration; not knowing where they were, they had to be cautious. With well-rehearsed movements, they made the Naga ready.

"We might be lucky, Zhampa," Fire Hawk said as the sound grew louder. "I hear gravel, not cliffs."

"What's that other sound?" asked Celeste. "Sounds like drums underwater."

"Waves crashing in a cave?" Zhampa said.

"Sharp eyes now," Fire Hawk said, looking into the murk. "And pull the center board, Zhampa. We're drawing deeper than we can see."

Fire Hawk readied a stern anchor in case they needed to hold off from the land, but when the low line of shorn-off buildings loomed out of the fog, he slammed the tiller hard to port.

"Good Christ," Zhampa said. Shattered walls of concrete and brick. Docks inching into the sea. A pod of boats resting on the gravel bottom, shifting against each other with the waves.

"Where do you think we are, Zhampa?" Celeste asked.

"Not the Kurils."

"What about water? Can we at least . . . ?"

"Not here," Zhampa said.

"You don't have any idea where we are?" Fire Hawk said.

Zhampa gave his tillerman an exasperated look. "Somewhere north of Hong Kong . . . and south of Vladivostok. Let's get out of here."

Sailing north in the light air, they stared at miles of ruined coast until at last Zhampa told Fire Hawk to pull off from the land. He went and sat before the mast. "Damn it," he yelled. "Damn it." And he spat over the side.

They sailed four days before they dared approach the shore again. This time they saw green hills and Fire Hawk made for a notch in the land. A mile from shore a fleet of fishing boats converged on them. They shrugged to show the captain of the first boat to arrive that they didn't understand his Japanese. But as soon as he saw Celeste, he motioned them ashore to their village. His wife gave them water to drink and to wash away the ocean. She served them dishes from both sides of the tide. To help them sleep, he served them tiny cups of rice wine. He and the other captains spent much of the night discussing what to do.

In the morning the captain came with gestures and the words "Inga leesa. Inga leesa." He bowed when arriving, when departing and when making a point that he was sure needed no rebuttal. Inga leesa was his attempt to say that he knew an Englishman who lived in a village up the coast. And when Zhampa understood, he allowed the captain to sail them there.

Charles Darby was an old man, an academic from Glouchester, England. Decades earlier, his wanderlust had landed him a professorship in Osaka Teachers University. And he was one of the lucky ones, he said, having been in the north of the country on holiday twenty-nine years before, as the south received a blistering assault from the main land.

"What you saw," said Professor Darby, "was payback—long-delayed— for Japanese adventurism into China one hundred and twenty years ago."

Though most cities on the big island had been destroyed, in the villages the centuries-old tradition of Japanese hospitality survived. Having not seen a westerner in some years—five or seven, the professor's memory was cloudy—he was happy for company. So his young wife Taka-ki prepared their quarters meticulously, down to the choice of folding screen for Celeste. When it became known that Celeste had nothing to change into,

Taka-ki returned from her sister's home with several things that fit her well enough.

They were guests for a week. Taka-ki and the Darby resources strained to accommodate them. Yet each day neighbors came bearing a basket of yams or a melon or vegetables from a garden. And in this way they eased the Darby's burden and got to see the foreigners up close.

Celeste noticed that being ashore changed Fire Hawk. After twelve weeks at sea together, she knew the sound of his breathing and his satisfied groans after eating fish—yet again—and his smile of triumph when the tinder responded to his coaxing of the coals. The image of him standing in the stern, feet braced on the gunwales and leaning into the wind, the tiller an extension of his body, was etched on her mind. She still felt the tingling in her arm where he had grabbed her during the storm when her bucket tried to pull her overboard. Once while Zhampa slept, Fire Hawk confessed his sense of adventure was wearing thin and that he'd begun to doubt being able to return solo, knowing he couldn't handle the Naga in a second storm. In passing, he mentioned continuing on with them to the Naked Red Lady Mountain, but she knew that it was because he felt pulled to provide; Crane being father to the child in her womb made her honorary sister to Fire Hawk. A mother should have a powerful set of hands at her beck and call, he'd said. It wasn't reasonable to think that old man Zhampa, all of fifty, could give her that. He'd told her that she needed someone whose best years were ahead of him.

But when the discussion in the village turned to readying the Naga for the trip to the mainland, Fire Hawk didn't speak. Disturbed, Celeste sought Zhampa's counsel but found him locked in conversation with the professor in the stone courtyard of the little teahouse. Through gaps in the bamboo fencing, she spied on them sitting close together in the shade of a wilderness of plants, both leaning in, as if under the influence of some near celestial body, the old man's frame aided by freckled hands, stacked on the handle of his walking stick. The professor knew his history and Zhampa was rapt hearing about other versions of the Unraveling. She listened a while, but became frustrated by trying to keep track of countless events and of the names of places and countries that she hadn't heard of. And she left them.

When they sailed for the mainland, the whole community came to see them off. Matsume, the linguist, was aboard. He guided them around the northern tip of the big island and through the Tsugaru-Kaikyo Strait to the mainland polyglot port of Kraskoli, a full day's sail south of Vladivostok. The port was part natural harbor and part river delta with the vessel depot being in the tidal portion of the river. Matsume knew that, being a foreign boat, the Naga wouldn't be allowed at the quay, so he picked out a stretch of shallow water near a rubble-strewn bank. Fire Hawk raised the centerboard and the Naga grounded softly in the mud with her starboard pontoon two feet from the high water mark.

Garbage and feces sloshed in the backwaters of the river flow. "It stinks," Celeste said. Zhampa nodded but was distracted. Though he had visualized walking across China, he hadn't ever considered the problems of the first ten miles. Beyond the waterside warehouses and shanties, the streets of Kraskoli buzzed—Chinese pushing or leading every kind of vehicle, White Russian shopkeepers calling from their doorways, Korean tailors working on the sidewalks, farmers unloading produce in the markets. The air throbbed with negotiations.

"I'm going to find you a guide," Matsume said. "And maybe someone who'll help fit you out for travel. This is the time to sell anything you don't need."

Zhampa looked instinctively to Fire Hawk.

"I'm staying with the boat," Fire Hawk said. He bent to coil the main sheet.

Zhampa acknowledged the loss with a nod. Selling the boat would have brought a great price, judging from the attention she'd garnered coming in. They could have bought a splendid wagon and hired guides to lead them all the way to Tibet. They could have paid for a midwife. But there was no use looking back.

At Fire Hawk's announcement, Celeste bent to pull bags from under the deck. They were too big for her, but she responded by pulling harder. When the handle of a skin bag tore off, she kicked it and caught her toes on a boat rib. She swore and turned away, but Zhampa turned her back around and held her.

"I hate to lose him, too," he said. "But now our main goal is to find a place for you to have your baby. Listen, if things don't turn out, we'll stop. We'll turn around and travel 'til we find the place where things make sense again."

"We could really have used him."

"I know, but he's got a different destiny."

Matsume returned in mid-afternoon with a tall man, blond hair poking like straw from under his cap. Hands in his pockets, he hardly broke stride coming down the rough bank to the Naga. He eyed the boat and Celeste.

"Is she for sale?" he said jutting his chin out at the boat.

"No," Zhampa said, waving a hand toward Fire Hawk, "she's going back with him."

"Too bad. Pyotr Sidirov," the man said offering his hand. "You're Zhampa? He says you want to go into China. I can take you, but I'll leave you at the first frost."

"How much?"

"Two ounces of gold now and one more at the far side of the coastal range. Two if we get to the banks of the Sung Ha."

Pyotr helped exchange the beaver skins, the ivory and most of the oils and soaps for precious stones, gold and mother of pearl. They sold the last Seradipan pistol behind a meat stall. The next day they bought a strong mule, whom they named Dun for his color, but they had to settle for a weary wagon to carry the new bedding, new pots and fresh herbs. When the time came, Fire Hawk and Matsume walked with them to the edge of town. It was less painful than having to watch the boat sail away.

Pyotr had learned English from his mother but not manners. He didn't help with the chores or with adjustments to the load. He satisfied himself telling stories of crossing the border many times.

"Border to what?" Zhampa asked.

"The Manchurians are slow to accept the change," Pyotr answered.

"Is there a government?" she asked.

"In their minds, yes. In any case we still have to pass through customs. Actually that's where the government begins and ends. At the border." He let out a loud laugh.

"What is it that they want?" he asked.

"Continuity," said Pyotr. "And money."

It was good to be in trees again. Even good to be going uphill. On that side of the range, the farms and villages prospered. They camped wherever they could set the mule to graze on the last of the summer's grass. Two days out, the traffic on the road thinned to wagons carrying logs or boards to and from sawmills on the tributaries of the river that fell into Kraskoli.

Celeste rested often and Zhampa brought her cool water from the creek. Her face was fuller in the jaw. Her hand fell naturally to her abdomen. It rained higher up and they passed children without shoes playing in the mud. An old man of mixed race hoed his garden with nothing more than a heavy stick. And as they walked, Pyotr taught them basic Chinese: food, verbs for buying and cooking, directions, landforms and numbers.

"Tomorrow the border," Pyotr said. "We want to get there before midmorning."

"Why's that?" asked Celeste.

"They're easier to deal with when they've recently eaten."

"How much money?" Zhampa said.

"They'll look you over to see what you're worth."

"Are they thieves?" she asked.

"Businessmen."

"And you say they wear uniforms?"

"Manchurians like uniforms."

At the highest point in the coastal range, they looked down on a still-green landscape of hills. Pastures quilted the valleys.

"It looks like Vermont," she said.

"I'll be damned," Zhampa said.

"Where's the border?" she asked.

"Over the second ridge. We'll camp tonight this side of it."

The next morning as they came to the border town, Pyotr said, "Go with whatever I do."

"What will you tell them about us?" Zhampa asked.

"I never know. It depends on who's there."

Short-walled houses of rust-colored brick closed in on streets of compacted clay. A small figure swaddled head to toe worked a willow broom pushing things ahead of her; she didn't look up as they passed. A brick wall cut through the middle of the town, west to east. At the sound of Dun's hooves, people milling in front of the gate that allowed passage through grabbed trinkets and pressed forward to sell them, jabbering. Laughing, Pyotr took the mule reins to allow Zhampa to fight them off.

"Like black flies, aren't they," Zhampa said.

"No. No. No, thank you," Celeste said. "Very nice. No, thank you."

A whistle blew and the peddlers pulled back for a little squad of men and women armed with rifles to parade from their post near the gate. They wore mismatched navy blue wool suits with bright red shoulder boards topped with gold stars. At a second whistle the squad came to attention, barring the way to China. A dumpling of a man with little black pupils made much of his few steps from the office to the head of his delegation. One hand rested on his sidearm holster, the other fit into the small of his back. He paraded left and right, barely looking at them. As Zhampa listened to Pyotr exchange little bursts of a singsong tongue with him, he saw the holster was empty and that the rifles were made of wood. Pyotr gestured, countered and suddenly grabbed Celeste, kissed her cheek and roped her with his free arm. Then he spoke again and patted her belly, beaming. She blushed and kissed his cheek. At which point the officer walked to the wagon and lifted a corner of the tarp.

"San bai," he said.

Pyotr looked aghast. "San bai?"

"Dui. Dui. San bai." And he stormed back to his office.

Pyotr followed pulling out a roll of paper money. He counted out six fifty-yaun notes and slapped them on the table. "Let's go," he said, coming back heated. The whistle blew again, but it was not for them. Another party approached the gate from the far side and the squad trotted off to defend their other border.

"What was that?" Zhampa asked when they had traveled down the road.

"A little game. A formality."

"But you paid him."

"Call it a fee." Then he laughed. "Those are old Chinese notes. They're worthless. He wanted to know who you were. I told him you were a Mongolian priest."

"Mongolian?" Celeste said laughing.

"Well, he doesn't look Chinese . . . or Mongolian. But it's the only thing I could think of. They're bigger than the Han."

"What if he'd known Mongolian?" Zhampa said.

"I would have told him you were a mute."

"You've earned your gold, Pyotr. Mostly by entertainment."

Pyotr swept off his hat and bowed. "Sometimes, though," he said, "they'll beat you. All part of the game."

"Now you tell us. Why not just go around the town?" she asked.

"Because if they find you in the hills, they kill you."

The nights got cooler. Farmers they met were happy to barter part of their bounty. Village markets were full—pigeons, cabbages, broccoli, grapes, grains. Mutton was available before noon, but the pigs were being saved for winter.

"I've never been farther inland than one hundred and fifty kilometers," Pyotr said. "No need really. It's just land like this. Not much that I want for trade in Kraskoli."

"What's beyond?"

"It gets dryer, I think. Deserts in the north, but I don't know how far or how big."

"Better to call her your wife in this country," Pyotr said as he was preparing to leave them. They had camped at the base of an inland rise and the first frost had killed the last of the flowers the night before. "They'll think you're lying if you say anything else. She looks odd enough to pass for Russian to them. Don't mention America."

"And the age difference?"

"That's no problem here."

They paid Pyotr a third piece of gold and then fell into a rhythm of traveling a day or so and settling in when they found a hospitable place. On their traveling days they passed home and hamlet seeing no one or just an old grandmother with the infants; the rest were working in the fields. But in the evenings, when the women saw Celeste's belly, they prevailed on their husbands to create a bed in their barns. And as the nights became colder, often as not, the door to the home was opened and they slept propped in corners of kitchens or were invited to lie on the sleeping platforms with the rest of the family. On those nights Celeste slept tucked into Zhampa, covered with his arm. Gradually Zhampa felt something in her let go.

It was Celeste who discovered they were accumulating things as they went. Little valuables were pressed into their hands as they were leaving or were tucked into their gear to be found later. Socks. A spoon. Some yarn. Zhampa figured they made a compelling sight: a light-skinned woman and a healer, heading west with barely any language. Winter and deserts before them.

"How are you feeling?" he said one October evening when they camped by a brook. "I mean about traveling?"

Lately she'd been calling the rest periods, using no words, just pointing at the spot that summoned her to sit. "Well," she said, "I can't do what I used to. Even riding in the cart ten miles seems like a long day now."

Zhampa nodded.

"I'm starting to think about making a nest. What are you thinking?"

"Of being smart," he said. "We want to choose our place. Not let the weather do it for us. The land seems to be leveling out. My gut tells me our winter home is behind us."

"Did you see it? A place that might work? Why didn't you say something?"

"No. But there are fewer villages out here. Fewer abandoned places too. The trees are smaller."

She nodded.

"So what I thought was to go on a couple more days, if you have it in you. To see if this is a flat region in the hills or if the hills are behind us. What do you think?"

"Maybe I can do a couple more weeks. It's hard to know."

They pushed over two more horizons and the land stretched before them with only the faintest contour. They passed through miles of fallow cropland where the hedgerow trees had all been cut. Then through the haze of dust, a city appeared in the distance, huge but without a wisp of smoke rising from it. Celeste pointed and they sat. They ate potato and carrot. Then they turned the wagon around and Dun pulled their load back the way they'd come.

"I think we should explore over there," he said pointing to some hills to the south.

"Looks like they're still a little green," she said.

"Maybe we'll get lucky and find an abandoned place."

"Yeah, one where they left all their belongings," she said.

He chuckled. "With a stream in the yard. And the hills full of medicine plants."

"With the table already set and a pig in the barn."

Celeste spied a large steel cauldron half-buried in the dirt. They dug it out and threw it into the wagon. "In case they haven't left us one of these," she said. "For when I'm screaming and you need to boil water."

They followed the widest tributary of the river that flowed from the hills and near sundown on the second day, they came to a settlement of some forty families stretched along its banks at a wide bend. When they were seen, a cry went from house to house. Women gathered their children. Men appeared carrying tools, taking stances both defensive and curious. But all eyes were on Celeste. Even though she was hooded, the sharp bone of her nose announced her as a foreigner. They stared and squinted at her marble skin. Then at her round eye sockets. Then at her belly.

"Celeste," said Zhampa without looking at her, "show them your hair."

But she was already freeing her scarf. When she threw back her hood and shook her mane, the people gasped and froze, then broke into a rolling laughter, covering their mouths. They pointed, all talking at once.

Finally when eyes fell on him, Zhampa said slowly and carefully, "I am a doctor."

"He's a doctor," Celeste said, nodding.

When Zhampa modeled the wish to sleep, tipping his head into his hands, suddenly everyone had an idea.

Thirty years past the Unraveling and forty since the harshest of the droughts, rains had returned to southeast Manchuria. Hay crops swelled out the doors of wood slatted barns. Sows bore huge litters. Children appeared like clusters of grapes. So the villagers along the river did not hold back. A simple meal and beds of straw were prepared for the guests. The next day, when Celeste pointed in her definite way to the ground and Zhampa rocked a make-believe baby, the village women understood. They yammered, pressing their husbands to create a solution.

First a shed, then a barn. A week later the town elder Wang Wu led them to an abandoned brick house a mile beyond the village. The barn was small and needed roof tiles, but Celeste clapped her hands; a little stream ran through the yard and the steel cauldron fit perfectly in the round hole of the cooking hearth.

She swept the house clean and arranged their belongings. Zhampa gathered fuel in the woods around the house. Everyday visitors from the village brought a sack of beans, some wheat or a piece of the day's slaughter. "For the baby," they would say with a gesture. One morning they heard whimpering outside and a man arrived with a boy, whose ear tilted into his shoulder. Zhampa laid the child out on the k'ang, the glorious, indispensable Chinese bed, which was heated by the kitchen fire on the other side of the wall, the social center of every home in winter. He felt for broken bones and finding none, he massaged the neck, rolled the head and gave it a sharp twist. The boy yelped as his pain vanished. On leaving, the pair bowed many times.

16

In a snowstorm, a strong hand rapped on the door. A woman stood there empty-handed and one look told Zhampa she wasn't ill. She pushed by him with a torrent of words and waved her arms, stopping only to peer into crocks and corners. All sparks and fire, like sun setting on a lake. Compact and proud. Her hair as black as Celeste's was red. Beautiful in every way, except for a slight harelip.

"Perhaps she's the previous owner of the land," Celeste said, "coming to claim her place. What are we going to do?"

The woman responded by throwing her hands in the air and collapsing by the k'ang. She heaved and grunted. When Celeste laid a hand on her shoulder, she shook it off, intent on rising again, but seeing Celeste's condition, she stopped. She stared at the swelled belly, then at Zhampa—his hair, his hands, his body. Her eyes glazed over and after a minute she nodded in agreement with her idea. Slowly her hands rose, mirrored the curve of Celeste's abdomen and came to rest upon it.

"Zhampa, I think she's a midwife."

The woman bade her lie back on the k'ang and lifted Celeste's chemise. She placed her ear near the navel, then smiled, drifting in thought. She shook her head clear and stood again, said a few lines in Chinese and as abruptly as she had come, grabbed her cloak, went through the door and headed up along the stream into the forest.

"We're saved, Zhampa. Someone in the village must have told her about us." She got up and straightened the blanket on the k'ang. "You won't have to do it," she said. "That's the best news. That's a relief to both of us, if you want to know the truth."

He turned to look out the one window and watched the figure disappear into the trees.

" . . . have you?" he heard her say, and realized he'd missed part of a conversation. She took him by the arm. "I asked you if you've ever seen her before."

He shook his head.

"Well, we have to find out where she lives. Look at the weather. I can't believe we let her go out in this weather."

"She came in this weather, Celeste. And she didn't exactly make hints at staying."

"We don't even know her name." She flopped down on the k'ang and covered her legs with the blanket.

"Are you cold?"

"Yes. Suddenly I am."

He went to the kitchen, broke more twigs for the fire and watched them curl in the flames. He returned with some tea, and when she took it, he said, "What's wrong?"

"We've let her get away."

"She must live nearby."

"It's not good enough. She was looking around to see if we had anything to pay her with."

Zhampa shook his head. "I don't think that's it."

"Don't just sit there. Fire Hawk was right. He'd be tracking her down right now. Snow or no snow."

"Fire Hawk?"

"Zhampa, please follow her. Now. Before her trail is lost in the snow."

"Okay," he said. He set down his cup, laced his boots, threw on his coat and went out.

He followed the tracks uphill two miles through the woods to a clearing and a clay brick building even more modest than his own. He knocked. With a smile, the woman let him in. The house was dense. Bundles of plants hung from the ceiling. Bowls and containers cluttered every surface. He saw tubers, seeds, bark, leaves and dried parts of animals. In the kitchen, cutting boards, graters and knives lay beside piles of mixed herbs. Bottles of liquids and scores of little boxes crowded the shelves. The air smelled of things fermenting.

"Are you a doctor?" he said.

"Yes. Like you."

"What is your name?"

"Liu Fang." But he couldn't understand what she said after that. He hiked his shoulders and shook his head. She nodded, holding up her hand and made space for him on her k'ang. Then she served him tea that brought heat to his hands and feet. Pleased, he pointed to the herbs and to his cup and raised his brows, wanting to know which plant it was. With a laugh, Liu Fang stood and waved her hand over some half dozen things in the room. Then with no invitation she kneeled down in front of him, close, to examine his eyes—the surface of them—shifting her head to see better. She said something, stood and forced her thumb over the lip of his clavicle. When he yelped at the pressure, she nodded, picked up a dried root and, talking to herself in the kitchen, chopped it with rapid strokes. When he rose to watch her, she was already returning with it in the cup of her hand. Undaunted, she made him open his mouth and packed a wad of bitter fragments under his tongue. She worked her cheeks to imitate sucking until he did it.

"Hun hao," she said. Then she held his coat out for him and buttoned it with hands so quick and light that he almost forgot why he'd come. He turned by the door and stammered, "Tomorrow, you come?" He used his hand to show Celeste's belly.

"Dui, Dui, Dui," she said turning him out. "Goodbye. Goodbye."

And true enough, she returned the next morning and every day after to listen, to watch and to feel. Instead of tantrums, she brought things for Celeste to eat and drink.

"For the baby," she said.

Over the days Liu Fang's visits became longer. She cooked with Celeste, teaching her how to prepare the foods and herbs she'd brought. She taught her the vocabulary of everything. Zhampa marveled at the chemistry between the women. Though he felt he was losing Celeste in some way, he consoled himself with the thought that Liu Fang's hands were confident in ways his would never be.

As for their first meeting, Celeste waved it off. Every woman has irrational days, she told him. And true enough, Liu Fang was steady in her kindness to Zhampa as well. She fixed him the tea that he found so pleasant at her house. Her food was delicious. Still, she was always encouraging him to get out to gather more wood. Manchurian winters always became fierce after the New Year, she said. Winds would sweep in from the deserts and the highlands beyond. And when people from the village stopped coming, she sent him there with the mule for meat, for eggs and for hay. It was then that he noticed a change in his reception by the villagers, a new reserve. He wished he knew more of their language. Perhaps by spring, Liu Fang's lessons would allow him to have real conversations. When he mentioned her name, they nodded. Yes, they knew her. But they called her by another name.

"Why do some people call you 'wupo'?" he asked Liu Fang.

Liu Fang jerked and then pushed a smile. "Where did you hear that?"

"In the village. That's their name for you."

"Of course." And she paused. "It means 'queen,'" and she held herself like an empress to show them. "Queen of Medicine. Sometimes they say it as a joke, because I, well, have my moods." And she laughed.

Celeste asked, "What are we going to pay her? She's giving us so much of her stores. And she's up for hours every night making things for me."

"I don't know what she wants," he said.

"We have to take care of her. She's a natural giver."

"Seems so."

"You would know. You haven't always gotten paid for what you've given."

"Things always come back around," he said.

She was thoughtful a moment. "Then we'll let her tell us when she's ready. But I have to say, I'm having such a good time with her. I love being pregnant."

"It shows."

"Liu Fang tells me it's a girl. She says she's dreaming of her at night."

"A girl? Good. I'll always have room for another girl."

In early January, Liu Fang moved into the house. "Going home is too hard for me now with the snow," she said. "Now I'll stay with you."

"Is the baby hun hao?" Celeste asked.

"The baby is very good," Liu Fang said. "Very good. She will come soon."

Liu Fang sliced and crushed the herbs she brought. She weighed them on a hand scale—a graded stick suspended on a string. She seemed to carry a thousand formulations in her head and used her sense of smell as the final arbiter for what she wanted. Things boiled on the stove. Concoctions brewed in glass bottles. Zhampa enjoyed watching her work and she smiled at his attention. She repeated the Chinese names of the herbs and he translated them to his paradigm the best he could. This species, that genus. Many things were easy, but some of her techniques and the plants she used were a mystery. He looked forward to seeing them in summer. In the meantime, she set him to work as her apprentice. And though much of what he made for Celeste tasted bad, she surrendered to it all with grace.

The night she moved in, Liu Fang fell asleep on the k'ang as easily as an old dog. But Celeste was restless. Finally she pulled soft bundles all around her, pushed herself back into Zhampa's curved torso and dozed. In the morning she awoke to the snapping of the fire and to Liu Fang working in the kitchen. The k'ang grew warm beneath her and as she lay there, she told Zhampa that with him at her back, she felt a primordial protection. She said she wished her mother could be there to see the new generation. She wished that Crane could know their love had born fruit.

Gradually the activity in the house slowed like a river in its delta. With the exception of trips to the yard to relive herself, Celeste lived on the k'ang. Ceding the kitchen to Liu Fang, she occupied herself making clothes—a cotton tunic with drawers to match and a hooded wrap of sheepskin. She sang the winter songs of the Tlingit and marked the dance steps she had learned with her first two fingers on the coverlet. She asked Zhampa to tell her all he could remember of Claire and pestered him to be accurate about her mothering skills. She reminisced about Little Bridge coming into the world. And she napped often.

Knowing that Celeste and the little one would have to ride to Tibet, Zhampa made alterations to the wagon. He enclosed the bed, so that they would be protected from the elements, and made a pair of shutters to cover the window in the front. As for himself, he didn't expect or care to ride. He was nearing the goal and could handle the desert and the mountains. In spring, grass for the mule would be plentiful. Yes, they would move more slowly. But the Naked Red Lady Mountain was within their reach before the next winter. The greatest obstacles were behind him, and the Chinese were proving to be practical people; they wanted to survive and understood the need of others to do the same.

Liu Fang did her chores with the attention of a watchmaker; she took pleasure in relating to each object, as if it were to be put away until the next year. She polished everything in the house, lastly sweeping and watering down the clay floor. Then she sat, watching the ripening of her project, teaching Chinese until Celeste's attention became overrun by a dreamy joy.

"Wake up. Wake up." Liu Fang rocked Zhampa's shoulder. "Water. Please heat the water." There was excitement in her voice. "The baby comes today."

Celeste was sitting up, her face serene, her nightclothes wet. "My water just broke," she said. "Are you ready to be a grandfather?"

He grinned, thrust himself up, dressed and went to the kitchen. The fire was almost cold. He had not awakened in the night. While he blew on the coals, Liu Fang guided Celeste through her first set of contractions.

"I can do this," she called out to him when it passed.

"Hun hao," Liu Fang said. "Very good."

Zhampa smiled. This would be his second birth in less than two years. His fathering would be transferred to little Sophia—if Liu Fang were correct about the baby being a girl. Celeste had liked the sound of the name and when she learned that it meant 'wisdom,' she would consider no other. Through the morning, he tended the fire and made the teas that Liu Fang had mixed in the previous days. When the cauldron came to a boil, he carried more water from the stream. But he was relegated to the kitchen.

"Here is women's room," Liu Fang said patting the k'ang.

Celeste nodded her agreement. "You're banished until further notice."

The rounds of her contractions gathered in intensity through noon. She was working more than New Moon did, but he knew first children came harder. He drifted between attention and contemplation, watching the fire, and checking, by the sounds, that Celeste's effort was keeping up with demands of her body. She was strong.

Later he jerked out of a dream. Liu Fang's breath was in his ear. "Bu hao. Not good. Bring more tea and come. I need you." Her eyes had lost their confidence.

Celeste lay on her side panting like a beast on a humid day. She was half-clothed, her skin glistening wet.

"The baby isn't coming," Liu Fang said. "It's stuck. Celeste's tired now."

The sun had already gone behind the hill and the light in the house was dim. Zhampa felt a cold brick in his belly. He helped Celeste sip from a cup, then smoothed her forehead. At his touch she let her head go. Encouraged, he placed both hands on her stretched stomach. Just beneath that skin, a being yearned to be born. She had already been in labor for eight hours with the hardest work yet to come. He asked Liu Fang what was happening and she used her body to show how she thought the baby was caught. This way or that way. Another flow of contractions came. But Celeste didn't push.

"I'm so hot," she said. "I'm so tired."

He ranged for ideas to shift the situation. If she were too hot to push, he had to cool her. Or he had to get a message to the fetus, to tell it to move and survive. He went to the door and opened it, letting the winter in and when the cold blast roused her, he thought, 'Let's try it.'

"Get up," he said. "Get up. We're going out."

She lay there, not understanding.

"We're going out," he said forcefully to both women. Then to Liu Fang, "Out. Out. Outside now."

Liu Fang was horrified. "You are crazy," she said. "I'm staying here."

"Of course," he soothed her. Then he modeled how the cold would make Celeste contract and twist. And as Liu Fang considered the idea, he gathered Celeste in his arms. "Take care of each other," he heard Claire say. The snow creaked underfoot. The air was bitter.

"I'm not dressed, Zhampa. I have no shoes." Her voice was soft and plainful.

"Stand. In the snow. Holler your baby out. You've got to get it out." He swung her feet down. She shrieked and hopped from one foot to the other. Liu Fang came from the house bringing her long coat to throw over Celeste.

"No," he shouted, pushing her away.

"You are a crazy man."

"Roll in the snow, Red. Roll."

Celeste looked at him in alarm, but she was present.

"Yes. For your baby. For your life. Roll in the snow."

She nodded, still hesitating.

"Do it. Before your next contractions."

"Do it with me," she said, grabbing his arm and dropping into the crystals. He followed her down. She rolled and the cold made her toss quickly. She whooped with the sting of it. He rolled, too. The ice on his face shrank his world. Somewhere in the distance, he heard Liu Fang shrieking. Celeste's next set began right there and she rolled up onto all fours.

"Now push, Red," Zhampa cried. "Both of you push."

And she did, roaring like a lion. Four times.

"It's coming," she cried. "I can feel her coming."

This time he didn't protest when Liu Fang covered Celeste with the coat. In the next contractions, Liu Fang was there to see the head come clean out and a moment later to catch the body.

Inside, the girl-child Sophia breathed on her own and after a few minutes she dropped off to sleep. Celeste worked to deliver her afterbirth, then, too, fell back exhausted. Liu Fang worked longer, cleaning up the bloodied sheets. In the end, only Zhampa stayed awake tending the fire. Sophia had Crane's coloring—light olive, a fuzz of coal-colored hair, brown eyes and, could it be? Asian lids.

In the morning Liu Fang was moody. Thinking she felt she had failed, Zhampa let himself become her student again. When she had him prepare a mixture of nuts and herbs to help milk production, he made it diligently. Celeste said it tasted miserable, but she drank it. They were all excited when Sophia tracked the nipple. But two days later, after she had taken all the colostrum, there was no milk to replace it.

Liu Fang frowned and disappeared into the kitchen. She made two more remedies.

"One more disgusting than the next," said Celeste. But nothing Liu Fang gave her seemed to help. Sophia was patient at first, taking the little drips her mother had, but eventually she tired. Worry settled on the household. In the night Zhampa awoke to stoke the fire and found Liu Fang in the kitchen with her blouse off, vigorously rubbing a scented cream on her breasts. She did not flinch at the sight of him.

"Our baby must eat," she said. Her breasts were large and moon-like in the glow of the fire. It was not impossible, Zhampa knew. Women have created milk for another's child out of sheer need. Part of the mystery. Liu Fang fingered her nipples taut and tried to insert them into her mouth but could not reach. Her eyes flashed in frustration. Finally she said, "Ching ni-yee, for the baby. For the baby," coming to him, sitting him down on the stool. She pressed his hand against her breast. She showed him how to twist and pull the nipple. Slowly at first, but then inspired by the possibility of helping the child, he let go of his awkwardness. When she felt him relax, she said, "Yes that's right." Then she took his hands away and pressed her breast to his mouth. "It's important for the baby. We have a family now. We have a family."

From that point on, Liu Fang nursed Sophia for a minute on each breast before handing her to her mother. This seemed to ease the strain on both women. And between feedings, she sat Zhampa down in the kitchen and removed her blouse. She was careless where she placed her knee and how she let her fingers hook inside his ears. He became flustered when he felt his charity quake and heat spread through his body. He denied it to himself and didn't speak of it with her. And he was relieved when he tasted Liu Fang's milk come in. Soon Sophia began to thrive.

"She has two mothers now," Celeste said, doing her best to sound cheery.

Zhampa admired her grace as she handed Sophia to Liu Fang. And for a few days all eyes were on the child, but then he noticed Celeste wasn't bouncing back from her delivery. He checked her signs and watched Liu Fang do the same. They agreed. Celeste's energy was low. Liu Fang gave her a new tincture, but it had no effect on the weakness. He stayed by the bedside until both women were tired of him and pushed him out, so he confided in the mule, walking around the stall for hours, talking and hoping for an idea. Liu Fang had Zhampa make another tea. Then another. Celeste had good days and bad days. Her improvements were always cut short by a steep decline. At the end of February she still needed help to go outside to relieve herself. March was better; she slept with Zhampa at her back and Sophia close to her chest.

Liu Fang worked to make the house smooth and restful. At Zhampa's request, she reviewed all the medicines she had—their names and which parts of the body they affected. He tasted them all, trying to link them with his own knowledge. Finally his persistence upset Liu Fang. Twice she made him stop and turned him out of the kitchen. A third time she pushed him hard away from the remedy she was making and got so furious that her hands trembled. "This is very hard work, trying to balance everyone's need," she said. "You just have to trust me, Zhampa."

When the snow melted, the wagon sat untended and unloaded. There would be no traveling in the near term. He waited for the plants to come up, but the arrival of spring was maddeningly slow.

Sophia, though, grew plump and attentive. She arched her back and responded to the movements of her two mothers. And Zhampa carried her in his arms for hours at a time. When the weather moderated, he took her out to examine the buds still tight on the trees and to marvel at the mule searching the yard for anything green. She delighted in the sounds of the stream, running fast with the melting above.

Early April brought two joyful events. Sophia found her laugh when Celeste blew on her naked tummy. For five minutes they conversed through laughter until Celeste became emotional and buried her face in the blankets.

And Sophia's new hair came in. It was red like her mother's.

"She's a perfect mix of Crane and me," Celeste said.

But Liu Fang wasn't happy. "Red hair is not good in China. Not natural. It will make problems for her." She made a disagreeable face.

Then Celeste caught the flu, though no one else did. Her cough lingered. "What do you think is the matter with me?" she asked Zhampa when Liu Fang had gone to her house for new herbs. "I have everything to live for."

"I can't figure it," he said. "Your symptoms move around. We treat one. It clears up and something else arises."

"Do you think it's . . . spiritual?"

"What do you mean?"

"Well, that I'm being paid back."

"Paid back? For what?"

"Killing those boys. They were boys, you know."

"You were sixteen. Minding your own business. Twenty-year olds are men."

"Well, what about Barker then?"

"You did what you had to. That was the best thing that could have happened to him."

They were silent a long time.

"What's happening in your dreams?" he asked.

She thought. "I've been having a recurring theme. It's not a dream with pictures, or, if it is, it's not one I remember. I can only tell you how it feels. I'm blocked in from the sides. And I hear the roar of life up ahead, vibrant and bright. There's no suffering. And I'm going home. But every time I go forward, I hit something I can't see. I bounce back. My energy's running out staying where I am." She thought some more. "It doesn't make sense, does it?"

It didn't make sense, but he felt pressured to say something positive. She'd never sought trouble. And if sickness were payback for bad actions, he should be the one ill. His voice soft, he said, "You've been as good as anybody could be in a world like this." Then, "I think the warmer weather might help."

But in the warmer weather things slid out of control. Her digestion became sluggish. She lost weight. Zhampa went looking in the woods himself, but plants that looked like ones he sought tasted quite different. He came in despondent. She was sitting up against the wall.

"Promise me," she said, "if I can't get through, that you'll take care of Sophia."

"You'll get through this, Red. We're all . . . "

"But if I can't travel . . . "

"I'm not going anywhere until you can come with me."

"What about taking Liu Fang? You could take her. She's healthy. She's strong."

"I'm not going without you."

"But if I don't leave here . . . " She didn't finish.

"We're family," he said.

Before death, a stillness. Signs of life become elemental: pulse, breath, sight, awareness, peace. Like the answer to prayers. For some, the stillness is brief. Celeste's lasted several days.

Then one morning she said," It's a beautiful day. Take me to the doorway." In the afternoon she said, "You keep being father to children who aren't yours." His cheek pulled in the direction of a smile. At dark she asked, "Do you think Claire will remember me?" He was incapable of answering. After stroking her arm, he went outside and laid his head on the mule's neck and listened to the animal breathe.

In the first quarter of the night, she lost interest in Liu Fang's tea. In the darkest hour, she spoke of lights the others couldn't see. Then she lay with Sophia asleep beside her. Breathing with her and nothing more. As dawn bled back into the hills, the first robin of spring lifted its head. It saw the light and inhaled to celebrate its arrival in its own home country. Celeste was beyond hearing. She had traveled on.

17

The mule pulled the corpse wagon to the cremation ground. Zhampa walked behind. Then came Liu Fang with Sophia bundled in her shearling wrap, followed by the whole village. They watched as he laid Celeste out on the pyre and as he placed spring's first blue flowers on her head. During Wang Wu's chanting of the traditional Chinese prayers, they stole looks at Liu Fang and the baby. Zhampa lit the pyre and all heads tipped up to watch the smoke ascend to heaven. After, in a few halting sentences of Chinese, he thanked them all.

As the gathering dispersed, Wang Wu approached with a married couple. "This is my niece and her husband," said Wang Wu.

"Yes, I remember you," Zhampa said. "You are kind to come."

The couple bowed. They seemed ill at ease and Zhampa hoped they didn't need treatment that day.

"We are sorry," the woman said, "that you have lost your wife, and that the baby has lost her mother."

"They have tried for years to have a child," said Wang Wu, "but they cannot. And they have asked me to say that they are willing to raise your baby and to save her from a difficult life—even though she has red hair."

Zhampa felt Liu Fang inching in beside him. She was quick to speak. "We are sorry for you, of course. Every woman should have a baby. But as you can see, the child is already well cared for." She turned Sophia for them to see.

The young woman barely glanced at Sophia and grated bitter words into Wang Wu's ear. A whisper, and not. Zhampa heard that word again. Wupo. Harsh. The woman's husband pulled her sleeve and Wang Wu furrowed his brow.

"Yes, he knows that I am a queen of medicine," said Liu Fang almost cheerfully.

"Yes," said Zhampa, "but even her medicines couldn't help. Don't be angry, please."

The young husband cleared his throat and his wife's mouth fell open. Wang Wu turned the couple around and hurried them away.

Liu Fang's demeanor dipped only slightly with the death of her friend, patient and sister. Sophia's needs were prohibition against grieving. Perhaps the child knew that some star had given out in the sky, but Liu Fang's presence let her know she still had a mother. Zhampa let Liu Fang carry on with the cooking and cleaning, but when she nursed the baby, he often had to leave. Then several days after the cremation, he began hollering in the yard. He took his ax to the covered wagon and using both the blade and the blunt face, he reduced it to splinters. After, he attacked a wall in the barn. Braying, Dun kicked down the boards of his stall gate and dashed into the woods. When Zhampa turned to the house, Liu Fang escaped up the hill to her own place with Sophia in her arms and a simple basket slung over her shoulder. Unimpeded, Zhampa thrashed the k'ang and the stone surface of the stove. Exhausted, he lay down where the bed had been and fell asleep in the cold twilight.

The next evening, Liu Fang summoned him to consciousness and led him up the trail to her house. She bathed his cuts in holly soap and made poultices for his infections. She plied the kitchen fire with sticks and laid him on her own k'ang, covered him with blankets her mother had made and let him sleep. She made him tea that tasted of raspberry and ginseng. And she waited.

When he finally asked for food, she made him some. She watched what he ate and what he put aside. Which medicines he drank and which not. What herbs soothed or agitated him. She let him leave the house when he wanted and welcomed him back. He rarely spoke and she did not press him.

In days, he began engaging the child again in ways to make her laugh. When Liu Fang noticed him listening carefully to her speaking Chinese to Sophia, she spoke more slowly. Some four weeks after Celeste had passed, he entered her kitchen to watch her again pulling herbs from leather pouches and copper boxes.

Then in a cool spell of weather she let the night fire go out. When he went to relieve himself under the stars, she placed Sophia in the warm nest where she had lain and moved onto Zhampa's spot. When he returned chilly, she held up the coverlet and said, "Come get under. I will make you warm." She had been so kind for so long and had asked for nothing in return that his skin ached for communion. He lay beside her. For two nights she ignored him, sharing only her heat. On the third she nestled into him as she had seen Celeste do. Her hair smelled of morning glory seed. He was tense at first; his restraint wrestled with his body, giving way through the hours in harmless steps to touching her in the guise of sleep until his hand came upon the freed button of her nightshirt and the smooth skin and warmth of her breast. She responded fully.

Through that summer Liu Fang became mother to a fattening child, and lover and teacher to Zhampa. Goats and two piglets ran in the yard. The mule was there, too. Zhampa's bundle of belongings sat vestigial on the chest behind the door. He was grateful for her grief remedies; they lidded his anger and kept his guilt at broken promises from rising in the night. Her question, "How are you feeling?" came to mean, "Do you need some more?" And he was honest about this simple thing.

She helped him realize that the past was better left in some attic, like old letters. He gathered stocks for tea and wood for the next winter. He hauled water without thinking of the Tlingit way. He repaired the corral in her barnyard and the stone walls in her pasture. He gathered herbs with her and repeated every word she said. He made love to her in the stillness of mountain nights.

"I have everything I have ever wanted," she said lying next to him, pacified.

"But I assume you want us to have a child of your own, making love this way. Or do you use medicine to stop your fertility?"

"I am dead here," she said, placing her hand below her navel. "No village man would marry me. But you have taken me the way I am. And I love you."

"Tell me," he said, "why don't you go to the village or have patients come to you?"

She rolled her back to him. "I used to," she said. "But some there think I'm not a good doctor." She lay a moment. "A woman died while I was caring for her. It's very hard to get rid of a bad reputation."

"I know," he said.

"People think medicine is magic . . . "

"Yes."

" . . . when, really, it's just an art to correct the injustices of life."

He nodded. "Illness doesn't listen to justice."

One evening in August Liu Fang pulled noodles for an evening meal. Zhampa carried Sophia to the corral to stroke the mule. She and the beast had a special connection. He watched the setting sun falling on her hair, a beautiful fluff and the phrase 'Red Lady Mountain' popped into his mind. It rolled easily on his tongue, but made no sense. It turned again and again. Something surfacing from the past. He saw the curve of the mule and then of the hills in the distance. With the phrase 'Hills like Women Lying Down,' he remembered the Hollow. And the farm there. And the stone walls. And Rinpo's cave. And the scepters.

He checked for the holster, but realized he hadn't been wearing it for months. Feeling dizzy, he put Sophia down to think more clearly. Where had he put them? Just then Liu Fang came to the door and called him for dinner. Seeing Sophia crawling in the dung mud inches from the mule's hooves, she ran out with a torrent of reprimands and gathered her up. The sound of her voice was of a metal spoon scraping the inside of a dry cauldron. He looked at the house and in that instant, saw it as squalid. His beautiful home in the Manchurian mountains was nothing more than a clay brick hut. He steadied himself on the mule's flanks until the spell passed.

When he didn't eat, Liu Fang showed signs of concern. "Are you all right?"

"Yes. Just not hungry."

She put her wrist to his forehead. "You're hot," she said.

"No, I'm just dizzy, is all."

"I'll make you tea."

He stood. "I don't want tea."

"But, you're dizzy. Something needs attention. That's what I am here for."

"I was dizzy. But not now," he said, annoyed.

She went into the kitchen and set to work. "Not too many," she said to herself.

"Not too many what?" He had come up behind her.

"Not too many times have you been dizzy," she said, palming the little pills she was counting and rolling a pouch closed. She got up on tiptoes and kissed his ear with the slightest inhale and passed over to the stove, tucking the pouch into the fold of her blouse. Zhampa picked up a black pill from the counter.

"What's this herb?" he asked, as he had a hundred other times.

Her voice came quick, higher. "A special herb. For dizziness, in case it returns."

"What's in it?"

"I'll show you tomorrow. Sophia needs to nurse."

He sniffed the pill, then licked it. It was familiar. He slipped it into his pocket. On the bench outside the door, he pretended to sip his nightly remedy and tossed it away when Liu Fang rose to get a cloth for Sophia. In the night he had wild dreams. All the next day he disposed of his tea and watched his pulses. They were erratic. After dinner, he passed out on the k'ang early and came to in the midst of intercourse. Liu Fang, possessed, rode astride him, hair flying, babbling something about justice and love.

In the morning he awoke with a stabbing pain in his stomach. When he went to relieve himself, his heart pounded, his hands shook. "What is it?" he asked himself. "It's like I'm drunk. No, coming off a drunk. Am I addicted to something?" He went to steady himself in the stable. His breathing was labored and his hand fell on the black pill still in his pocket. Without thinking, he brought it to his lips, and at the mere scent of it, he breathed easier. He licked the pill and a softening ran through his body.

"Black pills?" she asked. "What black pills?"

"You know, in the tea. What are they?"

"There are no black pills."

He thought a moment. "Why are you lying to me?"

Her eyes darted.

"I see," he said. "Is this how you show love?"

"What do you mean? You came into my life. You needed a woman. I am helping you."

He grabbed her wrist and dragged her to the light of the doorway. When he produced the pill, she shrieked and tried to break free. Sophia bellowed. He twisted Liu Fang's arm behind her and forced her to the k'ang. "Tell me what they are."

"They are nothing. Just pills to aid the chi."

"You call yourself a doctor. Doctors heal people. They don't drug them."

"I've healed many people," she said.

"That woman in the village—did you give her too much of something?" When she didn't answer, he said, "It wasn't an accident?"

Liu Fang kicked with all her strength to rise, but his free hand caught her by the throat. When her eyes turned submissive, he recognized the look. It was the murdered Curtis' look on a Chinese face. After a long moment, he released her. But when she stood up and started with a blister of cusses and screams, he chased her down in the yard and dragged her to the barn. With leather straps, he tied her to the central post.

"I can't find the scepters. Where are they? Liu Fang, answer me.'"

"I sold them."

"For god's sake why?"

"We needed to buy things," she said. "You haven't done anything for months, and I haven't been paid for any of my work."

"Who has them?"

"I don't know?"

"Who did you sell them to?"

When she was silent, he grabbed her jaw and barked at her. "Did you drug Celeste?"

She jerked. "Why ask me? You helped make her formulas."

"You witch. I can't believe I trusted her with you." He circled her three times, thinking. Since murdering Curtis, he had avoided violence. But if Rinpo were authentic, didn't delivering the scepters trump everything? His reputation? His belief in right or wrong? Was avoiding violence and its repercussions more important than delivering the dorjay back into the hand of the Enlightened Ones?

Only selfless action is worthy. So lean into events. Apply yourself for the good of all. Take the long view. . . . Take your place in the flow of things. Think beyond your valley. Do this for the welfare of all beings . . .

In English he said, "For the welfare of all beings, beating you is selfless action. Then you'll tell me who has the scepters. You'll tell me if you killed her. I'm leaning into events. I'm taking my place in the flow of things." He picked up the threshing flail—two tough sticks joined by a foot of chain and let one half dangle.

Seeing it, she gritted her teeth. "I've been beaten before," she said and looked away ready to receive the blows.

He circled her a fourth time, weighing her words. Beatings hadn't improved her. He hung up the flail.

"Beat me," she said. "It will make us both better."

"I'm sorry," he said. He untied her. "Nothing's that important."

He walked to the house, gathered Sophia in his arms and settled her. Liu Fang was slow to follow. When he told her that he would cook from then on, Liu Fang lost her appetite. When, with her worry, her milk dried up, he weaned Sophia onto oat gruel. Liu Fang was restless at night and babbled in her dreams, snippets about the scepters. Why would a man walk so far to deliver two pieces of metal? Had she missed their magic? When he felt her tension was peaking, he left with the mule 'for the day,' he said. He tied the animal a mile away, doubled back and caught her digging under the wood box for the copper tin in which she had buried them.

Her abilities were irreplaceable. She could share the workload of travel and food. She could tend his wounds and rub his aches. She could mother Sophia. With the language, she could negotiate the countless obstacles that lay ahead. But the next morning he again tied her in the barn.

He took his time. There was plenty of daylight ahead of him. He laid out his belongings. Just the essentials now. The hatchet, the fire bow, a hat, the canteens, one sharpening stone, the digger for roots, one pot, the scepters in their holsters, the amulet holding a lock of Celeste's hair. Sophia crawled over everything. Then she fussed. He walked her and bounced her until she fell to dreaming on his shoulder.

Liu Fang did not resist. During his trips to and from the house, during the packing of the bags, during the bridling of the mule, she apologized and begged to come. "Take me with you," she said. "I can love you in all the ways a woman loves a man. I'm your friend, your teacher, your support, your interpreter, your lover." Her shoulder rose through the cut of her blouse and it beckoned him. It asked forgiveness. It promised happiness. It promised companionship when he was old. When she said his name, her voice was easy and round. It made him remember her breath on his skin. It pulled on his bone marrow. He needed her. Yes, they agreed on all points about his predicament and how she could solve them all.

He fitted the mule with dual carrying baskets and loaded them. He fastened the securing strap into the right-hand basket, so that Sophia could ride without being bumped free or crawling out on her own.

"Zhampa," she said softly. "You have a right to be angry. I submit to you. But I want to come, for Sophia. At least you see the sense in that."

"Yes," he said. His voice was calm. He returned from the house with Sophia still asleep and set her in the basket. His eyes full of emotion, he slid his hand along the concave of Liu Fang's neck and fingered her bindings. His hands said he was sorry. His lips on her head were soft and slow.

"I'll send someone for you," he said.

The load on the mule told the villagers he was leaving. There was no woman with him, just the little redhead girl. They murmured to each other in their dooryards, resting from their chores to watch him pass.

Zhampa stopped in on Wang Wu. His hair was brushed back and his shirt was open in the heat of afternoon. He was playing a type of backgammon that Zhampa had never understood.

"You are leaving?"

"Yes. The little girl is with me. I left Liu Fang tied in her barn."

Wang Wu said nothing.

"Please cut her loose after I am gone."

Wang Wu's companion spoke under his breath, too fast for Zhampa to catch.

"Thank you for what you've done," Wang Wu said without looking up. He moved a few white stones across the board and smiled confidently at his friend.

"Release her, okay?"

"Dui. Dui. Dui. We will. We'll need her again, when you are gone." Wang Wu waved him out with the back of his hand. "Perhaps she'll behave herself now. Good luck."

Zhampa led the mule down along the river. A wet summer had led to it still carrying much water. The grasses were brown, many plants had gone to seed, but he figured he had three months until winter, a fattened animal, food, tools, and clothes for cold when it came. He descended through the foothills and out to where the land opened. He came to the place where Celeste had found the cauldron the previous November.

"Sophia, do you like mountains?" he said.

She brightened at her name. He took it as 'yes.' He led the mule west across the dusty land.

"That's where we're going now," he said in Chinese. "To the big mountains."

18

On the last days of Manchurian summer, the wind came thick with dust from vast deserts west of old cities like Changchun and Tongliao. Scattered across the land, clusters of farmers responded as they always had to the caprice of seasons, leaking roofs, children born without fingers, and the sow lying dead in her stall. Of the characters that traveled the road, a man with a redheaded child in a mule basket was the most unusual. Zhampa and the mule worked for what they received and women jostled to hold Sophia; those that were able nursed her.

Over the solitary miles, Zhampa admitted to himself that he had aided Liu Fang in her evil to his own daughter. He had misused medicine and she had bound him by his doing so. He might heal others, but he would never heal himself. It became clear to him how obstacles could herald safe passage and how good circumstances could threaten and kill. He'd seen death, both natural and not, and he knew reaching the mountains was not assured. His fate was to carry things. Nothing earth-shattering in that. Like a river doing what it does.

He lost track of distances. The water in the riverbed that he followed dried up. Three times they came to the husks of cities too vast to walk around, dense worlds of streets and buildings where nature was peeling the concrete coatings from mud brick walls, crumbling them into the avenues, burying hulks of automobiles and castoff belongings in elephantine mounds. Sunlight came in hues of gray. He saw footprints in the dust, and tracks of wheels and of things dragged. Finally he saw them, on the outskirts, gray-fleshed faces in gutted tenements, staring out.

The land beyond was drier still, a sea of shoulder-high shrubbery, with an occasional village. As October waned, he and Sophia spent most nights under the stars. He noticed when Dun's ribs began to show. The mayor of the Xangchen village shook his head.

"He's weak," he said about the animal, "and the land beyond has little food."

"Is there water?" Zhampa asked.

"Yes, in places. This was part of the Silk Road."

"But the mule . . . "

The mayor shook his head again. "He'll die out there."

Zhampa traded Dun for food and a tumbrel, a heavier version of his seed cart. But Sophia would not ride behind, so he pushed it through a landscape of pale gravel where the grass grew thin. He entertained her with stories of the Old Time, to which she listened until the rhythm of the wheels grinding on the road made her sleepy.

They traveled on a good highway for several days, sleeping once in an empty tavern, but when it verged northeast they took a small track west into sharp hills. On a bitter day, Zhampa spied a shepherd's hut standing alone on a slope, the door a heavy tarp, and inside, space only for a hearth and k'ang. Lacking fuel, he fed Sophia the last of the cheese and laid them both out to sleep.

They were awakened by a herd of goats, bleating, rubbing against the corners of the hut. When a stout billy pushed his way inside, Sophia clapped her hands.

By his own admission the goatherd Ping was an old man. "Fifty-three," he said proudly through yellow teeth.

"Very good."

"What's the matter with the baby?"

"She's hungry."

"Does hunger make her hair red?"

Zhampa blew a jet of air. "Her mother had red hair," he said. "She died last spring."

Ping expressed his regret by clicking his teeth.

"We're in your hut?"

"Yes."

Zhampa rose to leave.

"No, no. It's plenty big enough for all of us. We will eat. We will talk. First we need sticks for the fire."

Over the ridge they gathered all the willow wands they could carry. Ping knew which goat he wanted. Kneeling, he wrapped his arm over its shoulder and holding the front legs, he drew the knife across the neck. He roasted the meat on spits.

"So where are you going?" Ping asked.

"Tibet. Have you heard of the Naked Red Lady Mountain?"

Ping shook his head. "Except for my days in the army, this valley has been my home."

"Is this a valley? It seems flat."

"There are mountains." He pointed north. "The cold in the desert will kill you soon. You need a place to live."

"Is there a village nearby where we could stay?"

"Mine is too small for two more mouths. This is difficult land."

Zhampa pondered. "Why do you stay?"

"It's my home," he said picking up a piece of the dirt floor and grinding it into powder.

Zhampa nodded. Ping was lucky to live in the land where he was born.

"There is water in the mountains. Perhaps you can stay there."

"Do you know the way?"

"I've never been, but old Shi knows. We will find him tomorrow."

Ping hadn't underestimated his village—fields worn through, the river a muddy wallow. The houses were patched, and sores thrived on the children's lips. Yet old Shi hosted him. Afterwards, Zhampa walked into a gray headwind along miles of irrigation ditches—the wind filling them with sand and scouring them clean again—toward a towering line of upthrust rock. Old Shi had said to find the place where the face of the rock was smooth like a tipped-up table, then to push along the base for several days to where water poured from a canyon. The Communists had used it, he said, to run a crusher for coal before shipping it down to Baotou. Up that canyon were mine buildings and the remains of a temple.

Zhampa heard the water before he saw it. Lively, tumbling out, but disappearing immediately beneath the sand on the plain. Climbing the track beside the water, he met two men lumbering down with carts full of coal.

"Where are you going?" they asked. "You can't carry coal in that."

"To find a place to spend the winter."

"In the mine buildings? Well, people use them from time to time, but you'll see. They're pretty rough." They looked at Sophia.

"I've heard that there used to be a temple somewhere," Zhampa said.

They laughed. "Something grandparents say to stir magic in the minds of children. It exists somewhere between myth and memory. Don't waste your time. The season comes soon."

"Where are you going?" Zhampa asked.

"East to our homes. Near Huahotte."

"How far?"

"Forty-eight kilometers," they said.

Zhampa whistled. "Do you have any food?"

"What can you pay?"

Zhampa produced a piece of mother of pearl almost as large as his palm for which they gave him a block of cheese and some oats. He headed on. A mile higher he found a pile of tailings, and above it, the work complex and the mine entrance. The buildings were cold—concrete cells with interior walls black from open coal fires. He laid their bedding out and they ate. As the moon rose, he sang Sophia a Chinese song about a fish too smart for a hook.

In the morning he pushed the cart farther up the river hoping for a building with the glass intact. The canyon ended at the base of a large waterfall; a stair cut into the stone next to it had been destroyed. He hesitated, then strapped Sophia to his back and climbed hand over hand where the steps had been. At the top he found himself in a narrow gorge walking on granite blocks laid level and tight next to a smooth run of water. Ahead, a clear lake a kilometer across, a bowl in the mountains. The last leaves of aspens fluttered on the far slope that climbed to severe cliffs. At the edge of the lake, the path became stairs leading down into the water. He paused. He looked back to remember the top of the waterfall. Seeing there was no other path, he removed the sash that held Rinpo's text, put it on the child and her on his shoulders, then walked down the stairs. When the water came up to his chest, the steps leveled out. Sliding his feet forward more than one hundred paces around the bend, he came to another stair which led him out and which he climbed in switchbacks up a steep seam in the rock. Above him fresh snow lay in the hollows and below, teal-colored water along the shores dissolved into a central dark eye. The drop was dizzying. Many stairs more. And at the top, the iron bars of a great gate blocked the way. He knew that it was locked before he reached it. But his eye fell on the two greenhouses, the glass steamy with plants. And beyond, a tile roof with upswept eaves, intricately carved corner beams and an array of solar collectors. The bare tops of fruit trees poked above a stucco wall. Two mammoth spruces dominated the courtyard of fitted granite blocks with a chase for water that flowed out from the coy pond, which was filled by cisterns stacked up the hillside. Terraced garden plots. An ancient structure with the roof gone hid in the shadows of the steep stone face. Columns made of whole trees supported nothing but the sky. Zhampa stood motionless so long that Sophia became restless inside his coat. He raised her to his shoulders, so that she could see.

An Asian man shrunken in his clothes appeared from behind a tangle of vines in the arbor. "What is your purpose?" he called out.

Zhampa paused. "How did you know I speak English?"

"You talk to yourself. Sound travels uphill."

"Yes, I was talking to her. It makes my work easier. I'm looking for a place to survive the winter."

"How many of you are there?"

"Just the child and me. I heard about the coal and the water; two things a man needs."

"But you didn't stay down there?"

Zhampa shook his head. "The buildings won't do."

The man was silent.

"When I came to the falls, and saw the old stair, I knew something had to be up here."

"You and a child? Where are you going?"

"Tibet." And when the man looked at him strangely, Zhampa said, "It'll take a while to explain."

The man turned and walked all the way to the coy pond. He stood a moment and returned. "My name is Tatsuhei. I haven't had a visitor in years."

"It was a retreat for the Ministers of Trade during the Ying Dynasty," Tatsuhei said. "They called it the Dream Fortress. Later it was a Buddhist Temple." He pointed to the ruins.

"It just fell down?"

"Destroyed by the Red Guards."

They had finished their first meal. Sophia lay asleep on the bench next to Zhampa. "Your English is perfect."

"I was trained in London. As a cultural anthropologist. But forgive me. I have trouble remembering vocabulary. And you speak Chinese."

"Badly."

"Then let's stay with English. I speak only Japanese these days, since my wife died. To my fish and my plants."

"And your wife?"

"She was Chinese. My co-worker. Tsao, the love of my life. We came to study trends of economic growth on rural regions in China and heard the myth about this place. Abandoned. Home to rats."

"The Chinese weren't interested?"

"Not a priority. Sad how the communists abandoned their legacy of art."

"When did you come here? And why?"

"During the white lighters. We thought it would be safe. Far enough from Baotou."

"White lighters? Here? I thought only the Globalliance had that technology. China was a leader of the alliance wasn't it?"

"True. But after America imploded, the alliance fractured along old lines. China hit Japan. India hit China. The Indians invented white lighters, you know."

Zhampa shook his head to show his ignorance.

After a silence Tatsuhei said, "We rebuilt the house first." He laughed at a past memory. "Every single brick and piece of glass came up from down below. I stole the glass for the greenhouses from the mine buildings."

"You didn't build a boat?"

"Too risky. Then others could have easily come."

"Hmm . . . Why does the path lead underwater?"

"General Su Yung's idea, I'm told. To foil those who live by expectations. I see you weren't deterred."

"No. The path begged for me to come."

"Begged. That's good. But come, Mr. DiOrio. It is late."

He led Zhampa to his little guesthouse. As he was leaving, he turned back. "We'll have a winter of conversation. It is about all I'm good for."

Tatsuhei served them breakfast in the sunny courtyard.

"In our first years here, Tsao and I carried coal on our backs up from the mine. Then one night she had a dream." He stopped and smiled. "She dreamed that there was coal in our part of the mountain. In the morning she scoured the rocks behind the temple. It was like she knew where it was."

"It?"

"The tunnel. The miners had followed a seam from below practically into this opening. We dug together. Pick and shovel. For twenty-four days. Since then we just . . . I just go inside our mountain here."

"You have everything you need."

"My days are short," he said.

"You're in excellent shape for eighty."

"For eighty," he said, lingering with the weight of it. "Eighty is enough to kill anyone." Then he laughed until he coughed.

The monsoon rains of January came as snow on the peaks. It melted and filled the cisterns and the pond. It dropped into the lake below. Water rolled over the falls and past the mine.

"Tatsuhei," Zhampa said, "do you think we'll just go on creating suffering? People, I mean."

Tatsuhei rose and poked the coals. He refilled the teacups. He examined the shadows in the corners of the room. Finally he said, "Having a heart is a prize almost too difficult to bear. It genuinely loves. But love so easily sours into grasping, don't you think?" He looked out at the dormant gardens.

"The droughts?" he continued. "We could have dealt with them. With a little clarity about how fragile we are, we might have healed things instead of resorting to war. I mean the climate and . . ." he waved his hand to show something passing between them. " . . . each other. We could have lived with less. . . . From where *we* sit, these are simple choices, no?"

After a moment, Zhampa said, "I've traveled a long way, in the hope that things will be different someday. Am I wasting my time?"

"That's not for me to answer."

"So you think there's no cure for it?"

"What? The heart?"

"Yes."

"There's nothing wrong with the heart, Zhampa. It loves. It admires the road and the ride. It loves the feeling of air on the skin. It loves fatigue. It even loves being sick, right down to the last breath. The schemes and divisions that unravel us, they arise in the head. The head, this brilliant cognition, wants to own what the heart has."

He walked to the door and stood in the last of the daylight. He shrugged and turned to face Zhampa. "I'm old," he said. "What do I know?"

During the winter in the Dream Fortress, Sophia took her first steps. Zhampa gathered coal and helped prepare seeds from Tatsuhei's fall harvest. In the evenings he studied Rinpo's texts. When it was warm enough, Tatsuhei encouraged him to leave. "You will want to be out of the deserts by June. When the Fu Hi Sa flowers, you have three weeks before the temperatures will kill you. You must take care of that child."

When Zhampa said he worried for him, Tatsuhei waved the words off. "I'm meant to die here. Even the cliff stairs are too much for me now."

Zhampa cleared the cistern outlets and mucked out the coy pond. Then he pulled the wagon out of its hiding place at the bottom of the falls. His provisions included some new items, most notably the robes of a Chinese monk, altered for the machete.

"You may find these protect you better than anything else in some of the lands ahead," Tatsuhei said. "I've worn them myself on occasion."

When he bade Zhampa farewell at the Gate of the Wind, he said, "You may be the last person I see."

Sophia rode down on Zhampa's shoulders, one hand on his horsetail, the other gripping the machete handle. She giggled when he walked into the water and she leaned over to peer at the mirage-like bottom. Down by the wagon, he changed into the monk's robes and by nightfall they came to the desert floor. Fat, the river ran above the ground and flowers bloomed along its edge.

The mountains yielded streams and the cart rolled sweetly on rain-packed earth. But after fourteen days, the land sprouted countless little hills several hundred feet tall and a straight course through them was impossible. In the evenings he wrapped Sophia inside his coat and they slept next to twig fires. He loved the rhythm of her breathing and the still-fresh scent of her. During the day she seemed to understand the drama of their situation and kept her screaming fits short. He took them as a chance to rest and walked her in his arms, cooing in her ear. He pointed to plants and named the ones he knew in English and Chinese.

The land to the south leveled out where the Yellow River carved shifting courses through a great gravel bed. And he came to Muslim villages on the shores where he was able to trade for meat and flat breads.

Now in his sixth decade the strength of his body was leaving him in all directions like heat from a sun-warmed stone at night. He did not have much time. If they lived and delivered the scepters, he imagined Sophia saying to her children, "He spent his life walking." And behind the thought, he heard another voice from a day among tall maple trees some forty-five years before, the voice explaining the walk of the elephant. Rinpo's voice.

"Do you understand?"

The boy Zhampa shook his head.

"Like this, with no distraction. With no hurry. Complete confidence."

The boy copied his teacher.

"That's good, but where is your mind?"

Zhampa shrugged.

"Your mind is walking too. Body and mind walking together."

"You mean like when I feel the ground pushing up into my legs."

Rinpo grinned. "Yes. Like that."

"And feeling my legs lifting and swinging."

Rinpo nodded.

"It's easy," Zhampa said.

"Not so fast. Where is your breath?"

"I don't know."

"Well, look for it."

After a minute, he said, "It goes in and out."

"Yes, in and out. And every cell of you moves through space. When you feel all that with no distraction, you are walking. Really walking."

This was too much for Zhampa and he put his hands on his head trying to feel all his cells.

"Don't think, my boy," Rinpo said. "Just walk."

Zhampa had since walked thousands of miles, but hearing the words return, he realized he had never mastered Rinpo's instructions.

"It's time to begin," he said out loud. "It's time I learn how to walk."

He tried. And failed. Sometimes he was able to take two steps then, like a snake, his mind escaped. It would appear again, ahead or behind, imagining or reliving. Hoping to catch it, he slowed down. But Sophia was impatient with the change and jiggled in her wagon spot. Faster, her body urged, faster. He slowed down more. Still 'just walking' eluded him. When he vowed to only take a step when his mind was present, he was flooded with self-consciousness.

"This will never do. The more important I make walking, the more slippery it is. But if I don't pay attention, I'm not walking at all."

In the wind, he heard, "Just walk. No goal."

"I'm always walking *somewhere*. My mind is caught in thoughts of the destination."

And with that he felt the earth push up through his legs, as if it were a partner to his travel, as if it said, "You can't travel, if I don't push against you." He felt gravity and felt the dance of his body wrapped in space. He erupted in laughter. Confused, Sophia cried. But he scooped her out of the wagon and cavorted with her until they both laughed with delight.

From that point on, he and the land tried to walk together. Mind, body, earth and now. One hundred steps. One thousand steps. Each unique. Each clear and meaningless.

"A tree doesn't think of itself as a tree," his teacher said another day. "It just stands. Be like that."

So when Sophia called the journey to a halt, miserable, aching to be held, soiled or hungry, he took on the magic of standing. His mind rested on her needs and on the space. When she was ready, they traveled on.

. . . Take your place in the flow of things. Think beyond your valley. Do this for the welfare of all beings and for those who will come in the Next Age.

Still Rinpo's commands perplexed him. They outlined goals, but his instructions clearly said to let go of all results. Over the miles, Zhampa wrestled with the paradox.

19

When the big river turned south, Zhampa headed west. The sun beat down on wide valleys with brackish streams. There he came upon an immense flow of footprints going his same direction. Trouble. That many travelers would exhaust the vegetation and water on his route. At noon he crested a rise to see a gathering of travelers settled down, filling the land as far as he could see.

"Sophia, we must walk right through them, okay?"

"Okay," she said. "Okay, Papa."

He smiled and said, "Hun hao?"

"Hun hao," she said. And she stood in the prow of the cart like a bowsprit maiden. "Hello," she said. "Nee-hao." The people parted to let the cart through. Some waved a listless hand at the child, but many shook their heads. Their eyes were dull, their faces skeletal.

"Out in the desert too long," Zhampa thought. "I must be careful."

"What are you doing?" they said.

"I'm carrying things."

"We are too," they said. "Traveling west like you." But they hadn't heard of the Naked Red Lady Mountain and when Zhampa asked for their destinations, they gave out their places of birth. "Settle down with us," they said. "What's your hurry? There's nowhere to go. Stay at least one night." And as soon as Zhampa and Sophia had passed, they dropped their loads to the desert floor and milled about as before.

Occasionally he thought he recognized people, someone's shape, how someone turned to look at him: an elderly couple, a woman in a hood with a small child, a scrawny fellow begging for food from the others. But when he came close, he didn't know them. In the distance he saw a beautiful horse and the back of a man, like an old friend, and he tried to make his way over, but the path was blocked with bags and circling people. Finally, he walked alone up a long grade, reaching the top just after sunset. He turned to the east, as he sometimes would, to see the day's progress, and the multitude stood facing him with hands together. En mass they prostrated. Perplexed, he looked to where the sun had been but saw only sand and bushes stretching to the horizon. When he turned back around, the valley behind him was empty except for the wind.

"I'm not well," he said.

"Okay," Sophia replied.

They camped in the low ground beyond.

Several days later they found themselves in a throng of people and animals, crossing their trail in both directions, too pressed to take notice of them. People pushed or pulled vehicles or carried huge bundles on their backs. They collided with each other. The air choked with argument.

Zhampa stopped to help a woman who had cut her leg. She said, "Thank goodness you're here," and went back to her quarrel with a young mother holding two babies and a huge water jug. But when he touched the woman's leg, she cursed him and ran off. People scowled and bumped into him. Sophia screamed and as he picked her up, two Mongolian boys made off with the cart. Putting Sophia down to chase them, three barren women carried her off in the other direction.

"Come back," he shouted, running after them.

But the women played keep-away with the child until he collapsed out of breath. When he came to, Sophia was in his arms, but the women, the crowds and his things were gone. He retraced his steps down a path he didn't remember, and there behind boulders next to a fire pit sat his backpack. The cart was nowhere to be found. "At least I have an ax and a pot," he said. He fed Sophia water and a handful of goat curd. Then he mounted his pack, put the child on top of it and walked on.

In the mountains they lived on gruel of berries and shrub bark, one spoon to feed them both. One morning they were awakened by the trumpeting of youthful voices. The hills and his campsite were fluid with children running down the slopes, jumping over rocks and swirling like tongues of fire. Zhampa packed, grabbed Sophia and took off after them. But the children were always faster, like sandpipers on a beach.

"I'm no match for them," he said, putting Sophia down. Then he spotted one last little boy nearby, a Tibetan with unblinking eyes. Quick, Zhampa grabbed his arm.

"Who are you? Where are you all going?"

"Please, sir," the boy pleaded, "we mustn't talk with you. It'll confuse things."

"So you're not real?"

The boy shook his head to say 'no' and then beaming, nodded vigorously. Flustered, Zhampa relaxed his hand and the boy slipped away, prancing to where the trail led down to his companions. "Thank you, sir."

"Thank you? For what?"

"For walking." Then he made a cheerful sign, eyed Sophia carefully and raced off.

On the down slope of the northern desert, in the jagged hills that forced Silk Road travelers to opt for the swift currents of the Great Tributary of the Yellow, and north of the Chinese city of Lanjhou, Zhampa reached for his map. But it had traveled a million steps and it crumbled at his touch. To arrive at the Naked Red Lady Mountain then, he would have to use his memory. Rinpo had drawn the junction of the Yellow River and the Great Tributary, the Huang Shui. And around the city there, he'd drawn a circle and written the word 'avoid.' Beyond that, a line wiggled southwest through a smaller city and through some bumps for mountains, straight through grasslands and south through more bumps to the sketch of a monastery near a circled X. 'Naked Red Lady Mountain,' Rinpo had written. Zhampa had come some twelve hundred miles across China. There were six hundred more to go. If all went well, the end was in sight before winter. But everything was falling apart. Panicked, he undid his sash to check Rinpo's text. It was in good shape. He had memorized some of it in the Dream Fortress, but had ignored it since, working instead with walking and standing. Soon—he didn't know when—he would be greeted by Tibetan stock. In the end it would be Tibetans who would help him find the mountain monastery and deliver the scepters. So he reviewed some of the chapter headings. "What to Do." "How not to Take Offense." "How to Pass beyond Small Mind." "How to Lead: The leader in the new world will need at all times to keep in mind the following things: . . . "

"We'll be all right," he said to Sophia. "Okay?"

"Okay," she said.

"Yappo dughh?" he asked.

She looked at him strangely.

"It's time for us to practice our Tibetan."

The next day, he found a three-wheel bicycle almost as old as he was, with a basket in front, a platform in back and solid tires. The frame was bent, but it rolled. With Sophia in the basket and a paragraph of the text on his lips, he pushed and coasted the bike south, down the road to the Great Tributary, the main highway from east to west. In the lower altitude, they came upon people in great numbers—men with impeccably white brimless hats on shaved heads, women wearing black head scarves, girls wearing pink. Zhampa had never seen such markets as those in the river towns that grew around the ferry crossings, countless stalls under woven awnings along every street: bolts of fabric, parts of shoes to be fitted and sewn on demand, steel pots, clay pots, water vessels, old and new tools, rugs, hides, baskets, tea, fruit and herbs. Meat and cabbage were plentiful. With a gold ring that Tatsuhei had given him, Zhampa bartered for a new water flask and clothes for Sophia. Seeing the mountains on the far bank, he sold the bike and bought walnuts, cheese and grain. They ate noodle soup in a smoky restaurant and slept in an open-air hotel within sight of the river. At dawn, men and animals moved barges up and downstream. He and Sophia crossed on the ferry and disembarking, he asked the ferryman about the Naked Red Lady Mountain "In Tibet, somewhere to the south," he said.

"Don't know it," said the ferryman. "You have an accent. Are you from there?"

Zhampa smiled. People would always guess him wrong. "Yes," he said, "I'm Tibetan."

In the red clay valleys south of the river, Zhampa hitched rides on wagons returning from the quays to haul more brick from the kilns. Days on, white coal smoke announced the smaller city on Rinpo's map long before he saw the checkerboard grid of vacant six-story buildings. But life swirled in the old streets, kept clean by squads of sweepers. Sidewalk foundries and restaurant tents lined the lanes and wheelbarrow children collected dung from draft animals that hauled carts with the morning's marked sheep and the evening's hides. Shoemakers, bending over their treadle machines, worked next to the tanners, who emptied their toxic casks into the concrete chase that carried the trickle of river. Tailors sewed across from weavers.

Laundrymen saved their water for the paper makers. Surrounded by his apprentices, the copyist made careful documents in Chinese characters. In the street pharmacy, Zhampa met a new world of herbs—hair-like roots, rich-colored barks, seeds and bugs.

"Some from the Central Valley. Some from Tibet," the pharmacist said.

"Which ones are Tibetan?"

He waved a hand in the direction of boxes of dried mushrooms, grasses, flower clusters and containers of little pills "They are special," he said about the pills. "Made by hand. Made by monks."

"Who brings them to you?"

"Tibetan traders."

"Are there some in the city?"

"Go to the big circle by the bridge. You will find many of them."

Under the huge, rusting steel girders, Zhampa found a community of men with thick blue-black hair, different from their neighbors in every way: stockier, slower and always joking. Dirty, with layers of clothes and bright sashes. At the sight of Sophia, they stopped in mid-sentence.

"Are you Tibetans?" Zhampa asked.

They stared at him blankly.

"Tibetans?" he asked again.

A few of the men snickered.

"We are," said an older man with a face like a worn leather mitten, "but we don't speak Chinese." Then in Tibetan, he said, "Where are you from?" Zhampa paused to catch the accent.

"Where are you from?" the man asked again.

"America nay-yin," Zhampa stammered.

The older men pressed closer. "Nguh-nay? Really? America nay-yin-bay?"

"Yes, from America."

Next thing he knew a dozen hands were on him. In celebration they took Sophia from his shoulders and his pack from his back.

"American. He's American. Good friend. Friend of the Tibetan people." And that night, they fed Zhampa and Sophia boiled mutton and hot sauce, peppers and pork and a bread they called arhi. They drank countless little cups of a burning alcohol called chang. Yes, they would help him to the highlands. No, they hadn't heard of the place he sought, but their cousins higher up would know it.

At first light on little sleep, they set off with eleven ponies heading west, then south, every step higher than the last. They lashed Sophia upright on a saddle and jockeyed for position to walk alongside her and Zhampa. They spoke fast, their language like unlaced boots, but gradually Zhampa began to hear what Rinpo had buried in his bones. Two boys taught Sophia phrases: "It's good," "I like it," and "Are you happy?" And she took to shouting them out. They wrapped her head in a teal scarf and taught her to say, 'The Queen is coming. The Queen is coming.' Singing simple songs in minor keys, they urged their animals with the constant touch of switches and walking sticks. Higher up where the Chinese-built bridges had ripped free in landslides of aggregate clay, the caravan stretched out along skinny paths cut into the scree.

"Where are the Chinese?" Zhampa asked.

"Gone," said old Lodro.

"What happened?"

His hosts looked at each other. Finally Palden said, "Nothing stays the same. Do you understand?"

"Yes. . . . And no."

"We invited them to go home." His tone was complicated.

"Was there fighting here, too?"

"We suffered a long time under them." He walked some, then said, "Then they suffered." He held up a hand to divert a question. "It was not a happy thing. But Tibetans are free again."

In six days, they ascended the lower mountains that ring the Tibetan Plateau, passing villages cut into hillsides, entering a universe the Creator painted in three brush strokes: red for the clay underfoot, green for the fields and treeless mountain slopes, and azure for the heavens, which arched into the orbit of the moon. The air was as light as emptiness.

Most of the men in that party lived in the half dozen villages embraced by a huge mothering mountain, a south-facing Eden of terraces, pastures and streams. Of their number, only Sonam and DaDrin lived further on, and for them, their friends made a grand farewell. Palden's interior courtyard became paved with rugs, blankets and stools. Traveling clothes were dropped in favor of brocade coats. The women brushed their hair to glistening with ghee and accented their braids with precious stones and colored ribbons. Dutch ovens on dung fuel fires churned out fresh arhi. Butter tea flowed and mutton boiled. The gaiety just below raucous. Sophia was wide-eyed with the color and commotion—rides, running, teasing and holding. She loved having her hair braided and inlaid with tiny silver beads and silk streamers. She touched it over and over.

As dark came, more faces appeared in the bonfire light, soiled beaming faces, with teeth like polished ivory. After the feasting, a man with features of a raven and a beautiful woman put stories to song retelling the glory of former days. At the end, the woman, joyful with the chang in her blood, called Zhampa forward as another woman came bearing highlander clothes across her arms.

"Chinese monk robes are okay for China," she said. "But you must wear these from now on. They will protect you from evil forces. Take those off. And your trousers," she said gesturing seductively. When she had finished adjusting and pulling, Zhampa bowed and a great cheer went up.

"A story," commanded Palden. "A story about your travels. Tell us about things we will never see."

"Okay, I'll tell you a story. But Palden, you have to translate for me. I can only tell it in Chinese." He began, "I've been admiring your homes. They are clever. The strong earth walls, the rafters and the layers of sticks and straw, and the smooth coating of clay on the roofs. In my land where the hills are like women lying down, there is a creature that lives in the water who builds like you . . . "

And Zhampa told them about the beaver, about his face, his fur, his skill under water and his devotion to family: how each night he cuts trees with his teeth, how he floats the pieces to dam the stream, crossing limbs like a basket maker, how he fills the gaps with summer grasses, and how he finishes his work with a smooth layer of mud. How, like Tibetan houses, the homes have an inner courtyard and no windows. He told them about the broad, flat, hairless tail that he uses for a paddle and a trowel. Used to tales of strange and magical beings, the Tibetans visualized every detail and at each line they laughed harder, slapping each other in delight. The Americans, too, had an imaginary god, a force for good in the world.

That night Zhampa learned to never tell a good story in story-telling culture. Every voice demanded that he tell another. So he told them about salmon: the resolute fish that begins life as a peal in hosts of millions in upstream backwaters, that tumble in silver clouds down snow-melt fattened mountain streams to the oceans. And after years of traveling half the world and of escaping other fish, the powerful adult, swollen huge with rich meat, hears the call to finish his life's journey. He navigates thousands of miles like an eagle and fights his way upstream through fishhooks, nets, waterfalls, and feasting bears to the very place he was born. Turning a magnificent color of red, he fertilizes the future, and lays down his body for the mission. A true bodhisattva fish. Zhampa told them about the giant salmon that landed at his feet. They grieved when it appeared to die. And cheered when it came back to life, flicked its tail and swam on.

When he finished, the courtyard was silent, letting him think. That night it became clear to him that he would return to Vermont to die in the Hollow. Whatever it would demand of him, he would go home.

20

Before noon, Zhampa left Palden's village with Sonam and Dadrin. Their route south crested passes into ever-ascending stone-strewn valleys.

"In my village," Sonam had said, "we know a place called the Red Mountain Lady. If you come, I can help you find the way." But when they arrived, Sonam's confidence vanished. "There is Red mountain over there," he said pointing east, "and Great Lady Mountain that way." He pointed to the sunset. "I'm not certain which one is your mountain."

They had only traveled some two hundred miles from the Great Tributary. Rinpo's map seemed to place the monastery hundreds of miles further south, beyond some open area between mountain ranges. But Zhampa was at the point where he would have to rely on local knowledge and not a sketch.

"What is that way?" he asked pointing south.

"Mountains. Lots of mountains."

"What's the quickest way through them?"

"Go that way nine days to the plateau," Sonam said pointing west. "Then south."

"Do you mean go around?"

"I think it's the best way. And we'll go by the Great Lady Mountain. Maybe it's the right one."

Zhampa paused to translate to himself. "Are you saying you will come with us?"

"Yes, you need help. You'll get lost without me."

Higher altitudes called for a change of beast. Sonam put together a small caravan of three yaks and they headed west the next day. Like all highlanders, Sonam knew every plant and its qualities: which ones helped with fatigue, which ones promoted breathing in the thin air, and which ones raised body temperature. He knew what kind of rock formation was likely to provide shelter, and where the passes were by reading the movement of the fog. He knew to cross rivers in the morning before the sun swelled them with glacial melt and to rely on the yaks' instincts for safety. He and the animals moved slowly, placing each foot . . . like elephants, Zhampa noticed. Rinpo's methods of liberating the mind were fused into his culture by living on that land. As they walked, Sonam taught him more Tibetan. And over time Sophia grew to reach for Sonam's arms when they halted at the cairns on the passes to cheer in celebration and when stopping for meals.

On a gray day, they came to a solitary mountain farm made of clay and stone; steep slopes plunged to a slate-colored river gnawing its canyon deeper. Sonam asked the old lady spinning wool in the doorway if the Great Lady Mountain was ever called the Naked Red Lady Mountain. The lines in her face twisted and fell, and she hooted a toothless laugh.

"People from away call it the Great Lady Mountain," she said, "because that's how it looks to them. Here, we call it Big Gray One."

"Have you ever heard of Chokyi Lodro Ngawang Selpo, Rinpoche?" Zhampa asked.

"No," she said, "not around here."

When she saw Sophia, she rose and hobbled close with her hands together and head bowed. "A special child," she said. "Like Tara, queen of peace." From the darkness of the house, she produced some dried curd. Sophia thanked her in Tibetan, which made the lady glad.

"The queen is coming," Sonam prompted.

"The queen is coming," chimed Sophia.

"My grandsons are on the mountain," the old lady said, throwing a thumb over her shoulder. "Three days gone. There's a mountain cat causing trouble with the herds."

As they climbed beyond, Sonam called down, "If we see your grandsons, we will tell them you are well."

Her worn hand waved and returned to work.

It was mid-September when Sonam stopped at the top of a high pass. Thin grass lay battered by the wind as far as they could see. The land was huge and stark, the heights as rounded as the vales. Distance was difficult to gauge.

"This is where I leave you," Sonam said.

Zhampa coughed. He looked around.

"It's the plateau," Sonam said. "I'm only a mountain herder. This yak's name is Nying Dhak, the Pure Hearted One. He's a good friend of mine. Take him with you. Go south and good luck."

When Zhampa offered Sonam a small gold statuette that Tatsuhei had pressed on him, Sonam refused. "I have no need of that," he said and turned to walk back down the switchback trail to his home with the howling of Sophia in his ears.

Then Zhampa turned toward the noontime sun and, following Nying Dhak's wisdom, he proceeded at an even pace. He used the hours to study great sections of Rinpo's *Song of the Great Seal* in English and Tibetan. They camped with societies of migrating birds by tarns of glacial melt from peaks they rarely saw. Save for a shy blue flower that flourished in the lee of the grasses, the year's blooms had gone. And because the night cold pressed down on the plateau without mercy, he stooped to gather every dried chip of dung; it alone kept them warm until the three of them—man, child and yak—fell asleep in one spot.

They passed the summer camps of herder families and learned of the lands ahead. For a time they joined a salt caravan from the big lake on its way south. And later they camped next to three itinerant monks by a shallow lake that skinned over with ice before the sliver of moon set.

"I am looking for the Naked Red Lady Mountain," Zhampa said. "Do you know of it?"

The three looked at each other. "Oh, yes. Everyone has heard of it," they said.

"Really? How far is it? Am I going the right way?"

"Why do you want to go there?" the older monk said.

"I have some gifts to return for the future age."

"And you are taking them to the Naked Red Lady Mountain?"

"Yes, and I need to get there before winter. Can you help me?"

The two younger monks snickered and the older reprimanded them in a local dialect. Then he said, "We'd like to help you, but you've wasted your time."

"Why? You said you've heard of it."

"Everyone knows that the Naked Red Lady Mountain is a myth."

"A myth?"

"The old texts talk about it as a perfect place, where the world is born again. But no one was ever able to find it. It's a great myth." He laughed. And when his companions laughed with him, a poison memory impaled Zhampa: "You're not from here unless your grandmother was born here," the bullies in The Valley School said. "You're not one of us."

Perhaps it was the altitude or his fatigue, but without thinking which decade it was or which continent he was on, he said, "My teacher gave me a map."

The monks stopped laughing. Finally the one with the broken teeth said, "Show it to us."

Zhampa shook his head. "It wore out along the trail," he said. "It was very old and I burned the scraps for heat."

"I don't believe him," said the monk with curled ears.

"Give us the map," said the older.

"It's gone," Zhampa said. "Don't you understand? It's gone." His mind raced with panic. Could it really be that the Naked Red Lady Mountain was a myth and that he had been on a fool's errand? In the flickering light of the dung fire, he was only vaguely aware when the monk with curled ears stood up. But he heard the air move just as he felt a crushing blow on the side of his skull that brought him down next to the coals. The heat kept him conscious, but his head spun. Sophia screamed and he heard the monks tearing through his baggage. They laughed when they found the statuette.

"Some precious stones. Not great gifts," the older said. "He's a dreamer. A simple traveler. But he won't need them."

"Big dreams," he heard another say. They pounced on his body and rolled him out of his highlander topcoat. When they found his text belt, they hooted and cut it off him. There was no map, but seeing the Tibetan script, the older monk squatted in the glow of the fire to read it. He was close and for a moment, Zhampa thought of leaping up, grabbing him, perhaps throwing the pages into the fire. But his arms didn't respond.

"This is good," he heard the monk say. "It looks real. It will bring something in the idiot's marketplace. But this other one, I can't read. We'll use it to wipe our asses."

The monk with the broken teeth pushed his face into Zhampa's. "Where is the map?"

"It's gone," Zhampa said. "Yook-shagh."

They took to kicking him, at which Curtis, the murdered bully, and Rinpo appeared in his mind—placid, mute, watching to see what he would do. His assailants were poor. Their lives would never be good. And he knew that if they intended to kill him, they would have used their knives. So he settled in to take the beating to avoid, finally, the consequences of his anger. He would submit, he decided, unless they found the scepters. That would get him to fight; he'd use the machete. And if he had to, for the benefit of those in the Next Age, he would hurt them.

He didn't feel the kick that knocked him unconscious. When the sun was high enough to crack his eyes, he found Sophia nestled in with him under his coat and the two of them wrapped around the biggest rock from the fire pit. The thieves had taken everything that could be sold or traded: the compass, the statuette, his few pieces of gold, and Rinpo's text. They had ignored the fire bow. In the dark they had missed the herbs, the acupuncture needles and one of the bags of butter and tsampa. He found his water flask thirty feet away. The pot was upside down in the fire pit.

Losing the text was too much to bear. And the yak, too, was a devastating loss. But worse, they had stolen the Naked Red Lady Mountain. Alone, past the autumn equinox and at fourteen thousand feet, Zhampa's mission had vanished. When he reached to check for the scepters, he felt all his wounds. His arms were heavy and his body core was battered. One of his ribs was surely broken. His left eye was blurry. But the scepters were there.

Too bruised to travel, they stayed that day by the lake. Zhampa kept the fire going with dung he gathered. By the next morning, he decided he must travel or die. He filled the flask, slung the bags around his neck, broke off a big chew of the bark from the painkiller bush that Sonam had gathered and placed Sophia on his shoulders. His sense of failure followed close behind.

He walked south without talking. In the middle of the second day, out of the blue, Sophia piped up in English, "Sacred World." It was the title of the first chapter of Rinpo's text. And without thinking Zhampa answered with Rinpo's opening lines:

All difficulty flows from mistaking this world as evil.

"Evil," she repeated.

"That's right," he said. "All difficulty flows from mistaking this world as evil." He sighed. "I wish you knew the text, Sophia."

She looked at him with consternation.

Then he stopped. He repeated the line. And as he listened, the second was there waiting. He said it aloud and knew it was correct. The next line came. And the next. He remembered the first page and turned it over in his mind. There lay the second.

"Sophia," he cried, "it's not lost. I'm carrying it." He settled down and recited three chapters. After a short meal, he recited the rest. When he came toward the end, he heard Rinpo's words to students of the future:

Learning words like a parrot is not sufficient. It's better not to start at all. A true traveler must fill his heart with the view and act accordingly.

"I carry it. But now I have to learn it." He was almost shouting.

"Learn it," she shouted.

"Come here, you parrot." He hugged her until she squirmed. After, he walked with new energy. When it came time for food, he gave his share to her. For three days he carried on, passing through abandoned herders' camps, reciting chapters in English and Tibetan. He didn't feel the ache in his body, or the shrinking of his stomach. But when the food was gone, Sophia began to cry.

In the morning he tried to rise, but fell back in a faint. He dreamed the river of his life, the glories and the mistakes. His family and his loves and the loss of them all; Eric and Sumiko, Claire, Celeste, his dog Coco, and New Moon. He asked Curtis to forgive him. Rinpo rode past on a cloud shining like a second sun, saying nothing. He heard bells and felt the brush of bird wings on his cheek. And a snort in his ears. He opened his eyes to horns and fur. Yaks were sniffing him. Strings of mucus hung from their snouts.

"Aiy! Ke-Aiy!" he heard from somewhere. "Par-juu."

The yaks jerked and looked for escape. Their great hooves kicked and danced. Zhampa closed over Sophia to protect her. She stirred inside his coat.

"Tashi-la. Look," a woman's voice called. "There's a man here."

"Yes," Zhampa said raising a hand to shield his eyes. The sun was high. The frost was off the grass.

A wind-scoured face of a young herder woman bent over him. A man bent over, too.

"Are you all right?" she asked.

"We're hungry," he said. "Monks robbed us."

"Three monks?" the man asked.

Zhampa nodded.

"They're not real monks. Bandits. Bad men."

"Look, Tashi-la. There's a child," the woman said.

"Quick, Drolma-la. Bring tea. Tsampa, too."

Drolma fetched a jug from their gear and poured tea into patina-colored bowls. With hands equally brown, she added barley flour and butter and produced wads of tsampa for the travelers. Tashi pulled out three small rugs and laid them on the ground. Sophia focused on the food until it was gone.

"Where are you from?" Tashi asked.

"I'm a foreigner," he said.

"Den-den-rei," Tashi said. "That's for sure."

"I come from beyond China, beyond the sea." But he could tell that they didn't really know what that meant.

"Where are you going?"

He paused to think about his answer and his audience. "I'm returning to the monastery of my teacher."

"What is the place called?"

"The Naked Red Lady Mountain."

"Naked Red Lady Mountain? Where is that?"

Zhampa's moment of hope flickered out. "No one knows this place," he thought. "Rinpo was so precise about how to walk, how to breathe and how to live. Why was he so vague about his birth place?"

"May I walk with you a while?" he asked.

Drolma looked hard at Tashi, nodding. Tashi looked away.

"Tashi-la" she said, "we must take care of him."

"It's a difficult time, Drolma-la."

"Tashi." Her face has hard.

"Okay, Okay. We'll take you back to our camp."

"Thank you," Zhampa said. "Thank you."

"Thank you," said Sophia.

They walked a few hours south toward a swart blemish in an expanse of grass. Tashi's yak wool summer tent peaked at the height of a man's shoulder. Yurt-like, its radial guy ropes fluttered with prayer flags. Next to it, walls made of pie-shaped dung cakes served as the corral. As they approached, two fierce mastiffs came racing and cornered Zhampa with their snarls, pushing him up against the yak that carried Sophia. When Tashi yelled and swung at them with his switch, they shrank bank. Two little boys with woven peaked hats with the ear flaps buttoned up broke away from their games in the mud and came running. They bowed quickly and Tashi lifted them, one in each arm, and answered their many questions, which came too fast for Zhampa to understand. An older girl emerged from the tent and stood in the dooryard fingering the fabric, a still figure surrounded by flags.

Not all was well. A woman lay in the dark of the tent, feverish, struggling for breath.

"Her name is Lhamo," Drolma said. "She's my sister. Tashi's wife."

"How long has she been sick?"

"Eight days."

"What are you doing for her?"

"We pray, of course. And she drinks the youngest boy's urine in the morning. There is nothing else to do. We're too far from any lama doctor. But . . . "

"But what?"

Drolma lowered her eyes. "If she's going to die, we hope it is soon."

Zhampa furrowed his brow.

"Because we have to travel to our winter home. Before the snow." She looked at the sky.

Zhampa looked in at Lhamo. Her clothes were stiff with filth.

"Drolma-la, Tashi-la, I'm a doctor. This is not good. Yappo-min-dughh."

"You?" Tashi said.

"Yes. May I touch her?"

"How?"

"On the wrist."

Tashi's face twisted. But when Drolma pushed him as before, he relented. Zhampa bade Drolma and the couple's daughter Jikmay to bathe her. Then he had them wash her clothes and bedding, a labor that took all day. He made Lhamo a fever tea from herbs that he carried from the city in the lowland and he convinced her that the acupuncture needles were for health. He adjusted her spine to ease the pressure on the lung meridian. Then he let her rest.

In three days, Lhamo sat up, her cough clearing. On the fourth day, she was back at work. On the sixth day, she had a short talk with her sister and that night, when the dung fire glowed only weakly, Drolma lay herself down next to Zhampa. When he didn't know how to receive her, she showed him with straightforward hands. In the morning, pleasure curled the corners of her mouth. And Lhamo nodded at him. "Thank you," she said.

Tashi said, "Zhampa-la, thank you. Without my wife to milk and weave and harvest and cook and make fuel and to dress two boys, we would all be in danger."

"Yes, I understand. I lost my wife. A woman can't be replaced."

Tashi put his hand on Zhampa's shoulder.

When Drolma and Tashi were out with the herd, Lhamo set Zhampa to churn butter, but took the paddle away from him, because he was too slow. She had him thresh barley and pack it into bags and he sharpened their tools. The boys adopted Sophia, carrying her everywhere. At night the three of them slept in a pile on the rug nearest the fire.

In the second week, Tashi fell silent. He wouldn't answer when Zhampa asked him if he were all right. Finally Drolma said, "He's worried. We have to move to our winter home and we don't have enough food for you and Sophia. He wants you to go."

"Yes, of course."

"It's hard because he's grateful to you."

"I will talk to him. I will go. I'm feeling well enough to travel now. Winter's coming and I need to find the mountain."

"But wait."

Her look caught him. "Yes?"

"I told him I want to go with you."

"I don't know where I'm going."

"I can help you. But Tashi doesn't think it's a good idea. He knows you're not a good husband. You don't know how to live in the highlands."

Zhampa opened his mouth to both protest and agree, but she said, "Take me with you. There's nothing here for me. I am not the wife. I have no joy."

"But the monks took the last of my money. We would starve."

"I have my share of my mother's wealth. It's a lot."

"But that is yours."

"In the highlands, wealth belongs to women. Men work so they can be with us."

"But he's right. I'm not a good husband. I'm a traveler."

"And I want to travel. . . . Please. I'm stuck here. I will never be married, if I stay."

"I will think about it. And I will talk with Tashi."

Because the labor of a third adult made their lives bearable, releasing Drolma was a difficult prospect for Tashi and Lhamo. But they understood that Zhampa needed Drolma as much as she wanted to go. First they agreed to let Zhampa and Sophia accompany them to their winter home near the upstream waters of the Yangtse. Then they decided that their daughter Jikmay was old enough to fulfill Drolma's duties. They packed the summer camp on their forty-five yaks and two ponies and set out under gray skies. On the fourth day, the grasslands terminated at a large pole with guy ropes alive with prayer flags. Beyond, they headed down a steep pass into a mountainous world of grass canyons and stone houses.

"We go down for two days and back up for one," Tashi said. He waved his hand to show a valley beyond view.

"We love winter," Lhamo said. "There is less work." She took hold of Zhampa's sleeve. "I didn't think I would see it."

"I hope you live a long time."

"The lamas say we never know when we will die."

Zhampa nodded.

Lhamo's winter home was one of nine stone houses scattered in a steep notch between mountain slopes with a supply of dung cakes stacked outside the door just as they had left them. In between farm chores, Drolma and

Lhamo separated their belongings. Two days later Drolma braided her hair with ribbons and ropes of silver and turquoise beads. She wore cascading necklaces of ivory and amber. Massive pieces of red coral adorned her brocade chuba. She wore rings on her fingers, silver earrings and a chain-mail hairpiece of gold. She talked to her sister a long time in the barn. Then as Zhampa waited near the small herd of animals they would take, Drolma circumambulated the home three times.

"Zhampa, bring her back, if she doesn't want you," Lhamo said. She turned to do her milking.

"I will," he said.

The trails into Jekundo were jammed with young highlanders driving animals culled from the herds to be sold before the winter snows. The market and streets were chaotic with buying and selling. Behind restaurants that lined the streets, Muslims in aprons greasy with death butchered animals without stopping. When the sun appeared, the heavy topcoats came off and highlanders paraded up and down. Women in fine-worked chubas and brocade aprons eyed men swaggering in high black boots with thick heels, dazzling coats and black hair brushed loose to their shoulders. When the wind brought a bite, hats like winged crowns appeared, lined with furs of fox, lynx and highland gazelle. Drolma quickly sold all but two of her animals and paid in advance for three nights lodging. Then she freed a large amber bead from the draw around her neck and bought Zhampa a blue brocade dress coat and black fur-lined pants that piled on his boot tops in the highlander style.

"Now we can travel properly," she said. "It's time we find your mountain. Let's go visit the lamas. They'll know where it is."

The old monastery citadel overlooked the town from the mountain shoulder. New monastery buildings in the ancient style sprouted inside the ruins of the old walls. When Drolma offered a bead of lapis at the entrance gate, a monk in straw sandals ushered them past a row of eight stupas, past groups of monks in thick saffron robes debating points of enlightenment, past phalanxes of hand-carved prayer-wheels, and through the courtyards of the library and the main meditation hall with its towering gold-plated statue of the Buddha. On the tiled roof of the abbot's residence a golden ornament—a wheel flanked by a pair of deer—looked out over the valley.

"The gold is from Chinese teeth," the monk said. "It gains merit for their rebirths."

They met the abbot of the monastery in his library.

"You have a Tibetan name," he said, "but you're not Tibetan." He sipped his tea.

"No. American."

"Unusual."

"He needs to find his teacher's monastery," Drolma said. "It's at the base of the Naked Red Lady Mountain."

"Hmm. A secret place."

"You know of it?" asked Zhampa.

"Maybe. . . . Yes. . . . I don't know."

"But you know something." Zhampa leaned forward.

"Naked Red Lady is a secret practice. Not my lineage. I heard of it when I was a young monk in a Chinese prison. Very special. Someplace to the south." He picked up a crumb of bread from a cookie and offered it to his parrot between the bamboo slats of its cage. "Why do you want to go?"

Zhampa sighed. "It's good to finally be able to tell my secret to someone trustworthy. I have a gift to deliver. A scepter that belonged to Padmasambhava."

"The dorjay? Do you have it? That is one of the great missing treasures."

At that moment Sophia jumped up. "I want to go," she said.

Zhampa put his finger to his lips to quiet her.

"Do you have Padmasambhava's dorjay?" the lama asked again.

But before Zhampa could answer, Sophia kicked Zhampa hard in the shin. "Let's go," she said loudly in English. When the abbot laughed, she shook the legs of his side table and his tea bowl shattered on the floor. Zhampa grabbed her arm, but the abbot interceded. "No, Zhampa, no. She's only a child, and a cup is nothing."

At the calm of his voice, Sophia relaxed.

"Perhaps it is best if we meet again tomorrow," the lama said. "In the meantime I'll ask about your monastery. Come in the middle of the morning. Perhaps I will have an answer for you."

21

In the predawn cold, Drolma urged her yaks through the empty streets of Jekundo. Sophia rode tucked under a blanket in a saddle basket on the lead animal. Zhampa trotted behind in the slick mud, watching doorways and alleys for concealed eyes or maroon robes. He clenched his teeth with dread of the answers to questions that had kept him awake. "What kind of a world am I trying to save? How can this be the birthplace of the next age of wisdom?" Passing two small monasteries on the outskirts of the town, they saw no signs of life, and they were well up the switchbacks at the southern head of the valley when the first trace of day appeared. Taking a last look down before the arc of the mountain would hide them from view, they saw four men in maroon on five ponies heading up with great speed. Drolma cursed and put her switch to the hindquarters of her yaks.

The previous afternoon as they were making their way through the town after meeting with the abbot, Drolma had put her mouth to Zhampa's ear. "We're being followed."

"Followed?"

"Behind us. On the right."

Zhampa bent as if to reset his boot strap and, looking back down the street, got a glimpse of two stocky monks lunging into a doorway.

"They're from the monastery," she said.

"What could they possibly want?"

"You said too much to the abbot."

"About what? About the dorjay?"

She nodded.

"But they're monks," Zhampa said. "They take vows to avoid harm and to place all others before themselves."

"Desire can be stronger than vows." Saying this, she took his hand and Sophia's and led them into a busy market. She cut between two stalls, dashed through the back of a stable and across another street. Back at their place of lodging, they stayed indoors and left Jekundo in the third quarter of the night.

A snow squall on the heights concealed their escape down a little-used side route. The steep road led to a modest nunnery where they sheltered for the night. The abbess had heard of the Naked Red Lady practice from her grandmother, who had been a nun before the Cultural Revolution. It was a rare practice, she said, very powerful if it still existed. And she encouraged them to look in the wild country west of the Chenchu, a river beyond the mountains that formed her view.

The first branch of that river was too treacherous to cross the day they arrived. Mistaking Zhampa for a yogi, the ferryman gave them a one-room stone building for quarters. Waiting for the rain to stop, Zhampa spent hours polishing his recitation of Rinpo's text in Tibetan. He asked Drolma if she understood his accent and the words. She said she mostly did. And she said that she longed to learn meditation but that her life herding animals gave her no options. When he asked her if she wanted to become a nun, she fell silent. Late in the night, she wrapped her body around his. He lay in the dark, reflecting on how she had stopped in front of a floor-to-ceiling scroll in the meditation hall as they were leaving the monastery in Jekundo. In it, a buddha sat in naked union with a young woman. Her flying hair conveyed bliss. Drolma stood a long while. Then she pointed to the woman.

"This is me. Drolma, Goddess of Peace." Then she pointed to the Buddha, smiled mysteriously and poked Zhampa in the chest. It got him thinking. Had this young herder woman's society woven the full spectrum of life into her? Could simple chores like milking be linked to ultimate liberation of the soul? What other gifts had Rinpo carried out with him? Which were left unopened?

When the ferryman delivered them to the other side of the river, he would take no payment. He pressed Zhampa's hands to his forehead. "Think of me, great lama," he said.

As snow made the mountain route impassable, they traveled along the river. It brought them to a region of sandstone cliffs where, over the centuries, yogis had hollowed out caves for their meditation.

"What's the name of this place?" Drolma asked some girls who were driving sheep uphill.

"We call it Happy Valley," said one in a sheepskin chuba.

"But," said the other, "the lama calls it Sa-chay-par, the Place in Between."

"There is a lama here?" Zhampa asked.

"He comes and goes," said the first girl. "He's a great teacher. He lives in retreat. Sometimes on this mountainside." She pointed up above.

"In one of the caves? Do you know which one?"

She shook her head and pitched a stone to keep her flock from heading back downhill. "Lama Patrul doesn't live indoors. He says caves are like homes and lead to craving."

"Oh, yes. Lama Patrul," said Drolma. "He has a great reputation."

"Did you say he travels?" said Zhampa. "He knows the area?"

Drolma read his thought. "How can we find Lama Patrul?"

The girls laughed and shrugged. "He comes and goes."

Needing a place for the night, they sheltered in a large cave up the slope. In the morning, looking for a way to reach the other branch of the Chenchu, they followed a trail across steep meadows and over rocky shoulders. They met a trader, who gave them directions around the mountain and on the way down they came to a man wrapped only in a white cloth sitting upright in a slight hollow. Even the yaks stared at him.

"Do you think it might be Lama Patrul?" Zhampa whispered.

Drolma said nothing but pulled a sack of barley flour out of her baggage. She prostrated, then quietly placed the sack near where he sat. The yogi didn't respond for a long while. Finally he roused himself. "Ah!" He looked at Drolma. "Remember, mind resting in its own nature does not only stand still like these mountains." He lowered his eyes again. After a few minutes Drolma beckoned for them to leave. But as they turned to go, the yogi said, "You have a question."

Drolma pushed Zhampa forward. "Yes, he does."

Zhampa bowed. "I'm looking for a place called the Naked Red Lady Mountain. Do you know of it?"

"You're close now."

"How do I find it?"

"Keep going the way you have been."

Zhampa's hands felt cold. "Do you have directions?"

"Those are the directions." Saying this, the yogi turned to look at Sophia. Slowly his face expanded into a great smile.

Grinning back, Sophia rocked in her saddle. She giggled, then said, "The queen is coming."

"You have to leave her with me," the yogi said.

Drolma took a step forward. "She's only a child."

"I'm not referring to the child," the yogi said, turning to Zhampa. "My good traveler, you have to leave your wife with me."

Zhampa gasped. Drolma stood struck. After a moment her face softened. Then three times she prostrated full length to the lama. Before she was done, Sophia began to cry. When she kicked her feet inside her traveling robe, the yogi rose stiffly and walked to her. Sophia became quiet. She focused on an orange that appeared in his hand. Like a magician, he peeled it and popped a section into Sophia's mouth. When she reached for the rest, he gave it. "She's a special child," he said, "but she needs guidance to steer her from a life of suffering."

"Are you Lama Patrul?" Zhampa said.

The yogi held up his hand. "That's only a name. Keep going." He gestured toward the mountain across the valley. "You will know it when you see it. But there will be snow tonight. Stay here. Leave tomorrow."

They walked back around the mountain to a cave where they prepared to say goodbye. "You may keep my yaks and my wealth," Drolma said.

"No, no. I hope I may take one yak. But you should keep your wealth."

"I won't need it," she laughed.

"Drolma-la, I told your sister I'd take care of you."

"Lhamo's a good woman and a good wife. But she doesn't understand many things. Karma is bigger than promises. If you won't take my wealth, I'll give it to the shepherd girls, because they directed me here. But you must take this." She removed her gold hairpiece and with two smooth stones broke it into little weights. "These will help you," she said pressing them into his hand. Then she held him until morning.

They packed one yak with supplies for his journey and the other with her things, and set off through new snow to find the yogi. It seemed he had not moved from the evening before. The snow around him had melted out to a distance of six feet, as if he were a small sun.

As Zhampa contemplated this phenomenon, the yogi spoke. "Go with him," he said. "Come back when your karma together is finished."

Drolma opened her mouth to speak, then lowered her head.

"No," he said. "This is not punishment. The union path of man and woman is the most effective one. And the most difficult. But to progress upon it, you must throw away all notions of This and That, of Mine and Yours. Only then can you embody the luminous nature of being." He opened his eyes. "In the meantime, help this traveler."

Descending and ascending the slopes south of Happy Valley, Zhampa struggled to keep up with Drolma's drive. Near the top of the next mountain, both yaks refused to break through the deep snow until she made a trail for them by laying her body down again and again. The cairn on the pass was buried. And dusk had fallen when they came to a herder's hut on the far side. In the morning light, they saw spruce trees climbing the flanks of the mountains. Drolma beamed. She'd never seen trees before.

They forded the southern branch of the Chenchu and, having crossed three passes in four days, they took shelter in the remains of a stone village high on the west side of a mountain. Dawn heralded a warmer day, and leaving Drolma and Sophia to rest, Zhampa set out to explore the flora of the new terrain. He traversed miles of grassy slopes and crossed a formation of red sandstone cliffs. He found an active animal track that led toward a river in a farmed valley. Terraced fields, yellow and brown. When he came to a well-traveled road parallel to the water, he saw a group of men in the distance downstream. In the other direction, he saw two villages, one on each side of the river. Setting out after the men, he was warned off the road by a clatter of hooves from behind; three stiff Tibetan ponies decorated with ribbons and fine saddle blankets galloped past. Their riders hooted at each other and took no notice of him. While he rested, two old women in fine dress hobbled by with their walking sticks.

"Excuse me," he said. "What is this place?"

The women spoke loudly in each other's ear. Zhampa pointed to the villages. "What are their names?" he said loudly.

"Oh, yes. We came from there," one said to him nodding vigorously.

"Do you know the Naked Red Lady Mountain?"

The women talked and then laughed. Their accents were hard to grasp.

"You want to go there?"

"Yes," he said, nodding, "I want to go there."

The ladies' faces were wrinkled and round, their lips caved in from missing teeth. Finally, one pointed over the mountain he had just climbed down. "That way," she said. "But you'd be silly to go. Today is a great celebration in the monastery. Everyone is going there."

Zhampa was struck dumb. Somehow they had passed the Naked Red Lady Mountain. Disconsolate, he sat thinking how to tell Drolma they needed to go back. A pack of teenagers came along the road from the villages. They were singing and pushing each other in play.

"Come," they said, when they saw him. "Today is a special day."

"I'm tired," he said.

One of the girls stopped. Her head was a hive of fine braids. "Our tulku is coming today. Our reincarnate lama. Come to the gompa. Don't miss the festivity."

"Who is your tulku?"

"Marpay Yeshay. We'll be meeting his party at the gompa when the sun is straight up." Then she turned and scampered off to join her companions.

"How far is it?" Zhampa called after her.

She pointed up the mountain slope on the far side of the river. He squinted. Flags marked the edge of a treed ridge some miles away. He ate a little tsampa and refreshed, decided to follow them. People there could give exact directions to the Naked Red Lady Mountain.

The road was deserted where it crossed the river on tree trunks spanning boulders in the water. As he climbed the winding grade beyond, the breeze stiffened, bringing clouds and working the branches of the trees. The air smelled familiar to him, like home, and each switchback gave him more energy. Finally the gold gompa roof loomed sharp against the mountain. Hundreds of people holding white scarves lined the way to the high compound walls. They looked expectantly at the road behind him. Monks and nuns, farmers, people in official hats, school children, elders pulling rosaries with their thumbs. All stood patient. Wings of cold fog sailed close over their heads. Unnoticed, Zhampa walked the road. When he got halfway to the gompa, he asked a farmer, "When is the lama coming?"

"Soon," said the man, looking only at the road.

"I'm a traveler. Tell me. Who is Marpay Yeshay?"

"Our teacher coming home. He's been gone a long time."

"I couldn't have picked a worse day," he thought and he settled in to wait a hundred yards from the main monastery gate. An old woman touched him on the elbow and handed him a white scarf. "Offer this to Marpay Yeshay when he arrives," she said.

But Marpay Yeshay didn't come. Nor did anyone else. Clouds thickened and still the people waited. Becoming chilled and thinking that Drolma would worry, Zhampa stole outside the throng and headed down the road toward the river. Afternoon sunlight poked through the overcast in long spears. The fog swirled and lifted to reveal the red sandstone cliffs he had traversed in the morning and the mountainside that he and Drolma would have to cross again. A pair of vultures flew over the valley. And shifting his gaze to focus on them, for an instant it seemed as if a form loomed out of the sandstone. He froze and focused his eyes near and far until they held the rest of the world in a haze. And there in the air was the form of a woman, poised on one foot like a dancer, her other leg lifted as if she were wrapping it around a partner. Her thighs were full—her arms jubilantly spread, one above her head. Even the curves of her breasts and genitals were unmistakable. When he focused on the cliffs directly, they returned to their wild and natural state.

He hadn't run in years, but he took off down the winding track until he came to the log bridge. Out of breath, he looked up again at the cliffs. There was neither building nor field. "No one lives there," he said striking himself on the head. "Where are you going?" He turned again and began climbing back up the switchback road. But people and ponies soon filled it coming down. Recognizing him, a few tipped their heads in confusion to see him climbing again.

"Not today," some said. "Marpay Yeshay is not coming."

"Is this the Naked Red Lady Mountain?"

"Yes, of course. Over there."

When he made it to the level ground outside the monastery, he was alone and the great wooden gates were closed for the night. Behind him fog and gloom obscured the valley and the dancing red lady. It being too late to find Drolma and Sophia, he rapped a stone on the gate again and again. But no one came. Over the walls he heard the distant drones of deep-voiced chanting and the persistent thud of drums. Twilight shrank away.

"Damn," he said and leaned his back against the wall. "I'm here and they won't let me in." But from under all his aching cells, the irony of the moment surfaced as a snicker. Then as a chuckle. And then as a laugh. A blessed release, he let it come. And it did, in waves, building to an uproar until he was breathless and coughing.

When he settled down, he thought about Rinpo living on that land ninety-some years before. He imagined him mastering his wisdom there, a galaxy away from the land where he died. The young abbot had walked out under threat of death. Zhampa had walked back. "All for what?" he said aloud. "All because some leader wanted more gold, more wood and more territory." He despaired, and as he sank, his exhaustion washed over him.

When he woke, the moon was up, almost full, the mountainsides yellow in its light. He was cold. The image of monks finding his body in the morning got him up. Walking around the walls, he found a gate in each of the four directions. The southern and western gates hadn't been opened in years, but as he came to the northern gate, it swung open and two young monks pranced out in bare feet. They fiddled hurriedly with their robes and began relieving themselves.

"Tashi delek," Zhampa hailed. But in the moonlight the monks saw whatever it was that they feared most. They ran inside and bolted the gate. Finally his banging a stone on one of the heavy hinges brought someone to stop the racket.

"I'm very cold. I'm a traveler."

The monk assessed him with sleep-filled eyes.

"I've been traveling for years. Rinpo sent me from America."

"Rinpo?"

"Chokyi Lodro Ngawang Selpo, Rinpoche sent me . . . from America."

The monk's mouth opened and he flicked his fingers palm down in the Asian way of summoning and closed the gate behind him. He moved quickly through narrow lanes, past countless doors of monks' cells and around growling dogs. They climbed several stairs and crossed courtyards. Large roofs angled past in the moonlit sky. Finally, they stopped at an elaborate door. Zhampa had the sense of a great building above them. The monk rapped three times. Then again. The door opened a crack. Quick words flew in a rough dialect. When Rinpo's name was mentioned, the door opened wide. A stocky monk eyed Zhampa.

"I am sorry," said Zhampa.

But the monk held up his hand. "What do you want?"

"I am carrying gifts that Chokyi Lodro Ngawang Selpo, Rinpoche took from here nearly a hundred years ago to keep them from the Chinese. I've been traveling for more than four years."

The stocky monk spoke to the other without taking his eyes off Zhampa. They nodded together. "Do you know the key to mind?" the stocky monk asked.

Zhampa's thoughts raced. What was the key to mind? Had Rinpo ever told him the key? He had no idea. But afraid to say no, he spoke out without thinking. "It moves like a great river," he said, "but there's nothing there."

The monk thought a moment, running his tongue inside his lower lip. He spoke again to the messenger monk. Then he said, "Come," and he led Zhampa up a dark stair to a room with a bed and a thick coverlet.

"Sleep. Pema Rewo will see you in the morning."

He was aware of motion in the building. Gongs rang in the distance. When he rolled over, he felt that huge stones rested on every limb. The window was shuttered but had no glass. The room was below freezing. He heard a double knock on the door. At his reply, a monk entered with a cup and tsampa on a tray in one hand and an urn of steaming buttered tea in the other.

"Tashi Delek," said the monk.

"La," said Zhampa.

The tea revived him. Halfway through the tsampa, the monk returned with a washbowl of hot water and a rough towel. He placed it on the table and left without a word.

Sated, Zhampa stayed in his quarters, waiting for someone to call for him. The blowing of conch shells told of the functioning of the day. Feet in sandals clipped by outside. Finally, curious to know why he was being ignored, he pulled open the door. An old monk sitting on a thin mat sprang to his feet, pressed Zhampa's hands to his forehead and bade him to follow. To keep up, Zhampa had to scurry behind him down dark hallways, through fabric-covered doorways and up several flights of stairs. Finally they paused outside a pair of exquisitely carved doors, thick with red and gold paint. He signaled for Zhampa to wait, then slipped into the room. There were sounds of wood being dragged and bodies moving. Then all was still.

The doors opened together into a small, pillared hall with wide wood flooring contoured smooth by feet. Facing each other on both sides of a center aisle, two rows of four monks sat on red rugs behind low tables. At the far end, a small middle-aged lama sat facing him on a raised dais decorated with silks bearing Tibetan symbols. A kind face, a freshly shaved head and a graceful body. The walls were heavy with scrolls, painted wood statues on platforms and cases of brocade-wrapped texts. Massive wood beams capped the heads of columns carved to suggest clouds. All heads were turned to see the traveler. Faces weathered by wind and softened by introspection. The old monk who had delivered Zhampa motioned him to the empty cushion in the very center of the room. It had a brocade cover of peacock design on a yellow background.

"What is your name?" the lama on the dais asked. His voice was soft and sweet.

"My name is Zhampa," he said in his best Tibetan. There was hardly a twitch in the room.

"What brings you to this monastery?"

"I am returning objects that Chokyi Lodro Ngawang Selpo, Rinpoche took with him in 1959."

Several monks sighed.

"And where did you find these things?"

Zhampa had to think. Yes, he did find them. "I found them in a cave in America where he lived. And where he died."

"Did you steal them?"

"No. Rinpoche was my teacher. . . . He is my teacher. He asked me to deliver these things."

The monk on the dais leaned forward. "Please tell us your story."

So Zhampa did. Not of the journey but of his childhood with Rinpo. How the monk was his parents' teacher and how he had steadied them during the years of chaos when the climate started twisting. How, in turn, they harbored him during the religious repression that sprang from the panic about the changes, when Christian government became the law of the land. He told of his training in the maple groves and with the ink brush, writing Tibetan. And of his experience of Rinpo's magic on the retreat ledge. When he mentioned the Unraveling, the monks nodded. No one in the world had escaped the suffering. Then he spoke of finding the scepters and the map.

"I've traveled four years, almost five, to return them. Padmasambhava's dorjay and Lord Mikyo's keela which cuts three ways."

"So you have the scepters?"

Zhampa inhaled to say a triumphant yes, then stopped. He remembered the monks in Jekundo. Perhaps this was still not the right monastery. "First you must tell me who are you," Zhampa said to the lama.

"Very good," the lama said. "You are cautious. It shows you have traveled a long way. I am Pema Rewo, the abbot of the Dorjay Palmo monastery in the Kham region of Tibet. Your rinpoche was born in these mountains and educated here. If you would like proof, take a look at the scroll over there. It was painted by my grandfather in 1958."

Zhampa did as he was asked. There in the smoky hues of the scroll was the beaming face of young Rinpo. He was cavorting naked in the arms of a red consort.

Pema Rewo said, "So, may we see the scepters?"

Excusing himself into the antechamber, Zhampa removed them from the holster. Reentering, he laid them on the abbot's table. The abbot examined the dorjay, turning it in the light. Then he leaned over to a senior monk and pointed to the underside of the prongs. Taking hold of the keela, he unscrewed the head of the horse. A diamond and a fragment of bone fell out of the cavity. The abbot nodded to himself and to the others. He passed the scepters down the lines of seated monks. They nodded. When they had finished, they looked to him with great expectation.

"Now what else have you brought?" the abbot asked.

Of course. He had forgotten the text. He told of translating it, and of how it had been stolen by the false monks. Very carefully he recited the verses in Tibetan. The monks listened to Rinpo's wisdom. At the end there was a long silence. Finally the abbot spoke. "But isn't there anything else?"

There was nothing else, and when Zhampa said so, the mood in the hall sank. Minutes passed. No one spoke. Zhampa was devastated. Had he left the most important thing? No, Rinpo had said there were three gifts. Only three, and he had delivered them all.

"What is the matter with these gifts?" he said. At that cue, the abbot and the others each produced from their laps a dorjay and a keela identical to the ones he brought.

"You see these are ritual implements. We use them in our practice to transmute our confusion into wisdom. You have returned Rinpo's to us. This is indeed Padmasambhava's dorjay. It is very special to Tibetans. This is good, but it is only a thing. These are really just pieces of metal and gold. What do you think? That they are magical?"

"Rinpo parted the clouds with the dorjay. He ripped a hole in the sky with the keela. I saw him do it with my own eyes. These scepters are special. They have power."

Some of the monks pursed their lips and glanced at each other.

"Honorable Zhampa," the abbot said, "you've done well. You've returned the scepters. But for us they only identify you as the right person. Before the world burned, Rinpo sent my predecessor a letter. He told us to expect you. And our astrologer here"—he pointed to a fleshy faced monk—"told us this was a likely time. But," he said with a shrug, "we've had some false alarms before, when we expected you. Three to be exact." He looked around the room. "We were expecting you to bring something else."

Zhampa left the hall humiliated. Through the day he retraced his journey with a dark heart. Guesses of what he had failed to bring chased the pain of his losses.

They allowed him to stay another night, but it was a measure of his state of mind that he did not think of Drolma and Sophia until waking the next morning. In his distraction heading back, he nearly slipped off one of the log bridges over the river. He traversed the red sandstone cliffs without thinking of the vision they supported. He allowed himself several screaming fits on his way up the slopes. But at dusk, he found no sign of life at the abandoned village where he had left them. In despair, he wedged himself into the swale where the three of them had slept two nights earlier and fell asleep with a stone at his back. A glacier of air settled on the mountain. Wind poured through the stones of the house wall. His mind sired dreams of failure. But nothing woke him until the sun brought a feeble heat back to the land. He lay blinking and listening to the rattle of his breath. Finally, thinking that Sophia might be in danger, he groaned and sat up. Irritated at finding his flask frozen, he flung it against the wall. It shattered and he cursed. He tracked them northwest to the river. By late morning at the first of the two villages, he asked if anyone had seen a woman, a child and two yaks.

"Yes," someone finally said, "we sent her to the other village."

There he was told they had set out for the monastery early that morning. If he walked fast, he could reach them by nightfall. He cut a flake from a weight of Drolma's gold for a flask of hot tea and some day-old arhi. Rejuvenated, he took off at a brisk pace. At sunset, the red cliffs came into view. At twilight, he crossed the log bridges. In the dark, he felt his way up the switchbacks. The monastery gates being closed, he circled to the northern gate and hammered on the hinge as before.

"Back again?" said the monk.

"I'm sorry. Now I'm looking for a woman and a child. They would have come today."

"There were several parties that came today. Follow me."

They went through courtyards and alleyways. There were conversations with other monks. Eventually he again found himself climbing the stairs in the abbot's house. This time the attendant led him past the hall where he had met with Pema Rewo to a smaller chamber. The attendant put his finger to his lips and gently pushed the door open a crack. Butter lamps lit the room. Three lamas, the abbot among them, squatted on the floor by a miniature throne. They spoke in low voices to a tiny monk in glorious robes. The little monk looked over a tray of different colored rosaries. He reached for the one of crystal and played it through his hand like an old man. The lamas showed their pleasure. Next they offered him a tray of old eyeglasses. The little monk examined them carefully.

"Take your time," the abbot said. "Choose the set that you used to wear."

The little hand reached for a black-rimmed pair and when he put them on, the abbot beamed at the selection. In response, the little monk chortled, and Zhampa heard Sophia's voice. He looked again. The little monk on the throne was Sophia, wearing a brocade crown, her hair all tucked into it, her face scrubbed clean for the first time in months. When the door drifted open on its own weight, Sophia caught sight of him.

"Papa Zhampa," she cried out.

The abbot turned and saw him. "Well done, Zhampa. Well done. You did bring what we expected after all. A girl child with red hair. This child fulfills all the signs and prophecies. And by properly selecting objects used by her previous incarnation, she is passing our tests of recognition. She is Marpay Yeshay, Red Wisdom, the reincarnation of Selpo, Rinchoche. Gone a hundred years."

22

The festivities surrounding the enthronement of Marpay Yeshay lasted eight days. They culminated on the full moon with feasts, lama dancing and, lastly, the ritual blessing of the throng by the new incarnation. Sitting on a high throne, the two-year-old tulku placed Padmasambhava's dorjay on the bowed head of every monk and nun, and every farmer and dignitary. As was customary, great teachers and their entourages came from distant corners of the Himalayas to file by and receive her blessing. When Zhampa offered the crown of his head to Marpay Yeshay, she made him stay bent a long while. Finally, she thumped him hard enough with the dorjay for welts to linger on his head for a number of weeks. Her stroke, and the laugh she gave doing it, established for him her true identity. In the following months, hundreds of boyhood images emerged from his memories, pointing out to him that most of Rinpo's instructions still lay unexplored. He walked around the compound with his head slightly tilted, periodically shaking it. They took to calling him 'headwagger,' which he came to receive with humor.

Drolma, too, was in the line that snaked forward for blessing and she stayed the winter in Zhampa's little house in the village closest to the monastery. Pemma Rewo gave her meditation instruction but did not shave her head, as it was clear she would follow the path of a yogini. In the spring she gave half of her wealth to the monastery, saving the rest for the shepherd girls, and departed with her yaks to find her lama.

Seeing her go and seeing the roads fit to travel got Zhampa thinking. Pemma Rewo said, "Before deciding to leave, it's good to consider the conditions that brought you here."

"I walked. I can return the same way."

"Yes." The abbot slurped his tea. He looked out at the garden through the open shutter of his study. "But I was suggesting a deeper level."

"Rinpo asked me to."

"He wrote you the letter."

"Yes, he wrote a letter telling me that he wanted me to return the scepters."

"And why did you agree to that request?"

"Because I murdered someone."

"And you wanted to atone? Is that all?"

"Because he showed me what the scepters could do, and said they were needed here."

"And now you want to go home?"

"Yes. No. I mean it seems impossible to just leave Sophia."

"Marpay Yeshay."

"Yes. Marpay Yeshay."

"So your job is done."

"Yes."

"And what more do you have to accomplish in your life?"

"Not much. That's the problem."

"And you think by going home, you will live in peace."

"It's the dream I have."

Pemma Rewo pursed his lips. "You may be surprised with what greets you there."

Zhampa thought of finding his house in ruins and grew silent.

"Do you think Selpo Rinpoche asked you to carry the scepters because you happened to be there? That it was a random request?"

Zhampa didn't answer.

"Who gave you your name?"

"Rinpo did. That's what my parents told me."

"Who taught you what you needed to know to come here?"

"Rinpo, of course."

"Yes. Chokyi Lodro Ngawang Selpo Rinpoche. . . . Have you ever considered that Selpo Rinpoche might be your father?" The question hung in the air. Then Pemma Rewo said, "He sent a letter to the previous abbot here foretelling his reincarnation. Marpay Yeshay. Almost fifty years ago. I've seen it. You were a little boy."

Zhampa threw up his hands and let them slap his thighs. "Well, if he could send a letter, why didn't he just send the scepters? Why did he need me to carry them?"

Pemma Rewo tipped his hand palm up to return the question. Zhampa's eyes flitted in rushing thoughts. He shook his head. "I know it's off the subject, but there's something else. How come Marpay Yeshay is a girl?"

Cradling his teacup, the abbot lifted and reset the porcelain cover several times. His voice was soft. "Everything that arises disappears. Do you understand?" His gaze caused Zhampa to avert his eyes. "There's a great shift underway, Zhampa. Creating order from the outside in, by force of intellect, has been dominant as far back as we know. And the world has suffered for lack of another way. Now the momentum of a new voice is building, a voice to lift this Dark Age. One that speaks of creating order from the inside out. It's the voice of community."

After a long silence Zhampa said, "So is it women who will open the gate to wisdom?"

Pemma Rewo chuckled and shook his head. "Women *have* come to a different viewpoint. They have good ideas. But, Zhampa, at its essence, wisdom is beyond gender. The pendulum is soon to swing away from outside in. And it will move toward inside out. But the ultimate state, of course, is the balance of the two energies. Cutting and allowing. Both things. In every being." He paused. "This world desperately needs to be managed in a new way. Nature is generous. Even here on the top of the world, there's enough to go around to provide a decent life for every creature. We must learn how to go along with her. Individuals or tribes or nations taking the lion's share is not a workable idea." The room was quiet like a closed book.

Finally Zhampa said, "But the momentum of creating order from the outside-in is still dominant. It's all most people know. It doesn't listen to or like things coming from the inside. How will Sophia . . . Marpay Yeshay, how will she learn to deal with the force of it? How will she survive?"

"A plant knows how to guard its seed in a drought. When conditions become right again, the seed is there and ready, correct?"

Zhampa understood seeds.

"Marpay Yeshay's not alone. The conditions are coming for inside-out wisdom to ascend."

Zhampa thought of the Lake Clan and the We People, and of the ways they divided up their world and work. He thought of the Tlingit. And of the hierarchy in Drolma's yak herding culture. "But," he said, "who will protect Marpay Yeshay when she is young? Who will teach her?"

The abbot's eyes softened. "Look at me," he said. "Look closely. What do you really see?"

Zhampa saw the abbot's round head with soft flesh behind the ears and under the jaw. He saw a balanced mouth and supple skin. Soft lips. Pemma Rewo's hands were small and graceful.

"Pemma Rewo, are you telling me you're a woman?"

Pemma Rewo's head dipped in a subtle nod. "I came from another monastery with papers naming me as Pemma Rewo, Lotus Mountain." She smiled. "A nice monk's name. Soon it will be time to reveal this secret." She let Zhampa ruminate a long while, then interrupted. "You've always been returning like this. It's your karma. Rinpo knew you'd find him in America. You've always found him. Birth after birth. And you've always done the impossible things he's asked." She got up and walked to the scroll between the windows. The central figure was Chokyi Lodro Ngawang Selpo, Rinpoche in monk's robes sitting on a lotus throne. She pointed deliberately to another figure, a small one in the foreground, an old man kneeling in homage. She didn't say anything.

"What am I supposed to do now?" Zhampa said. "The only thing I know how to do is walk. I've been walking away from a murder I committed thirty-one years ago. I can't change the past. I'm a murderer, Pemma Rewo. There's no place for me in a world of enlightened beings."

Pemma Rewo was about to sit. Instead she moved to a bigger scroll. The main figure was nothing but skin and bone, slightly green with a hand cupped to his ear, as if listening to something faraway. "Zhampa, this is Tibet's greatest yogi, Milarepa. When he was young, he caused the death of an entire village. To wear out the consequences of his actions, his teacher made him build a stone tower and then commanded him to move it eight times. Finally Milarepa was ready. He opened and, through diligence, became enlightened."

"I'm too old," Zhampa said, "to build any more with stone."

The abbess Pemma Rewo laughed a long laugh. "Milarepa built towers," she said. "You pulled a cart."

Summer came. Zhampa rose and fell with his moods. Pemma Rewo kept an eye on him. He came to her at different times to find a way to escape the relentless weight of his lifetimes. He still longed to understand the scepters. "But I saw Rinpo change the color of trees by waving that dorjay. He cut the sky with the tip of the keela. He poked holes in the clouds with it."

After a long pause she said, "The power of the dorjay is *real*. But it comes from knowing what it is not. If you conquer concepts, Zhampa, if you conquer their hold on you, then the whole universe is delivered into your hand. Anything becomes possible."

A month later he agreed it was finally time to look without making any assumptions about what he would see. And with that he began to feel he would stay there in the Naked Red Lady Mountain monastery.

"Selpo Rinpoche wanted you to sit where he sat when he was young," she said in late summer, "where he trained in the illusory nature of things. It's not much, his place. A little rammed-earth retreat hut up above in the hills. One door and one window looking south. We've kept it clean and ready for you. It's humble, but it's a perfect place to find riches."

Zhampa panicked when she took him there. He knew the rigors of meditation baffled the best yogis.

"I'm not ready for retreat," he said. "Perhaps I could start with the preliminaries, with the novices."

"Preliminaries are for the young, because they are exploding with self-interest. But people like you and me, well, there's not a lot of time." She stopped to let the words sink in. "I think pulling carts across half the earth and losing everything you love has worn down some of your anger and your pride."

When Zhampa sat in Rinpo's retreat hut, she gave him meditation instruction. "Be. Simply be. Body and mind as they are. Clear and pure. In the beginning, at best, you will only imitate simply being. That is not bad. When you catch yourself imitating, release trying. Then you'll come to genuine experience."

"Then I don't have to try?" he asked.

"That would be too easy. There is no way to get there by not trying."

His mind leapt the other way.

"And," she said, "there's no way to get there by trying either."

The two ideas reminded Zhampa of the boy who had to hold his head when Rinpo was teaching him how to walk like an elephant.

"There's no hint of laziness in it," she added. "Remember, if you think it's happening, it isn't."

In the early months of his practice, Zhampa was completely discouraged. Pemma Rewo said, "It's all directed to one simple thing. The mind that makes progress is the problem. Stop pulling the cart."

"But you ask me to pull it," he said. "Every day. Sit. Sit. Pull. Pull by not pulling." His eyes were wild. "*Rinpo* asked me to pull the cart."

"Yes," she said. "That was to get you ready to not pull it."

The seasons went by. Out the door he saw sky and mountains. The Naked Red Lady danced in her permanent stride over the valley, her leg raised in exultation. She mocked everything that was important to him, including the sky and the mountains. When he took the time to see her, he stopped pulling the cart. When he stopped seeking progress, his mind opened.

He saw Marpay Yeshay now and then. She loved to break away from her tutors and take walks with him on the slopes all around and down to the river below. She ran like the wind and spoke several languages. English with him. Her hair was long. In it, he saw her mother and her grandmother. And his heart was pulled both ways, as only loss wrapped in the promise of children can do.

When she turned six, Pemma Rewo said of her, "She's doing very well." And the way she nodded told him that Marpay Yeshay would master creating order from the inside-out. It was a world he wouldn't live to see.

A year. And another year, in spring. Zhampa sat in the meditation hut of his master. There, between his sessions of practice one day, he ruminated on the lives of salmon. How they are conceived and arise in the millions in an environment where anything except survival is assured. He pondered how they grow first in one world and then in another, how they travel by instinct, by passion, and on currents, awake and blind at the same time. How they drive out and how they are called home. He visualized their final journey against the rush of the river—pushing, losing weight, changing color, evading predators, leaping over falls, dashing against the stones, falling back and trying again. Never giving up. Drawn by a scent. Or is it a sense of something?

After a supper of butter tea and barley flour, he thought again of his meeting the old fish heading home from the sea. He wondered what it might have realized after spawning, swimming in water too shallow to enjoy and too fresh to drink. Had it ever understood its place in the flow of things?

In the quiet shallows upstream, as death approached, had his old salmon seen that it had spent a lifetime in nonstop exertion? Had it seen that it had made a choice with every flexion of its glorious body? Had it been able to grasp the wisdom even in that? Zhampa began to laugh, and over the months his laughter became uproarious. It boomed in the space of his retreat and escaped on the wind, so that those in the halls and valleys below heard the music of the yogi recognizing truth.

The air around the cave was thin and he knew his time was short. He had offered himself for some cycle that he couldn't fully see. He wondered if there were a way to impart to at least one person that . . . that, what was it? That life was like the print a bird's wings leave on the sky; magical, full of purpose and unseen. Neither good nor bad. When he looked at it honestly, wasn't that all it was? If so, there was no point in struggling. There was nothing to fight over. Trying to grasp the notion brought laughter. Nothing more. Only the bird can touch the essence of a bird's life, he concluded, and only as it flies. Only the fish in the water as it swims, only the man pulling a cart and only as he pulls it. But if the bird or the fish or the man measures how high it flies or how deep it swims or how far he pulls, then he misses the essence and lives not at all.

The End

The author believes that elements of the Path of Dharma that appear in this text are accurate in their presentation and takes responsibility for any mistakes, but he cautions the reader that they are not complete as a basis of instruction to practice meditation or as a vehicle to understand the view. If a reader feels inspired to explore or enter this path, the author recommends she or he study with an authentic and accomplished Dharma teacher.

Acknowledgements

This book was made possible by a long list of collaborators. Early on, the stories of teachers and journalists sparked investigation of societies and social orders. While researching far-flung locations, the kindness of many strangers ensured my survival. Translator and language teacher Xu Zi Wen collected me upon arrival in Beijing and gave many days without thought for herself. Lergiatr Lergiatr (a name so powerful it bears repeating) settled me in Tibet and opened the way for me to live in Tibetan villages at 10,000 feet. Dirap Lama and Rinchen introduced me to the vast magic of KumBum Monastery. Tashi Chintso and Limao Zhuoma guided me overland to hidden valleys and finagled invitations to the inner sanctums of working monasteries. Their parents Lergiater and Lhamo generously let their daughter and niece travel with an American man, and their meals and smiles awaited me at their home in my base camp city of Xining. Sonam, my guide to the most remote Himalayan regions, modeled the equanimity toward his captors that is indicative of Tibetans who spend time in Chinese prisons. Inner Mongolians Aruna and Ge-guntuya offered me Huahote. Erka Erdenetseg scooped me up in my excursion to Mongolia. Liu Ying rescued me in Changchun.

I give special gratitude to Ilse Mattick who heard the story before a word was written and who strongly encouraged me to follow through when the goal seemed allusive. I am grateful to the generosity of my readers who kept me on the path: Margot Page, Paul Birnbaum, Judy Meloy, Margaret Clark, Kathleen James, Ilse Mattick, Chris Morrow, Jari Chevalier and Tim Noonan. Joel Wachbrit's stinging critique made me reach for the highest bar and reveals his true friendship. Justine Cook steered me through coral reefs of style and usage points. Finally, without the brilliant, dogged and kind work of my editor Philip Russell, this endeavor would have languished in confusion.

July 2009
The Mettowee Valley, Vermont

299 POP   11/09

The Trouble With Wisdom

Thomas Henry Pope

	DATE DUE		
	JAN 30 2010		
	MAY 22 2010